A Valentine's Day Romance Anthology

Lexi Aidyn

R.K. Fultz

Myria Wild

Nan Sampson

Love, Hope, & Second Chances: A Valentine's Day Romance Anthology

Stories included in this anthology:

Published by Ravens Call Publishing
Cover and formatting by Nydia Pastoriza

Paperback ISBN: 978-1-951608-21-7
e-Book ISBN: 978-1-951608-20-0

Contents

A Heart Ready to Hope

by Lexi Aidyn

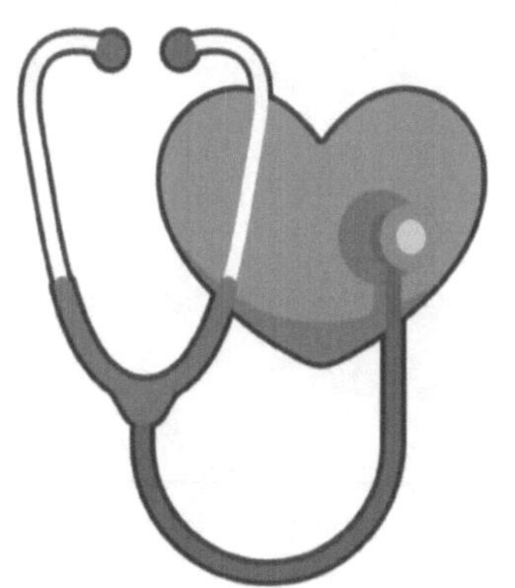

Chapter 1: Strangers at 30,000 Feet

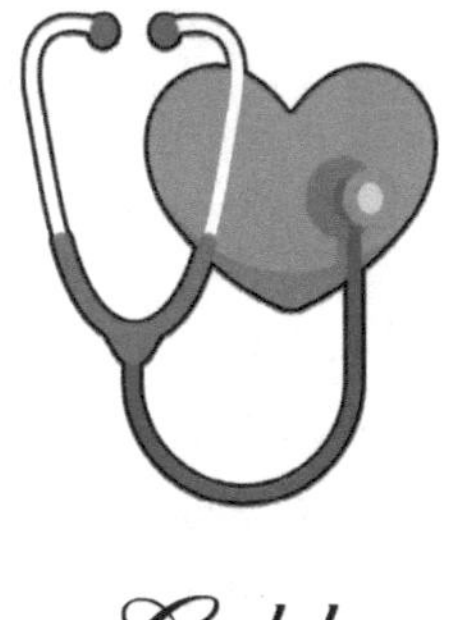

Caleb

"Yes, Mom. I promise I'll let Dr. Monroe know you said hi," I assure my mother for the fifth time since I arrived at the airport.

"Good. He's a wonderful man. And remember to call me when you land."

"I will," I say, trying to keep the impatience out of my voice.

"They're calling my flight to board. I'll talk to you later. Love you." Finally, I hang up, exhaling as I approach the boarding gate.

I step into the line, grateful I only carry a small bag for this quick trip to Charlotte. I'll be there just a few days to catch up with Dr. Monroe and maybe reconnect with a few buddies from my high school days, and then I'll be back home.

As I inch forward in line, I notice a woman standing off to the side. "I'll be fine, Mom," she says, her phone pinned between her shoulder and ear as she rummages through her oversized bag.

"No, you and Dad don't need to come. I'm a big girl." She rolls her eyes as she finds what she's looking for—her ticket. "I'll be fine. Tell the boys I love them. I'm boarding now. Love you."

With a dramatic sigh, she tosses her phone into the abyss of her bag, no doubt destined to get lost like her paper ticket.

I chuckle softly. Moms, they're all the same. It doesn't matter how old we get; they'll always worry. It reminds me of the conversation with my mom just a few minutes ago.

The agent waves me forward, and I scan my ticket on my phone before heading down the jet bridge.

I find my seat, a window seat. I'm thankful, since I didn't select my seat when I bought my ticket. I stow my bag in the overhead compartment and settle in. No one is next to me yet, and hopefully, it'll stay that way. I get as comfortable as I can being a six-foot-three man in a coach seat. Earbuds in, I lean back and let Maroon 5 fill my head with "Beautiful Mistakes." I'm hopeful I'll get some sleep and, for now, forget about the next few days, which will not be easy.

I've just closed my eyes when I sense movement beside me, a subtle shift in the air as someone steps into the aisle near my seat.

I open my eyes to find a woman, about five-foot-five, standing in the aisle, her brow furrowed in frustration as she wrestles with her carry-on. She rises onto her tiptoes, attempting to shove the bag into the overhead bin, but the angle isn't quite right. The bag catches on the edge, teetering precariously.

Without a second thought, I remove my earbud from my ear, unbuckle my seatbelt, and stand. "Need a hand?"

She exhales sharply, a mix of relief and stubbornness flickering across her face. "If you don't mind." She steps back just enough to let me help.

With a nod, I take her bag, adjust my stance, and push the bin open. My own carry-on is already tucked neatly inside, leaving just enough space. I shift a few things around, making room before securing her bag beside mine.

“Thank you,” she murmurs as she slides into her seat and gives me a smile bright enough to knock me off balance. She has these striking green eyes framed by long lashes, and her blond hair is tied up in one of those messy buns like my female co-workers at the station wear when they don’t want to deal with it.

I nod, sitting back down and slip my Airpod back in my ear, as she settles beside me. It takes me a second to realize she's still talking.

"Sorry," I pull out one of my AirPods again. "I didn’t catch that."

"Oh, I was just saying thank God I’m not sitting alone. I don’t fly a lot," she admits, fastening her seatbelt and glancing at the flight attendant moving down the aisle.

“It will be fine. Like being in a car.” I realize she’s the same woman I’d notice while standing in line earlier. When the flight attendant begins reviewing the safety information, I take the chance to put my other AirPod back in and close my eyes, hoping to fall asleep.

Not long after, as the plane lifts off, I shift in my seat, trying to get comfortable. My eyes flicker open for a second, and that’s when I notice her. Her fingers grip the armrest in a vise-like hold, knuckles pale against her skin. She swallows hard, her breathing quick and uneven. Shallow inhales that barely fill her lungs before slipping out in shaky bursts.

“Hey, are you okay?” I ask, keeping my voice low.

She turns to me, her eyes wide and glassy under the cabin lights. Her breath stutters, and she blinks rapidly, barely moving, frozen in place, as though any shift might crack her.

“I’m absolutely petrified of flying,” she whispers. Her voice trembles and she starts to ramble. “I’ve only flown once before, and that was with my family, and I was much younger.”

I offer her a reassuring smile. “It’s going to be fine. What’s your name?”

“Chloe,” she says. She shuts her eyes tightly for a few seconds, but at least she loosens her grip on the armrest.

“Hi, Chloé. I’m Caleb.” I subtly curve my lips, trying to keep things light.

"Hi, Caleb." She gives a small, nervous laugh, her hands still clenched. "Sorry, It really... really terrifies me to fly."

"It's going to be okay, I promise. So, is your final stop in Denver?" I ask, hoping to distract her a bit.

Her response is hesitant. "Unfortunately not. I have one more flight to Charlotte. You?"

"Same." She's still gripping the armrest, but the color is starting to return to her knuckles. Progress.

"So, are you from Seattle?" she asks, clearly trying to stay in the conversation to keep her mind off the flight.

"My family is, but I was born in Charlotte." I relax in my seat, hoping she'll do the same.

"Ah. I've only been to Charlotte once before." She loosens her grip a little more.

"Is that the one time you flew"

"Yeah, but my brothers were with me, and they kept me distracted." Her gaze drops to her hands as she finally lets go of the armrest.

"It's always easier with company." I lean back and close my eyes for a moment.

"Thanks, Caleb. Actually, could you... talk to me a little more?" Her voice is soft, the tremor in it unmistakable. My heart tightens as I sense her anxiety creeping back. I turn to meet her gaze, offering a look filled with genuine warmth and understanding. I'd planned on catching some sleep, but after her soft request I'm more than okay to stay up and keep her company.

I keep my voice gentle, but firm. "Of course. What do you want to talk about?"

Chapter 2: Between Takeoff and Touchdown

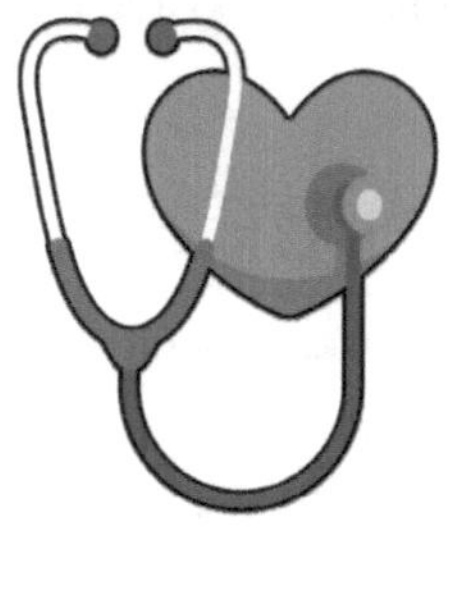

Chloe

I'd probably feel embarrassed about my behavior if I weren't so terrified. But once the plane took off, my anxiety hit like a tidal wave. Flying unnerves me. I know it might skew my test results at the doctor's appointment in Charlotte, but this fear refuses to let go.

"What do you do?" I ask Caleb, hoping to continue distracting myself. He's been so kind, and talking to him steadies my racing heart. He probably just wants to sleep, but I need something—anything—to keep my nerves from spiraling before we reach our destination.

"I'm a firefighter," he says, smiling warmly. His long legs almost touch the seat in front of him, easily marking him over six feet tall. As I glance at him more closely, his build becomes evident even beneath sweatshirt, broad shoulders, lean hips. His striking blue-grey eyes stand out against his darker skin. They're intense yet kind.

"And you?" he asks.

"I'm a teacher. Not nearly as exciting as firefighting," I reply, unable to stop my smile. "The most exciting thing about my job is getting marbles out of five and six-year-olds' noses."

He laughs, shaking his head. "No way. Teachers are the coolest. Trust me, I know. I live with one."

"Your wife?" I sound like I'm fishing for details, and maybe I am.

"No." He grins. "My mom. She was a middle school teacher before she retired."

"Ah, now she's the real hero," I say, imagining the patience it must take. "Middle school can be brutal."

"What grade do you teach?" Caleb leans in slightly, giving me his full attention.

"First grade. I don't see myself going past third. The older the kids, the more drama." I laugh, meeting his gaze, and his smile widens.

"Middle school is rough," he agrees. "But my mom was a no-nonsense type of teacher. I even had her for math in seventh grade. It was... an experience." He shudders theatrically, and I can't help but laugh.

"I can't imagine teaching my own kids."

"Do you have kids?" he asks.

"Nope. Just nieces, nephews, and my students. You?"

"Not yet." He glances out the window before looking back. "Maybe someday, but for now, it's firefighting and rescuing kittens."

I shake my head, smiling "You rescue a lot of kittens, I bet."

His smirk deepens, but the flight attendant interrupts us to offer drinks.

"Thank you for keeping me distracted. I really appreciate it," I say after the attendant moves on.

He meets my gaze, and in the quiet pause that follows, his expression softens. "I'm glad I can help," he replies gently. "You mentioned brothers. How many do you have?"

"Four brothers." It always surprises people when I share that I'm the only girl of five kids. "Yep, I'm the only girl."

"You're kidding!" His eyes dance with amusement. "That's... a lot."

"Tell me about it." I grin. "But it worked out. I got out of a lot of chores. What about you?"

"I had a sister," he says quietly. "But... she passed a while back."

My heart sinks. "I'm so sorry. I can't imagine..." My voice trails off, unsure of what to say.

"It's all right." He gives me sad smile. "It was a long time ago."

We spend the rest of the flight in light conversation, sharing stories about work, books, and music. Caleb no longer feels like a stranger, and I realize I'm not just comforted by him but genuinely attracted. By the time we land in Denver for the layover, my fear of flying has melted away, and the purpose of my trip to Charlotte isn't even top of mind.

As the cabin lights brighten, Caleb turns to me. "We have a three-hour layover, and it's past lunchtime. Do you want to grab something to eat?"

I'm surprised, because I assumed he was just being polite during the flight.

"Sure!" I say as we both stand. He helps me with my bag as he did when I boarded in Seattle, and we disembark from the plane.

"We don't have a lot of options in this terminal," he says as we stop to survey the area, "but I've been through Denver a few times and know some decent spots. What do you feel like eating?"

"Anything. I'm not picky."

"Okay. I know a place with little of everything." He smiles and grabs my carry-on bag. "Follow me."

We walk toward a cozy restaurant, and Caleb adds our name to the short waiting list. As we wait, my phone rings. I glance at the screen and sigh, it's my mom. Again.

"I have to take this," I say, slightly embarrassed, and he nods. I step aside.

"Hey, Mom," I say as soon as I pick up the phone.

"Hi, sweetheart! Did you land safely?" she asks, her voice immediately laced with concern.

"Yeah, I just landed. Sorry I didn't call right away," I reply.

"How are you feeling? Was the flight okay?"

"I was a bit frightened at takeoff, but the rest of the flight went fine."

There's a brief pause before she asks, "And what are you planning to do during the layover?"

I hesitate. "I'm just grabbing something quick to eat. Nothing heavy, I promise."

Her voice softens with that familiar blend of worry and care. "Alright, just remember to take care of yourself. Text me as soon as you get to Charlotte, okay?"

"I will, Mom. I'll be careful."

"Good. I worry about you, you know that, right?"

"I know, and I appreciate it," I say, feeling a mix of exasperation and gratitude. "Love you, Mom."

"Love you too, darling. Call me if you need anything."

The hostess signals our table is ready, and I quickly end the call. "I have to go, Mom. I'll call you later."" I end the call with a relieved sigh.

"Ready?" Caleb asks as I rejoin him.

"Yeah, I'm starving." I tuck my phone away, my stomach fluttering for reasons that have nothing to do with hunger.

Chapter 3: The Space Between Strangers

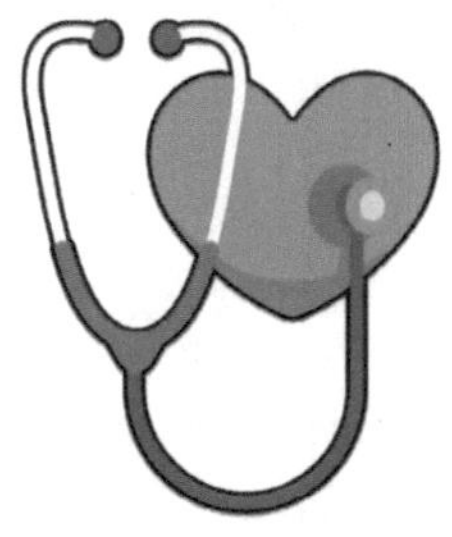

Caleb

"What are you in the mood for?" I ask Chloe as we examine our menus.

"I think I'm going to try the Cobb salad. What about you?"

"I'm going to have the mushroom cheeseburger." I spot it on the menu and remember when I ordered it during a skiing trip with my friends. "If my memory serves me right, the sweet potato fries are really good here."

She looks up from the menu. "I've never had sweet potato fries."

"Really?" She nods, smiling at me. "You have to try them. I'll share them with you."

The waiter takes our order, leaving us with water to drink.

"So, you've been to Denver?" she asks after taking a sip.

"Yes, I've been here with some friends, skiing and snowboarding."

"I bet that's fun." She looks down at her hands with a wistful look that makes me wonder if she's never really experienced the exhilaration of skiing, even as she imagines it.

"It's a blast. You've never been?"

She shakes her head and changes the subject. "Did you always want to be a firefighter?"

"Not always. I met some fantastic first responders in high school who influenced my career choice." For a split second, I let my mind wander to a day I rarely speak of, a day that left me with a hidden, lingering emotional scar, its echo still felt in quiet moments. I shift the conversation. "Did you always want to be a teacher?"

"I did. I've been obsessed with it since I met my brother Luke's first-grade teacher." Her green eyes get brighter as she shares the memory. "I would make my brothers play school with me, even though they're all older than me." She giggles, and for some reason, I don't want to think about why I'm enjoying it so much.

I laugh with her. "It sounds like you had them wrapped around your little finger at an early age."

"Kind of. We're all pretty close." Her sharing about her brothers reminds me of my own little sister and how I would have done anything for her.

"How long are you going to be in Charlotte?" I ask, pushing that thought to the back of my mind.

"Just a few days. What about you?"

"Same. Do you have any fun plans?"

"Not really. I'm meeting a family friend." She shrugs. "I hope to check out a few museums or go shopping."

"There are some great museums in Charlotte." The waiter returns with our food, interrupting the conversation. We eat in silence for a few minutes.

"Okay, you've got to try these. So good." I push the basket of sweet potato fries toward her.

"Aren't they…weirdly sweet for fries?" She eyes them skeptically.

"Trust me, they're amazing. And bonus points, they're technically a vegetable, so it's like eating a salad." I grin.

"That's a stretch, but fine. One fry." Chloe picks up a fry, cautiously takes a bite, and pauses.

"Well?" I watch her intently.

Chloe nods slowly, surprised. "Okay, not bad. It's kind of…crispy and soft at the same time. Still sweet, though."

"In the best way, right?"

'Better than I expected." She puts the rest in her mouth. "Now I feel like I should share some of my salad."

"Not necessary, but take as many as you want. Sharing is caring." I take a few extra fries and slide the basket closer to her.

While we eat lunch, we learn more about each other's jobs. I share amusing calls we've gotten at the station, and she shares the funny things that come out of first graders' months. By the time we're done, she tries to pay the bill, which I had taken care of before we even finished our meals.

There was something magnetic about her that commandeered my attention like nothing I'd experienced before. I couldn't explain it, but I knew it was there.

We headed back to our gate with an hour to spare before boarding and it dawns on me that we might not be seated next to each other.

"Hey, what's your seat number on the Charlotte flight?" I ask her as we reach the terminal.

"Let me see." She digs through her bag just like she did in Seattle. Pulling it out, she looks at it. "15B.,You?

I check my boarding pass on my phone. "I'm in 22C." "Let's see if they can move one of us to sit together, if that's okay with you."

She nods, smiling. "I'd like that a lot."

We walk over to the gate desk together. "Excuse me." I address the agent.

"Can I help you?" She looks up from her computer.

"I was wondering if my friend and I could have our seats changed so we can sit together."

"It depends on whether the flight is full." She looks down at the computer. "Let me check."

I smile at Chole as we wait for the agent.

"You guys are in luck. We might be able to. Do you have your tickets?"

We both reach over the counter, me with my phone and Chloe with her paper ticket.

"Okay, it looks like I can move you to 12A and 12B. How's that sound?" she asks as she glances between us.

"Perfect!" we both reply. The agent prints two new boarding passes and hands them to us.

"Thanks again."

"I'm so glad we were able to change our seats," Chole tells me as we find a spot to sit and wait to board. "I hate to be alone or beside a stranger given how much I don't like flying."

I fail to stifle a laugh.

"What?" she asks.

"Technically, I was a stranger back in Seattle."

"Yeah, but you were so kind. I'm sure it would have been much different if I had to sit next to another person."

Within the next hour, we board and take off to Charlotte.

Our conversation flowed effortlessly as we swapped stories about art, music, and our favorite artists. Before long, Chloe began reminiscing about her brothers' wild antics growing up.

"They were always up to something," she says with a laugh, though a hint of wistfulness softens her eyes. "I didn't really join in on their schemes. I always felt like I slowed them down."

I tilt my head, curiosity piqued. "Really? That doesn't sound like much fun."

Chloe waves a hand dismissively. "Oh, it was nothing. They were so overprotective that they'd hold back whenever I tagged along."

"They sound like good guys."

"They are. Overbearing but good."

When we land in Charlotte, I realize I spent the better part of the flight simply enjoying her company. I hadn't anticipated feeling this comfortable with someone I just met. Her laughter lingered in my mind, a soft echo that felt strangely familiar. I found myself replaying moments in my head; the way her eyes sparkle when she talks about her favorite musician, the little wrinkle in her nose when she laughs, and the way her voice softens when she speaks of her brothers.

As the plane doors open, a rush of warm, pressurized air replaces the hum of the cabin. Chloe and I step into the aisle, moving in sync as we grab our bags from the overhead compartment. Neither of us speaks, but the silence between us isn't awkward, it's comfortable, the kind that lingers when you don't need to fill the space with words.

We walk side by side through the jet bridge, the rhythmic shuffle of passengers around us blending into white noise. Every few steps, I glance at Chloe. She looks relaxed now, her shoulders no longer tense like they were during takeoff. As we step into the terminal, the bright lights and bustling energy of the airport feel jarring after the quiet of the flight. Chloe slows her pace, pulling her phone from her bag. She taps the screen a few times before glancing at me.

"I'm just ordering an Uber," she says casually.

I nod, watching as she tucks a loose strand of hair behind her ear while focusing on the screen. The realization settles over me: I don't want this to be the last time I see her.

We continue through the airport, reaching the automatic doors. As they slide open, a sharp breath of February air rushes in, cool and dry against my skin after the sealed, recycled warmth inside. Chloe pulls her coat closer as we step outside, weaving around travelers clustered near the curb, shoulders hunched against the cold. She glances at her phone, checking the status of her Uber.

The sun hangs low in the winter sky, pale and distant, casting a muted gold across the city. Long shadows stretch over the pavement, light glancing off windshields as cars creep through the pickup lane. The air smells of exhaust and cold asphalt, clean and brisk, with none of the softness summer brings, just enough bite to remind you it's still very much winter in Charlotte.Chloe squints at her screen, her face illuminated by the soft light. "Five minutes away," she announces, tracing the edge of her phone with her thumb. The movement is casual, but there's a trace of hesitance in her eyes, like she's not quite ready to say goodbye either. "Well, here we are," she says, pulling her carry-on bag closer. "Back to reality."

"Yeah." I shove my hands into my pockets. "Guess this is where we part ways."

She hums in agreement, eyes flicking to her screen. I nod, shifting my weight from one foot to the other, stalling. I don't know why, but I feel like I'm about to let something slip through my fingers. The past few hours; meeting her, talking, laughing, felt easy in a way that nothing has in a long time.

She stares at me, hesitating for a second before saying, "I, uh, just wanted to say thanks again. For helping me stay calm on the flight. I didn't realize how much flying would affect me, and talking to you made it a lot easier."

Something warm settles in my chest. "You're welcome. But honestly, I think I got the better deal. I really enjoyed your company."

She smiles, something soft and almost shy about it, and I feel the moment stretching out between us, thick with a kind of anticipation.

"You said you wanted to visit a museum," I say. "I could show you the Mint Uptown. Maybe dinner after, if that sounds good."

Chloe's smile is slow, thoughtful. "Dinner sounds good."

"I might know a place with sweet potato fries," I add.

She laughs softly. "Okay. I'm in."

Relief flickers through me, and for the first time in a while, I actually feel like I have something to look forward to. "Great. There's this place I know, with a great view of the city."

Her eyes brighten, curiosity flickering there. "You already have a place in mind?"

I shrug. "I've thought about it."

She laughs, the sound light and melodious against the evening air. "Alright, museum and dinner sounds perfect."

Just then, her Uber pulls up. She glances at it, then back at me, and for a second, I think she might say something else. But instead, she rests a hand on the card door handle, giving me a playful look.

"I'll call you?" I ask, suddenly wishing I had something better to say.

She smirks. "You better."

I reach into my pocket, pulling out my phone. "Here," I say, unlocking it and handing it to her. "Put your number in."

She raises her hand, and takes it without hesitation, her fingers move quickly over the screen.

"There," she says, passing it back. "Now you have it."

I glance at the new contact—Chloe—and something about seeing her name on my screen makes me smile. Before I can say anything else, she opens the car door and slides inside.

She waves out the window as the car pulls away from the curb, disappearing from view, and I watch until it's gone, that spark of anticipation glowing within me. For the first time in a long time, tomorrow feels like something truly worth looking forward to.

Chapter 4: More Than Survival

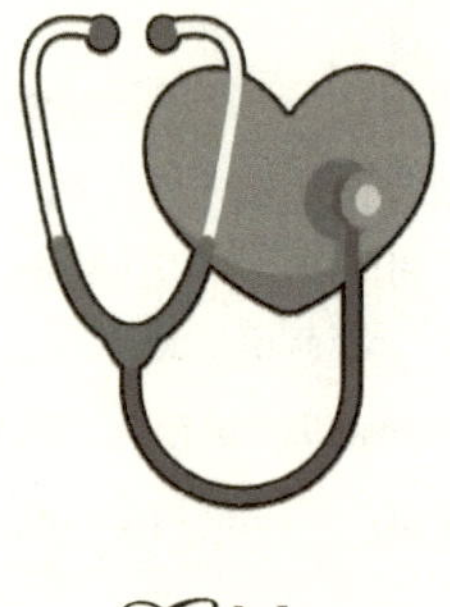

Chloe

After confirming my destination with the driver, I glance back one last time and wave again. Caleb stands there, takes his hand out of his pocket, and waves back, a steady presence against the blur of bustling travelers. As the car pulls away, I watch his silhouette grow smaller, finally disappearing from view. A warmth unfurls in my chest, a fragile yet thrilling notion that this trip might mark the beginning of something more.

At twenty-two, my life hasn't exactly been typical. Diagnosed with cardiomyopathy as a child, my heart has struggled for as long as I can remember. By the time I was ten, I couldn't keep up with my classmates. Running during recess felt impossible. Even walking up the stairs sometimes left me breathless.

The heart transplant at twelve was supposed to be my second chance. It saved my life, but the scars it left behind weren't just physical. Recovery was long and grueling, filled with medications, hospital stays, and the constant shadow of my overprotective family, who seemed to watch my every move. Dating, or even considering it, seemed like a foreign concept in a world where staying healthy felt like a full-time job.

But as I consider my appointment in the next few days, a check-up that might finally clear me to live a little more freely or start looking for a new heart, a flutter of hope stirs within me. If all goes well, could I dare to think about more than simply surviving? Could I dream of building something beyond the walls of caution that have kept me safe but lonely?

I unlock my phone and text my mom, letting her know I've arrived safely. The day ahead looms large, but for the first time in what feels like forever, I'm allowing myself to think of the future not just as a string of health milestones, but as a life filled with possibility. Now, I want more than just to be okay; I want to live.

As the Uber weaves through Charlotte's city streets, I stare out the window, my phone resting in my lap. Caleb's name is in my recent messages since I texted myself from his phone.

I think about tomorrow, our date, the easy way he makes me laugh, the way he seems to see me, not just as some fragile person who needs to be handled carefully, but as someone worth knowing. I don't think I've ever felt something like this.

And then I think about what comes next.

Charlotte is temporary. In a few days, I'll be back in Seattle, back to my routines, back to my life living with my parents and having my brothers hover over my every move. Caleb lives there, too. That thought lingers, curling around my mind like something warm and dangerous all at once.

Would seeing him again be possible? Could this—whatever this is—be something real?

I exhale, leaning my head back against the seat.

My family will have opinions, a lot of them. My mom will probably be happy, hopeful even, but my dad and brothers? That's a whole other thing.

My brothers, have spent most of my life acting like bodyguards rather than siblings. Always checking in, always watching me like I might break. Like if they let me out of their sight for too long, I'll disappear. They mean well, but sometimes their concern feels suffocating.

How would they feel about me dating? About me opening myself up to someone new?

I sigh. It doesn't matter yet.

Everything depends on my appointment. On what my medical team says. On whether or not my doctor thinks I'll be fine or if I leave with new worries weighing me down.

For now, all I can do is wait.

And maybe...just maybe, let myself look forward to tomorrow.

Chapter 5: A Piece of Emily

Caleb

The Uber ride to my buddy's house stretches out before me, the city's glow casting fleeting patterns across the window as we speed through the night. The engine's humming provides a backdrop to my thoughts, but they're anything but calm. Meeting Chloe had been a welcome distraction, an unexpected moment of brightness, but now my mind returns to why I'm really in Charlotte. The weight of it settles over me, heavy and inescapable.

I pull out my phone, scrolling through my contacts until I find the name: Dr. Monroe. For a moment, my thumb hovers above the screen. He isn't just a doctor; he's the one who handled everything when my sister, Emily, was on a ventilator. The man who walked my family through the organ donation process after the unimaginable happened.

The phone rings twice before he picks up.

"This is Dr. Monroe," he says, his voice calm and professional.

"Hey, Doc, it's Caleb," I say, steadying my voice. "I just made it. We're still on for Thursday morning?"

"Of course," he replies without hesitation. "Come by the hospital around ten."

"See you then, Doc." I hang up and let my phone drop into my lap, then stare out the window mesmerized as the city drifts by.

The lights flicker and stretch, but they can't distract me from the knot in my chest. I think about Emily; her laugh, the way she used to tease me about my inability to win a single board game against her.

The hospital room, sterile and suffocating, with its constant beeping and hum of machines. The decision that tore through my family like a storm. My mom had made the call to take Emily off the ventilator, a choice I couldn't reconcile with. I fought her, pleaded for more time, but the decision was final. And just like that, Emily was gone.

Even in my anger and grief, I remember how steady Dr. Monroe was, how he assured us that Emily's gift could save lives. And it did, five people, to be exact.

One of them will be in to see Dr Monroe this week. That's why I'm here, but I haven't decided whether to meet them. Dr. Monroe will facilitate the connection but tells me I don't have to. Meeting someone who carries a piece of Emily feels both comforting and overwhelming, like a doorway to closure I'm afraid to step through.

The car makes a sharp turn, pulling me out of my thoughts. The GPS voice announces we're close, and my chest tightens. I glance at my phone again, tempted to text Dr. Monroe and cancel. But I can't shake the thought of what Emily would've wanted. She was always the generous one, the one who saw the good in everyone, even when I couldn't.

As the city moves beyond the car windows, my focus is inward. The next few days hold a decision I'm not sure I'm ready to make. If I choose to meet the recipient, will I find peace? Or will it only reopen wounds I've tried so hard to heal? I don't know, but the question won't let me go.

Chapter 6: A Heart Reawakened

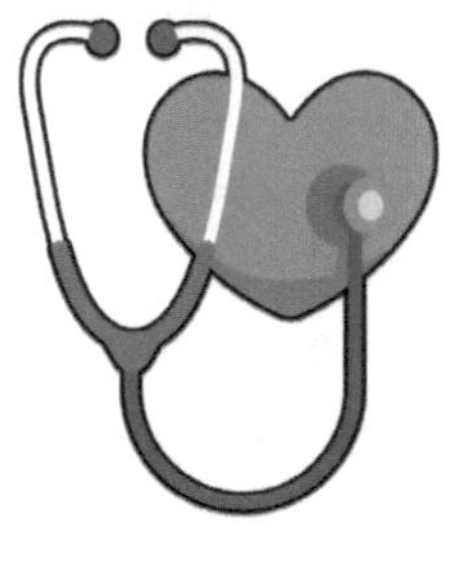

Chloe

I'm still in bed when my phone buzzes on the nightstand, the sharp vibration cutting through the quiet of my hotel room. I glance at the screen, my heart giving a slight, unexpected flutter when I see Caleb's name.

I hesitate for half a second before answering. "Good morning," I say, my voice still laced with sleep.

"Morning." Caleb's tone is warm and a little amused. "Did I wake you?"

I sit up against the pillows, rubbing my eyes. "No," I lie. "I was already up."

He chuckles, and I can hear the smile in his voice. "Sorry if I woke you. I wanted to let you know I made a dinner reservation. As promised, they've got sweet potato fries."

I smile, pulling my knees up to my chest. "Sweet potato fries automatically put you in the good decision-making category."

"Good," he says, then adds, "I should tell you though... it's Valentine's Day."

I sit up, the word settling between us. "Oh."

"Yeah. I didn't realize it at first, and most places were already full." He pauses. "But someone canceled, and the host made it work for us."

Something about that lands deeper than I expect. Not the reservation, not the fries, but the fact that he moved forward anyway, even knowing what the date carries. That he didn't treat it like something to avoid.

"That actually means a lot," I say quietly.

"I'm glad," he says. "I also got us tickets to the Mint Museum. Thought we could make an afternoon of it."

The way he says us makes my stomach flip. I lean my head against my knee, letting myself feel it. "That sounds perfect. Where should we meet?"

"In front of the museum," he says. "Noon?"

"Noon works for me. I'll see you then."

"Looking forward to it."

For a moment, neither of us hangs up. The silence stretches, comfortable in a way that surprises me.

Finally, he exhales. "Okay, I'll let you wake up now."

I laugh. "Thanks."

"See you soon, Chloe."

"See you soon, Caleb."

I end the call and stare at my phone for a moment, my fingers still curled around it.

Tickets to a museum. A walk around downtown Charlotte. And dinner, just Caleb and me. This sounds like a real date.

I bite my lip, trying to temper the growing excitement bubbling in my chest. But as I lay in bed, I know the truth. I'm already looking forward to it more than I probably should.

I stretch and roll out of bed, padding across the plush carpet of my hotel room. Sunlight spills through the sheer curtains, casting golden streaks across the crisp white sheets. My stomach growls, and I grab the room service menu from the nightstand, flipping through it absently as I settle back onto the bed.

A stack of pancakes sounds tempting, but since I'm having dinner with Caleb later, I decide on something light. I dial the number and order an omelet and fruit instead. As I wait, I grab my phone again, hesitating for just a second before hitting FaceTime on my mom's contact.

She answers on the second ring. "Chloe! Sweetheart, how are you feeling?"

Her face fills the screen, warm and familiar, framed by the soft waves of her light brown hair. She's sitting at the kitchen table with a mug of coffee in her hand.

"I'm good, Mom," I say, smiling. "I just woke up and figured I'd check in."

She narrows her eyes slightly. "You're not nervous about tomorrow, are you?"

I hesitate. "Maybe a little."

"It's understandable. Just don't forget to ask the doctor about your medication schedule." Her concern is etched between her brows. "I've read that some long-term heart transplant patients need adjustments after ten years."

"I've got it, Mom." I try to sound more confident than I feel. "I'll ask about the meds."

"And the scar tissue," she presses, leaning closer to the screen. "You read that article I sent you, right? Scar tissue around the heart can—"

"Mom," I interrupt gently, holding up a hand. "I'll ask about the scar tissue, I promise."

She sits back, but her expression doesn't ease. "And new treatments," she adds, the words tumbling out in a rush. "There's that post-transplant therapy they're testing. You need to ask if you're eligible."

I suppress a sigh. "Okay, medication, scar tissue, new therapies. Anything else?"

She pauses, and I brace for the flood. "Physical activity!" she exclaims. "Make sure he tells you what's safe. And find out about travel—can you travel more?

You've been wanting to see more places. And ask if your immunosuppressants—"

"Mom," I say, softer now. "I'll ask. All of it, I promise."

"Good," she says, her voice wobbling slightly. "I just want you to have all the answers, sweetheart. It's been ten years, but I still worry. We all do."

In the background, I hear Dad's deep voice, a soothing counter to her nerves. "Tell her we love her!"

For a second, we sit in comfortable silence, the familiar sounds of home filtering through the call, the faint clatter of dishes, the murmur of the morning news. Then, as if remembering something, Mom asks, "So, what are you up to today?"

I hesitate, but only for a second. "I'm going to check out a museum."

Her eyebrows lift slightly. "That's nice. Which one?"

"The Mint Museum. Figured I'd get a little culture in before my appointment."

She nods, then the concern creeps back into her voice. "Just be careful, okay? You know how your father and brothers worry."

I smile. "I know."

Right on cue, I hear a voice in the background, a deep and slightly exasperated. "Is that Chloe? Tell her not to wander off alone."

I roll my eyes. "Which one was that?"

"Ryan," Mom says, turning her head to answer him.

I laugh. "Tell Dad and the boys that I love them."

Mom shakes her head with an amused sigh. "You know Ryan hates it when you call him that."

"I know," I say, grinning. "That's why I do it."

She chuckles and takes another sip of her coffee. "It's good you're getting out, though. I was a little surprised when you mentioned sightseeing. You usually don't like going out on your own."

I shift slightly, hoping she doesn't notice the way I hesitate. "Yeah, well... figured I'd try something different this time."

Mom studies me for a moment, something thoughtful in her gaze. "Chloe, is there something you're not telling me?"

I force a casual shrug. "Nope."

But if I told her the whole truth, that I'm actually meeting someone, that I have a date—it wouldn't just be worry in her voice. It would be shock.

Because I don't date. I never have. Not really.

Ever since my surgery, my family has watched over me like I might break at any moment. And maybe, for a while, I let them. I never gave them a reason to think otherwise, never showed interest in anyone, or let anyone get close enough to even try. Not because I didn't want to, but because it always felt... complicated. Like something I wasn't ready for.

And yet, here I am, about to spend the day with Caleb.

If my brothers knew, they'd probably be on the next flight to Charlotte, demanding to know who this guy is and what his intentions are.

I shake off the thought and force a small laugh. "Relax, Mom. I'm just taking in the sights. I'll be fine."

She sighs, clearly not convinced but knowing better than to push. "Just be careful, okay?"

"I will," I promise.

We say our goodbyes, and as the call ends, a knock sounds at the door. Time to eat.

As I sit down to eat, I let my mind drift back to Caleb. To the day ahead.

Chapter 7: Artful Connections

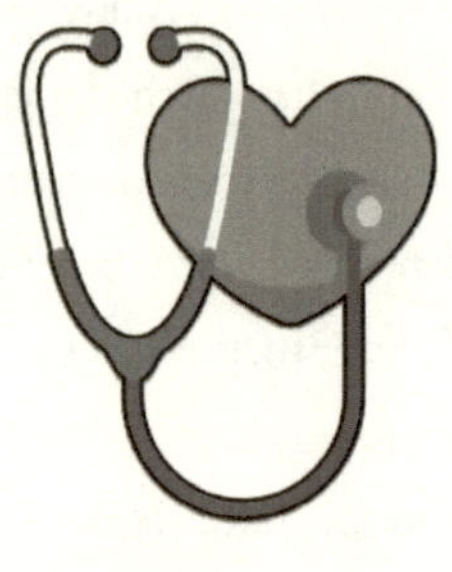

Caleb

I spot Chloe before she sees me, standing near the entrance of the Mint Museum with her back to me, studying the banners above the doors. The cool morning light catches in her golden blond hair, the loose strands lifting slightly in the breeze, and for a moment I just watch her, surprised by how familiar she already feels.

When I booked our tickets, I read that the museum, housed in a sleek, modern building in the heart of Charlotte, is known for its impressive collection of American, contemporary, and European art.

Then, as if sensing me, she turns. A slow smile spreads across her face, and damn if it doesn't make something tighten in my chest.

"Hey," she says.

"Hey. Ready for some culture?"

She grins. "Absolutely. Impress me with your deep artistic insights."

I chuckle. "I make no such promises."

We head inside, moving through the grand, open atrium before making our way to the galleries. The first exhibit we walk into is full of abstract paintings with bold colors, sharp angles, and layers of texture that seem to mean everything and nothing at the same time.

Chloe tilts her head as she studies a particularly chaotic piece. "This one reminds me of my classroom after an art project. Just... pure disaster."

I smirk. "That bad, huh?"

"Oh, you have no idea. Glitter stays in the air for weeks."

We move through different exhibits, stopping every so often when something catches her eye. Chloe points out pieces she loves, sharing what she'd tell her students about them.

"This one would be great for a lesson on colors and emotions," she says, gesturing to a painting that looks like a sunset melting into the ocean. "I'd ask my class what feelings it reminds them of; happiness, sadness, nostalgia. It's amazing how much kids pick up on."

I watch her as she talks, the way her eyes light up, the way she gestures when she gets excited. It's easy to see how much she loves what she does.

She steps closer to the next painting, her fingers hovering just above the canvas as if she can feel the brushstrokes without touching them. "You're really good at this." I follow her gaze, trying to see the artwork through her eyes.

Her lips curve into a soft smile, her focus never leaving the painting. She tilts her head, examining the vibrant colors that swirl together. Without looking at me, she moves to the next piece, her movements graceful, effortless. I fall into step beside her, the faint scent of her perfume lingering as we weave through the gallery.

She glances at me. "At what?"

"At seeing things. At making connections."

She pauses, her fingers brushing her chin as she considers another painting. "It's all about the emotion." She speaking more to herself than to me. "If you can feel it, then the artist did their job."

I'm captivated by the way she absorbs each piece. She's not just looking, she's experiencing it.

She glances at me, her eyes bright with excitement. "Come on, there's more in the next room." She's already moving, a lightness to her step as she leads the way.

I follow without hesitation, my heart thudding as I realize I'd follow her just about anywhere.

By the time we leave the museum, the fading afternoon light stretches across the sidewalk, casting long shadows that trail at our feet. The air is cool now, crisp against my skin, carrying the muted smells of pavement and distant traffic. The sky shifts through soft grays and pale golds, the first stars appearing sooner than they should, tucked into the early evening.

My stomach growls, and I realize just how long it's been since lunch. I glance at Chloe, who's still buzzing from the last exhibit, her eyes sparkling as she recounts her favorite pieces.

"I hope you're hungry," I say as we stroll down the sidewalk, weaving through the early evening crowd. "Because I'm about to make sure neither of us eats for the rest of the day."

Chloe laughs. "Sounds like a challenge."

The air is cool but manageable, the kind that makes the walk feel good instead of rushed, so we head to Church and Union on foot. Inside, the space opens up around us. High ceilings, warm wood floors, and a long marble bar anchor the room, while modern chandeliers and sweeping floral installations hang overhead. Everywhere I look, there are subtle reminders of the date. Couples leaning closer in their booths, candles glowing a little softer, the low hum of the room edged with intention. Valentine's Day, present but not loud about it.

It's busy but not overwhelming, and we manage to snag a table near the windows. The soft interior light settles between us, warming the space in a way the evening air outside never quite could. I catch her watching the room, taking it all in, and something about sharing this night, of all nights, feels deliberate in the best possible way.

The second we sit down, Chloe raises an eyebrow at me. "So, what's the over-the-top order you're planning?"

I grin, leaning back in my chair as I flip open the menu. "It's going to start with a big basket of sweet potato fries, obviously."

She grins, her eyes dancing with amusement. "Obviously."

I signal the waiter, who arrives with a friendly smile. "We'll start with the sweet potato fries," I say confidently, then glance at Chloe. "And two iced teas, please."

The waiter jots down our order before looking at us expectantly. "Anything else to start?"

Chloe glances at the menu, her lips pursing in thought. "You know what? Let's add the crispy Brussels sprouts."

I nod, impressed. "Good call."

When the appetizers arrive, the sweet potato fries are piled high, golden and perfectly crisp, with a side of cinnamon-sugar dip that smells like heaven. The Brussels sprouts are charred just right, tossed in a balsamic glaze that makes my mouth water.

We waste no time digging in, each fry a burst of sweet and salty perfection. Chloe's eyes widen as she dips a fry into the sauce. "Oh my God," she says around a mouthful, her eyes rolling back in exaggerated bliss. "These are dangerous."

She continues between bites. "So, where exactly do you live in Seattle?"

"Montlake," I answer, grabbing another fry. "You?"

"North Queen Anne."

I pause mid-chew. "Wait. Seriously?"

She nods.

I pull out my phone and open the maps app. "You realize we're, like, fifteen minutes from each other, right?"

Chloe leans in to get a better look, her shoulder brushing mine as she peers at the screen. "Really?"

Her closeness sends a jolt through me, but I keep my focus on the map. "Yeah. I thought for sure you'd be on the other side of the city."

She tilts her head, studying the screen. "That's... weirdly convenient."

I chuckle. "I'm starting to think fate's trying to tell us something."

Chloe leans back, considering. "Or maybe it's just a small world."

I chuckle, setting my phone down. "Small enough that running into each other again wouldn't be impossible."

She picks up a fry, twirling it between her fingers. "Maybe not impossible," she agrees, her tone thoughtful.

Something about the way she says it makes me glance at her again, watching as she takes a slow bite, her gaze flickering to mine before she looks down.

The thought lingers between us, unspoken but undeniable.

Fifteen minutes apart.

Close enough that when we get back, this doesn't have to end.

Chapter 8: A Hope for More

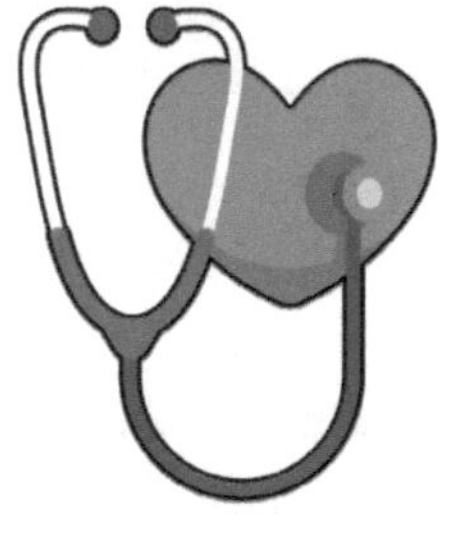

Chloe

We step outside the restaurant, the sky dark now, brushed with the last traces of fading light. City lights glow along the street, reflections catching on windows and passing cars. The air is cool, sharp enough to make me tuck my hands closer to myself, but not uncomfortable. The kind of cold that feels awake, like the night still has something to offer. My Uber is already on the way, but I almost wish it wasn't.

Caleb steps out beside me, hands tucked into his pockets, his breath faint in the cool air. Inside, the restaurant hums on without us, but out here everything slows. We've spent the day talking, wandering through art, and slowly getting to know each other. Now, standing just outside the door, there's a pause that lingers between us, like neither of us is quite ready to be the first to walk away.

I stare up at him. "When do you head back home?"

"A few more days," he says. "I'm catching up with some old high school friends while I'm here. Mostly an excuse to eat barbecue at our old hang-out and pretend we haven't all grown up."

I smile. "Sounds fun."

"What about you?" he asks, turning toward me.

"I leave in two days. I'm visiting a family friend tomorrow, then flying back the next morning."

He nods, rocking back on his heels. "So... when we're both back in Seattle, do you think—" He pauses, like he's considering his words. "Would you want to see each other again?"

The question is casual, but there's something behind it, something that makes my heart beat a little faster.

For the first time in my life, I let myself admit that I want more. That I'm not just open to the possibility of something real, I'm hoping for it.

"I'd like that," I say, my voice softer now. "Yeah."

He lets out a slow breath. "Good," he says. Then, quieter, "I'll text you when I get back to Seattle."

Just then, my phone buzzes with a notification. Your Uber has arrived.

I exhale, glancing at the car pulling up to the curb. "That's me."

Before I can move, Caleb steps closer, his hand grazing my arm as he leans in. My breath catches, and then—soft, warm—he presses a kiss to my cheek. It's brief, a few seconds, but it leaves my skin tingling and my heart racing.

As he pulls back, our eyes meet, and I know he felt it too.

"Have a safe flight, Chloe," he says.

I hesitate for just a second. "You too, Caleb."

And as I slide into the car and it pulls away, I already know one thing for sure.

This isn't over, I don't want it to be.

As the city moves past in a blur, I barely see it. My fingers rest lightly against my cheek, the spot where Caleb kissed me. It's still warm, still buzzing with something I don't fully understand.

I close my eyes for a moment, replaying the way he leaned in, the way his touch sent a slow, sweet ache through me. It wasn't just the kiss—it was the way he looked at me after, like he felt it too.

I exhale, shaking my head as I drop my hand back into my lap.

I like him. That much is undeniable. I like the way he listens, the way he teases, the way he sees things. And the attraction? That's been there from the start, from the moment he noticed how terrified I was during takeoff.

I can still hear his voice, calm, steady, pulling me out of my fear, distracting me just enough to keep me from spiraling. But now, after today, after hours of easy conversation and shared laughter, it feels like more than just enjoying his company. It feels like he's starting to matter.

And that scares me.

Because how is this supposed to work?

I've spent so long keeping people at arm's length, avoiding anything that might turn into something real. It's not that I didn't want to date; I just never wanted to deal with the inevitable moment when I'd have to tell someone the truth about me.

Would Caleb see me differently if he knew? If he knew about the scar running down my chest, the medications I have to take every single day, the doctor's appointments I can't miss? Would he pull back, like so many others have, afraid of what being with me really means? Would he see the expiration date stamped on my heart and decide it's not worth the risk?

Or worse. Would he see me as something fragile, something breakable?

My family does.

I swallow hard, pushing the thought away, determined to hold on to this moment just a little longer. Even if our time is short, right now, it feels limitless.

I press my lips together, staring out the window as the Uber navigates through the city. I know my parents and brothers love me, that they only worry because they almost lost me. But their concern has always felt like a cage, one built out of love but confining all the same.

I don't want that with Caleb.

I can't have that with him.

But I don't know if I can have nothing either. Not when my heart is still racing from the way he looked at me, from the way I still feel that kiss long after it happened.

I close my eyes, leaning my head back against the seat.

Maybe it doesn't have to be complicated yet. Maybe I don't have to think about all of this tonight.

The problem is, I know I will.

Chapter 9: Heartstrings

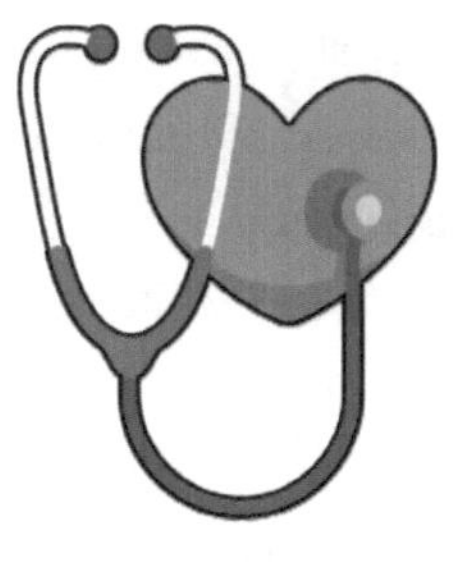

Caleb

The morning of my meeting with Dr. Monroe is finally here. I sit in the sterile, white room, my fists clenched in my lap. The Charlotte skyline sprawls into the distance through the large windows behind Dr. Monroe.

Dr. Monroe leans back slightly in his chair, his expression calm and attentive. His presence feels steady, just as I remember it from years ago when every decision felt like a battle against fate.

"How are you doing?" he asks, his voice gentle yet probing. "And how's your mom holding up?"

I exhale, glancing again at the cityscape before answering. "She's doing great, all things considered. She's staying busy. After she retired, she started volunteering at a women's shelter, which gives her purpose. And she's found a good church community. It's been great for her."

Dr. Monroe smiles warmly. "I'm glad to hear that. She's always been strong."

"Yeah." A smile tugs at my lips, thinking of my mother. "Helping others has helped her cope."

Dr. Monroe nods knowingly. "It's a beautiful way to channel strength. And how about you? How are you holding up?"

I move my hands, flexing my fingers against the chair's armrest. "I'm managing," I admit after a pause. "It's been a long road. I'm still trying to make sense of it all."

He leans forward, resting his elbows on the desk. "Meeting the recipient of Emily's heart can be a powerful part of healing. It reminds us there's meaning in loss. Your sister's death wasn't meaningless."

I nod, my jaw tightening. "I know. That's why I'm here. But it's a lot. They are walking around with Emily's heart. Emily isn't. I don't know if I'm ready for that."

Dr. Monroe leans back again, understanding in his expression. "It's normal to feel that way. This isn't easy. But most families find that meeting the recipient brings peace."

I let out a sharp breath. "I'm here, so I'll do it. I owe it to Emily."

Dr. Monroe nods approvingly, glancing at a file. "The recipient will be here today for routine tests. She's been doing remarkably well with the transplant, even after 10 years. If she's comfortable meeting you, we'll set a time."

I swallow hard, my gaze darting back to the window. "What if she says no?"

Our eyes connect. His show compassion. "Then we respect her decision. But I don't think that will be the case. Most recipients are deeply moved by the chance to meet their donor's family members."

I exhale shakily and lean back. "Okay."

"I'll let you know her answer."

The words hang in the air and my heart pounds. The girl with Emily's heart will be in the same room that I'm in. The thought overwhelms me, but I feel like I'm stepping forward and moving on for the first time in years.

Dr. Monroe stands, his voice steady as he says, "I should have her answer by the end of the day."

I nod, standing, and follow him to the door. As we step into the waiting room, the cool air feels harsh against my skin, pulling me out of my thoughts. My gaze drifts, and then I see her.

It's Chloe.

She's sitting by the window, flipping through a magazine. Sunlight hits her hair, and I almost think I'm imagining her. But then she looks up, her green eyes meeting mine, and recognition flashes on her face.

"Caleb?" Her familiar voice holds uncertainty.

"Chloe?" My voice cracks. "What are you doing here?"

Before she can answer, Dr. Monroe's curiosity interrupts. "You two know each other?"

I glance at him, then back at Chloe. "We just met on the flight to Charlotte."

Dr. Monroe raises an eyebrow and nods, looking thoughtful. "Well, I suppose the world is smaller than we think." Then he turns to Chloe. "I didn't realize you were already here. I'll call you in shortly." My stomach drops, wondering why Chloe is here.

She smiles politely at Dr. Monroe, then looks back at me. There's uncertainty in her expression, and it makes a knot tighten in my chest.

Dr. Monroe gestures for me to follow him out to the hallway. "Caleb, I'll reach out later today, okay?" he says, shaking my hand.

I nod. Is Chloe Dr. Monroe's patient? I want to ask so many questions, but my feet feel rooted in place. He turns and walks back to meet with Chloe in the room where she's waiting.

Chapter 10: The Weight of a Heartbeat

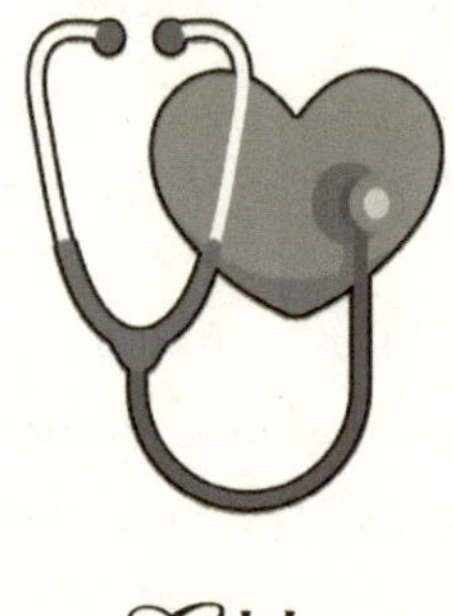

Chloe

As I wait for Dr. Monroe to call me back to his office. I think of Caleb's eyes, the way they seemed to be searching for something. Curiosity? Realization? He followed Dr Monroe, walking past me. My pulse races. Is he a patient here too? What are the odds?

"Chloe, come in," Dr. Monroe calls gently. I follow him to his office, shutting the door behind me, and sit across from him.

Dr. Monroe folds his hands on the desk and leans forward slightly. "So, you know Caleb?"

I nod, gripping the arms of my chair. "Yeah, we just met..."

He exhales. "Under normal circumstances, I would wait until the end of your appointment to bring this up, but the fact that you two have already met makes this situation a bit different." His voice softens. "So let's just talk about it now. Caleb is the brother of your heart donor."

My stomach drops. Her heart pounds in my chest, its rhythm steady but now impossible to ignore. "Her… brother?" I repeat, my voice barely audible.

Dr. Monroe nods. "He reached out to me a few months ago, hoping to meet one of his sister's organ recipients. Legally, I can't share your identity or any details without your explicit permission." He pauses. "Knowing your appointment was today, I invited him in case you wanted the opportunity to meet him. As things stand now, you still have the power to decide whether you'll share that you're a recipient."

I sit frozen, my hands trembling in my lap. Caleb doesn't know. Of course, he doesn't.

"I want to tell him," I say finally, my voice shaky but resolute. "I think… he deserves to know." My heart races. Not with fear, but with something more complicated. "Can you arrange for him to come back? Maybe after all my tests are done? We can tell him together?"

Dr. Monroe nods. "Sure, I'll have the nurse contact Caleb and ask him to return around 4:00 PM. That should give us plenty of time to complete all the tests."

I return the nod, but my relief is fleeting, quickly swallowed by a storm of anxiety. How will Caleb feel when he hears the truth? He'd seemed excited during our date and about connecting in Seatlle, but will he still want to after learning I have his sister's heart?

My thoughts spiral. Will he even want to be friends with me? Was the connection I felt between us real, or was it just fate's way of connecting him with a piece of his sister?

I press a hand against my chest, over her heart, and try to focus on the steady rhythm. I'm not just carrying her heart, now I'm carrying everything that comes with it.

Chapter 11: Crossroads

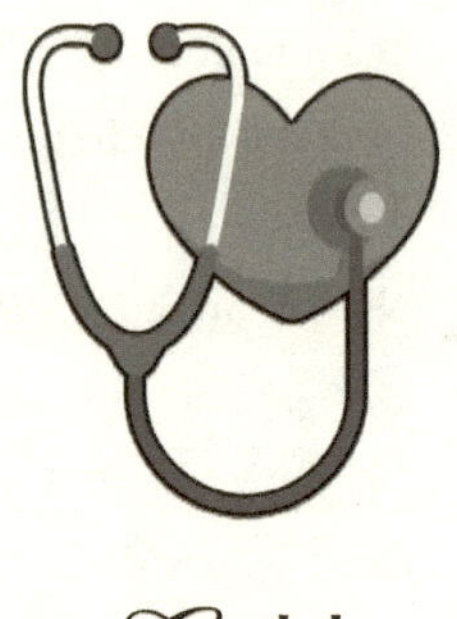

Caleb

It's 1:15 in the afternoon when my phone buzzes. I glance at the screen and see it's Dr. Monroe's office. My stomach tightens. I'm sure it's Dr. Monroe letting me know if the recipient of Emily's heart might be willing to meet me. I swipe to answer, bracing myself.

I push thoughts of Chloe out of my mind, forcing myself to focus on the reason I came here: closure for the loss of my sister. I owe it to Emily to see this through, no matter how much my heart is tangled up somewhere else.

"Mr. Williams? I'm calling from Dr. Monroe's office," the voice says.

"This is he."

"Can you come in at 4:00 p.m. today?"

"Uh, yeah, I can." I try to keep my voice steady. "Is this about—"

"I'm sorry, I don't have any details," she cuts in quickly. "Dr. Monroe will speak with you then. Have a good day."

The call disconnects before I can push further. I stare at the phone, feeling a mix of anticipation and frustration. Why couldn't the nurse say more? I'm sure it's about the heart recipient. But Dr. Monroe has made it clear that he can't reveal anything unless the recipient agrees. No names, no details, nothing that could lead me to them.

I let out a slow breath, trying to ground myself, trying to remember why I started this journey in the first place. Closure. For Emily. For me. But right now, all I have are more questions.

I shove my phone back into my pocket, leaning back. My thoughts drift, unbidden, to Chloe. The woman who's been occupying my mind since our date yesterday.

I shake my head. Focus, Caleb.

I pull up my mom's number, deciding she might help clear my mind. After two rings, her familiar voice answers, cheerful as ever. "Hi, honey! How are you?"

"Hey, Mom. I'm good,"

"I was just about to call you. How's Charlotte treating you?"

"Same as always," I say. "Listen, I wanted to talk to you about something. You know Dr. Monroe reached out to the recipient of Emily's heart."

There's a pause on the line. "Yes. Did you hear back?"

"I'll learn more at 4pm. He asked me to come back but didn't say why." I admit.

There's a soft hum on the other end of the line before she responds. "How are you feeling about it?"

I rub the back of my neck. "I don't know. Nervous, I guess. I keep thinking about what it'll be like to meet her, to know a piece of Emily is still alive in someone else."

"It's a big decision, Caleb," Mom says gently. "But it might bring you some peace."

"You sound like Dr Monroe."

There's a pause, and then she says, "Because he's right. When I went to Charlotte a few years after we lost Emily, I met the recipient of her kidneys."

I blink in surprise. "You did?"

"Yes. He's a young man, about your age. We've kept in touch over the years. It's been comforting to see him live his life, knowing that Emily's gift made that possible."

"Why didn't you tell me?" I ask, a hint of hurt creeping into my voice.

She sighs. "Because I knew how you felt about the decision to donate Emily's organs. You were so angry back then, Caleb. I didn't want to reopen that wound. You needed time to grieve and heal in your own way."

I sit on the bed, her words sinking in. "I've been thinking about that a lot lately. About how wrong I was to fight you on it."

"You were grieving," she says softly. "We all were. But now that you're considering meeting the heart recipient, I think it's a sign you're ready to find peace with it. To see the good that came from such a terrible loss."

I nod, even though she can't see me. "Maybe you're right." The words feel foreign in my mouth. "I just... I don't know what to expect if I meet her."

She doesn't rush to fill the silence. Instead, she lets me sit with it, just like she always does. Finally, she says, "Whatever happens, Caleb, remember: This is your choice. Meeting them doesn't have to be about closure; it can just be about connection. That's what it was for me."

"Thanks, Mom," I say, meaning it.

We talk for a while longer about her garden, my job, and the little things that ground us. But when I hang up, my mind is still spinning. The clock on the wall says 3:30. Time to head to Dr. Monroe's office. As I wait for my rideshare, my thoughts wander beyond just the heart recipient.

I think about Chloe.

She was at Dr. Monroe's office this morning, sitting in the same waiting room where I'd been sitting earlier. Her face is clear in my mind, her soft green eyes that seemed to carry both curiosity and a hint of worry, her blond hair pulled into a loose braid and just a hint of makeup that made her look effortlessly natural.

Why was she there? The interaction was so quick, almost like Dr. Monroe was rushing me out. And now I can't help but wonder if I'll have the opportunity to ask him about her visit to his office. The thought gnaws at me, equal parts curiosity and concern.

As the Uber drives me to the hospital, the question of meeting the heart recipient looms large. The car rolls to a stop outside the building. After thanking the driver and stepping out of the car, I take a deep breath and steady myself. Whatever this meeting is about, Emily's heart or Chloe, something tells me it will change things.

Chapter 12: Heartbeat of Truth

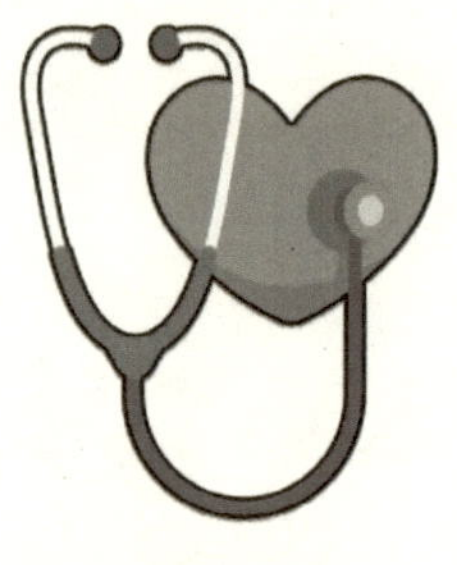

Chloe

By 3:30, I finally complete all the tests. The poking, prodding, and relentless questions exhaust me, but I know it's necessary. Dr. Monroe had warned it would be a long day, and he wasn't exaggerating. Back in his office, I sit across from him, waiting for the verdict.

Dr. Monroe leans forward, his expression warm. "Chloe, I'm happy to say everything looks great. Your heart is strong, and as long as you maintain your health regimen with exercise, medication, regular checkups, I think you can expect a normal, healthy life."

Relief rushes through me so completely I almost laugh. My shoulders fall, and I melt into the chair, all my worry disappearing in light of the news. "That's wonderful. Thank you."

"There are still a few pending results," he adds, "but so far, it's all positive. You've done an excellent job taking care of yourself."

I nod once more, the pressure easing from my chest. "That means everything. I can't wait to tell my family. Thank you."

Dr. Monroe's tone shifts, casual yet curious. "You mentioned earlier you and Caleb just met?" I nod. "How did you meet, if you don't mind sharing?" Dr. Monroe would ask.

"On the flight here," I say lightly. "It was a coincidence. We ended up sitting next to each other and got to talking."

Dr. Monroe raises an eyebrow but lets me continue.

"During a layover in Denver, we grabbed lunch. He was so kind. He helped calm my anxiety during takeoff, actually. I thought my nerves would ruin my test results." I don't share much more.

Dr. Monroe nods thoughtfully. "Did he mention why he was here?"

I shake my head. "No, and I didn't share why I was in Charlotte either."

Dr. Monroe studies me, then says gently, "You're in control, Chloe. Share as much or as little about your health as you feel comfortable. My role is to facilitate the introduction."

My fingers twiddle nervously. "I appreciate that. I've been thinking a lot about what to say."

"It's understandable. Meeting someone in this situation stirs emotions. For you both to meet by chance adds complexity, it brings up questions neither of you might be prepared to face. You're not just strangers; you share a history without ever having met. That kind of connection can be overwhelming

I nod, my thoughts spinning. I don't tell him about my fear, our date, how much I like Caleb, our plans to see each other again when we get home, or my terror that everything will change when he learns I carry his sister's heart. Instead, I manage a small smile. "Thank you."

He smiles kindly and stands to escort me to the next meeting. "Let's go meet Caleb. Remember, I'm here for support."

Chapter 13: The Changing Beat

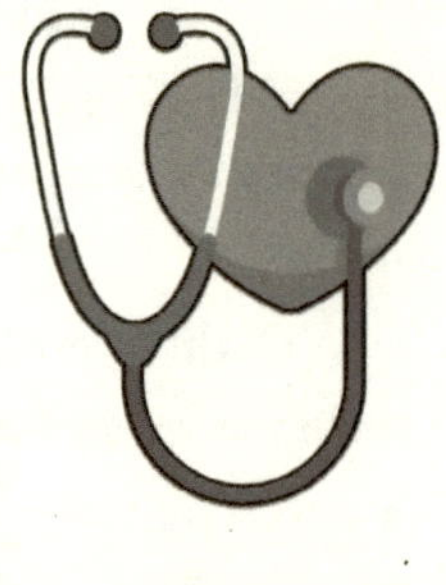

Caleb

I check in with Dr. Monroe's receptionist, who directs me to a small meeting room. Sitting there, my hands tremble uncontrollably, and I clasp them together, trying to contain the movement. My whole body feels like it's vibrating and my heart thuds loudly. The room feels smaller with each breath, the walls closing in as the gravity of what's about to happen settles over me

What am I doing?

Why did I agree to meet this girl?

My stomach churns, my palms sweat, and I almost want to bolt for the door. To distract myself, I stare out the window. Cars glide by below, their headlights slicing through the dusk. The skyline stretches in the distance, bathed in the warm hues of a setting sun, but even that serene backdrop can't ease the tension clawing at me.

The door clicks open behind me, and I turn, expecting Dr. Monroe. He steps in, but it's the person behind him that makes my stomach drop.

Chloe.

My mind races, trying to process what I'm seeing. What is she doing here?

Did Dr. Monroe want her to talk to me before the meeting with the recipient?

My throat goes dry as she steps inside, avoiding my gaze. She looks different now, not like the confident, playful woman I spent the day with yesterday, but hesitant, almost vulnerable.

I shift in my seat, trying to piece together what's happening. Then Dr. Monroe clears his throat, his expression gentle but serious, like he's preparing to tell me something life-altering.

"Caleb," he says, "the recipient of your sister Emily's heart is Chloe."

The words hang in the air, heavy and unreal, refusing to sink in.

Chloe.

The woman I met by chance on a flight. The woman I had lunch with in Denver. The woman I spent the entire day with yesterday. The woman I haven't been able to stop thinking about.

And now this.

She carries Emily's heart.

My sister's heart beats in her chest.

I look at Chloe again. Her eyes remain lowered, her fingers fidgeting restlessly at her sides. A wave of emotions surges through me: shock, disbelief, even anger, though I can't pinpoint the reason. And beneath it all, a sense of connection I can't explain but can't ignore.

I sit there, the shock crashing over me in waves.

This was the same Chloe I'd met by pure chance, the woman I'd been looking forward to seeing again.

My voice comes out rough, barely controlled. "Did you know?" I ask, turning to Chloe. "Did you know it was my sister's heart you received? That it was Emily's?"

Finally, Chloe looks up at me, her eyes wide and uncertain. Her lips press together before she takes a breath, steadying herself. "I didn't know when we met," she says softly. "But Dr. Monroe told me earlier today."

I stare at her, trying to absorb her words. Earlier today. She's known for hours.

My chest tightens, and I shift my gaze to Dr. Monroe. "Why?" I demand, the edge in my voice unmistakable. "Why did you wait all day to tell me?"

Dr. Monroe folds his hands, his expression calm but serious. "Caleb, when I learned about your chance meeting, I needed to confirm with Chloe first. She still had to decide if she wanted you to know. This is a deeply personal matter, and I couldn't take that choice from her."

I glance back at Chloe. Her face is flushed, her hands resting on her legs, visibly shaking.

Dr. Monroe continues, his tone measured. "The fact that you two had already met made this unusual. It's not every day that someone crosses paths with the donor's family without realizing the connection they share. I wanted to approach this with care for both of you."

I shake my head, running a hand through my hair as I try to make sense of it all. Complicated doesn't even begin to cover it.

I sit across from Chloe, the weight of the revelation pressing down on me like an unyielding tide. I notice the tremor in her fingers. My mind is a cacophony of emotions; grief, confusion, anger, but above it all, one truth echoes louder than the rest: a piece of Emily lives on inside her.

This woman, who I've felt drawn to from the moment we met, carries a part of my sister. The connection is no longer just chance; it's something deeper, something I can't ignore.

"I don't know what to say," her voice barely above a whisper. Chloe's eyes glisten with unshed tears as she looks up at me.

"It's... overwhelming," I admit, struggling to find the right words.

She nods, her voice trembling. "When Dr. Monroe told me, it felt like the air was sucked out of the room. I didn't know how to face you... what to say."

We sit in silence for a moment, the air between us heavy with unspoken words. Finally, I ask, "How do you feel about this? About... us?"

Chloe hesitates, her teeth catching her bottom lip. "I don't know," she admits. "But what I do know is that meeting you didn't feel random. I felt it the first time we talked on the plane. Like there was this... pull. Like you understood me in a way no one else ever has. And now, knowing why—" Her voice catches, and she shakes her head. "It's overwhelming, but it also feels... right. Does that make sense?"

I nod, my throat tightening. It makes too much sense, and that's what scares me. "I feel it too," I admit. "But I'm scared, Chloe. I'm scared that this connection—Emily's heart—it's too much. That it'll be a shadow over everything."

She reaches out then, her hand tentative as it touches mine. "It doesn't have to be," she says, her voice steady now. "Emily's heart brought us here, but what happens next is up to us. We don't have to know what it all means right now. We can take it one day at a time."

Her words ground me, and for the first time since the revelation, I feel a sliver of clarity. Maybe she's right. Maybe we don't have to have all the answers today.

What matters is that Emily's heart isn't just a source of grief anymore. It's alive. It's beating. And it brought Chloe into my life.

I squeeze her hand, a small smile tugging at my lips. "One day at a time," I agree.

Her smile mirrors mine, tentative, but real. "I think that's all we can do."

Dr. Monroe observes us, a subtle relief evident in his expression. "I'm pleased to see how you're handling this," he says, his tone thoughtful. "I'll be honest, I wasn't certain how this conversation would unfold. But it's clear that the bond between you two is stronger than I anticipated. It's commendable that you're both choosing to navigate this together, despite the complexity of the situation."

Chloe and I stand, both turning to him. "Thank you," she says softly. I nod in agreement.

Dr. Monroe gives us a small, knowing smile. "Take care of yourselves."

As we step outside, the afternoon breeze brushes against my face, calm and steady, anchoring me in the present. For the first time in years, I don't feel like I'm carrying the weight of the past. The grief is still there, it always will be, but it no longer crushes me like it used to.

Emily is gone, and nothing will ever change that. But her life, her love, and even her loss have shaped me into the man I am now. I used to think that moving forward meant letting go, but I see it differently now. Moving forward means carrying her with me, not as a burden, but as a part of me that still matters.

Chloe, too, has changed me in a short amount of time. She doesn't even realize it, but the way she sees me has given me something I didn't know I needed, a reason to live, not just exist. A reason to hope for love, real love, and the possibility of forever.

I squeeze her hand, feeling her fingers tighten around mine. She looks up at me with her soft, steady green eyes, and for the first time in a long time, I don't feel lost. I know exactly where I'm supposed to be.

"Ready?" she asks, her voice light yet full of meaning.

I look at her... really look at her.

"Yeah," I respond, breathing in the moment. "I am."

And for the first time in a long time, I actually mean it.

About Lexi Aidyn

Lexi Aidyn is a sweet romance author who writes from the heart, shaped by more than 30 years of love, marriage, motherhood, and a deep belief that second chances can be just as meaningful as first ones. By day, she is a creative director; by night, she is a storyteller drawn to quiet moments, emotional connection, and love that feels real. Her stories feature relatable, resilient characters finding their way to happily-ever-afters that feel honest, comforting, and earned.

Connect:

- Website: https://www.lexiaidyn.com/
- Amazon.com/author/lexiaidyn
- Facebook.com/lexyaidyn
- Instagram.com/author_lexi_aidyn

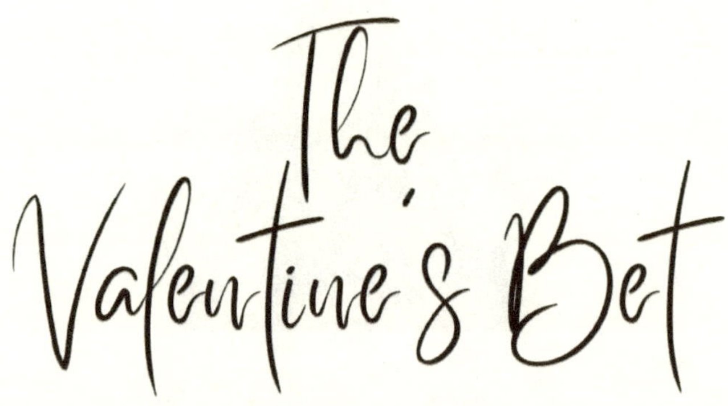

by R.K. Fultz

Chapter 1

Scarlett

I can't believe I have to do this ridiculous dare because of my sister. In my defense, she caught me after a long shift at the hospital and pounced while I wasn't thinking clearly. Amanda is way too excited, sitting in an overstuffed chair with her feet propped up on an ottoman outside my dressing room door.

I raise my voice so she can hear me through the door as I try on another one of her outfit choices. "Why are you holding me to this? You know you took full advantage of me."

It takes her maybe a nanosecond to start laughing. I know that laugh from years of her getting me into situations exactly like this.

The typical roles of an older sibling and a younger sibling are reversed in our case. She's five years older, but certainly not the wiser. Amanda is spontaneous, lives for the unexpected, and takes pure joy in being the ringleader. Her husband, Danny, is a saint and tolerant of her abundance of plans and spur-of-the-moment ideas. I love him, but don't quite understand how he hasn't grown tired of her minute-by-minute nature.

We have totally different styles, and even though I'm way out of my element with this whole bet, watching her sitting outside the dressing room with her feet up and hands gently rubbing her pregnant belly, spurs me along. The entire family is excited that in less than two months, she will give birth to my first nephew. Amanda has always been pretty, but she's currently glowing, and I can't help but be a bit jealous. She deserves happiness, and I hope I can find it someday, too.

"Letty," she calls to me, "you are going to have a fantastic time and potentially meet the man of your dreams."

"I seriously doubt a blind date photo shoot is going to land me the man of my dreams." My sigh is extra loud for her benefit, but it doesn't affect her in any way if her giggling is any indication.

There is zero chance she is letting me out of the dare. It seems Amanda promised her friend Madelyn that I would be part of her first pairing for a Valentine-themed blind date photo shoot. Her business has been doing well since she started a few months ago. The idea of a blind photo shoot is a newer concept, and she hopes it will be a hit in our town. I am happy for her, but I hate the fact that my sister volunteered me to be the first. My dad started the whole family dare idea years ago. He is a huge basketball fan and would have Amanda and me predict the scores of the local games. It had always been a fun family wager, and Amanda has carried on the tradition, except she doesn't always make the wagers fun. They are more embarrassing, at least it seems that way when I lose.

"It's been two years since you and Justin broke up, and you haven't had a single date. I'm tired of watching you build your emotional wall, layer by layer. You're a phenomenal woman, and I know any guy would be lucky to date you. But it's hard to meet anyone if you never go out."

"That's not fair. I go out," I protest. But it's true because I've sworn off men since my ex-fiancée cheated.

"Yeah, right. Going to work and Sunday dinner with Mom and Dad doesn't exactly put you at the top of the list for eligibility."

It's annoying to feel like the family project. My heart was shattered last year after I found out Justin had been cheating with his co-worker. We met in college and were pretty much inseparable. We were both busy starting our careers after college and spent long hours apart. I have a small apartment in the city near the hospital where I work, and he rents a small two-bedroom house twenty minutes outside the city. I thought we were happy, and I was caught off guard when he announced he had fallen in love with another woman.

Amanda chattered on. "I've got a good feeling about this photoshoot, and Madelyn says she has a perfect match picked out for you."

My head whips in the direction of her voice. "How does Madelynn know what kind of guy would be a perfect match for me?" I open the door to stare at my sister, waiting for her explanation.

"I helped with some specific details to pick the right guy, and I watched out for red flags. The cool thing is it's a Valentine-themed photoshoot and you know I'm a sucker for romance." Amanda stands up and pulls a red dress off the rack of clothes the salesperson rolled into the dressing area for me to try on. She pushes it into my hands and turns me back toward the door of the dressing room. "I love the color red on you. This dress will look adorable with some authentic cowboy boots. The boots will be perfect since the photoshoot is at her family's farm."

Amanda should do the photoshoot. She's way too excited about dressing me up. My usual attire is scrubs for work and comfy clothes when I get home. I close the door of the dressing room and hang up the dress Amanda handed me. It's stunning, and as I run my fingers across the delicate fabric, my stomach flutters. I shake off the sudden thought that the stranger I meet might be the one for me. I figure the red dress is the reason for my flutters, not the idea of potentially standing across from my soul mate in it.

Chapter 2

Noah

"Madelyn, I agreed to the photo shoot on the farm today, but at no point did I agree to being a tour guide."

My sister marches into my office and sits in the chair directly across from my desk. I've been happy with my choice of making an office for myself in the big barn after renovating this farm, but right now I'm second-guessing that decision. My sister is three years older than I am, but she never lets me forget I am her kid brother. I think Mom and Dad decided to have another kid to take the heat off them with her incessant bossiness.

"Noah, it's not exactly being a tour guide. It's more of a VIP escort from the front gate. I need every minute to prep and double-check my lighting. This could lead to big business with more sessions booked. Besides, you know it's way too cold to have her walk all the way to the big barn."

I don't understand why anyone would willingly sign up for a blind date photo shoot. I think blind dates are bad enough, but to be blind folded and have pictures taken is bizarre to me. Maybe Madelyn had the same reservations. She did look anxious and like she might throw up any second.

"Fine," I groused. "I'll pick her up at the front gate, but don't expect anything other than that. I'm slammed today and don't have time to waste on your romantic photo sessions."

She laughs uncontrollably. "Noah, when was the last time you did anything romantic?"

The farm is my life, and I love living here. The hard work and sacrifice are paying off. My business is thriving, and I'm currently in the process of buying an adjacent property to expand. The only downside is that I'm doing it alone. It's been over three years since I bought this property with the idea of starting my own family and growing old. But my ex felt different, and I ended up doing it alone. I don't mind getting up when the rooster crows, but after Meredith, I'm just not sure if I'll find anyone who feels the same way. "I don't have time for romance right now. This farm is a full-time job, and honestly, that's okay."

She rolls her eyes and is about to respond when her cell phone rings.

"Hey there. No problem. I'll have someone meet you at the front gate and escort you to the big barn, where our shoot is today. That works. See you in a few." She turns to me with her hands folded in the universal prayer gesture. "My model is early, actually, too early since I'm not fully set up. Could you take the long way back to the barn and give her a quick tour of the place?"

I cringe when the request slips from her mouth. I knew this would happen. It always does with her. It's always just one more thing. If she weren't my sister, I'd boot her right off the property. "You have got to be joking, Madelyn. I just told you how busy I am today. Now you need me to entertain her?" My irritation grows second by second. This is just another one of the countless situations she's gotten me into. You'd think an older sister would steer you in the right direction, but not her. She is impulsive and doesn't think things through.

Madelyn tucked her flyaway hair behind her ears, something she did when overly excited. "I have faith in your ability to entertain. This place is amazing and pretty much speaks for itself as you drive around the property. Just show her the highlights, and I will text when everything is set up."

I grumble under my breath as she hugs me, smiles, then races out. I shove out of my rolling chair, grab my truck keys, and follow her outside. My brain can't process the idea of someone willingly signing up to meet a stranger, then having their photo taken at the event. I know it's been years since I've had a Valentine's Day date or even just a Valentine, but this doesn't seem like anything I would ever do.

The drive to the front takes about five minutes, and as I make the turn around the circular drive at the entrance, I notice a white four-door car sitting outside the entrance gate. I hit the open button on my cellphone app to let it in. The vehicle pulls through, turns left in the lot, and parks. I wait to see the driver step out of the car. My phone beeps with a new text message, and I know without looking that it's from my sister. I read the message and start chuckling.

BE NICE!

She knows me too well. I set my phone down and look up to see a woman standing right outside my truck in big purple curlers. She doesn't look happy to see me. She certainly isn't dressed appropriately for the colder temps. She's wearing black yoga pants and an oversized gray sweatshirt with white tennis shoes. I don't see a jacket, but she is holding several large bags and tapping her foot, as if she's mad at me. My sister owes me big time for this.

Chapter 3

Scarlett

I didn't think this day could get any worse, but I was wrong. Amanda assured me that she would come with me for support and make sure I didn't chicken out. She sent me a text message right before I left to pick her up to let me know that she had a migraine. I told her I would cancel, but she begged me to go and support Madelyn. I've lost count of the total times she's driven me crazy with her antics, but I can't think of anyone I want more by my side. My head is filled with second- and third-guesses on my choice of wardrobe. Madelyn sent me instructions on what outfits to bring: two casual outfits and one dress. I'm having significant anxiety over the red dress that Amanda talked me into. It's way out of my comfort zone, much less wearing it for a stranger.

Madelyn texted me to say she'd have someone meet me at the main gate. The views along the main road leading up to the gate are captivating. Despite it being late January, the area looks straight out of a Hallmark Movie. I consider myself more of a city girl, but I feel like I could get used to these rolling hills. The chill in the air is adding to my current discomfort. I figure I'll take a couple of minutes and give myself a pep talk as I pull into the driveway outside the main gate.

I'm irritated to see a silver truck on the other side. So much for a few minutes to pull myself together. "You can do this, Scarlett," I tell myself. "It's only one day out of your life, and you've endured worse."

The main gate opens up, and I drive through to a small parking area. I hop out and gather my bags, thankful not to be encumbered by a large coat. I look towards the silver truck, hoping to see the driver coming to help me with my stuff, but instead, he rolls his window down and yells, "Hey! You can put your things in the back seat."

I'm shocked by his lack of manners, and then I watch as he proceeds to roll up his window.

My irritation grows as I wait on the passenger side for him to at least be chivalrous enough to open the door.

Again, he rolls the darn window down and says, "It's unlocked."

My temperature is rising, and not because of any outerwear. "Ummm, thanks, Einstein, but it's a bit hard to open the door with my hands full. I refuse to put my stuff on the ground, and I doubt your boss would approve of your bad manners."

He stares directly at me, and I simply raise my eyebrows. He rolls the window back up and climbs out of his truck. I watch as he approaches, and I'm caught off guard by his size. That usually isn't the norm for me since I'm five feet seven inches tall. This guy has to be every bit of six feet four inches. He's wearing an old, blue, weathered ball cap, well-worn jeans, brown work boots, and about a week's worth of beard growth. Many women might consider him ruggedly handsome, but right now, I consider him just plain rude.

He opens the rear passenger door and, with a low, southern drawl, says, "My lady."

I turn at the comment and see a huge smirk. I toss my things onto the back seat and squeeze in beside them. I refuse to sit up front with this jerk. He laughs as I grab the door handle and yank the door closed. I do some deep breathing to calm myself while he strolls back around the truck. I sure hope Madelyn is better at picking blind dates than she is at hiring staff.

As he starts driving, the tension in the truck is uncomfortable. I don't do well with silence. I wish I did because he's the last person I want to talk to. "Madelyn said you're taking me to meet her at the barn."

He looks back at me in his rear-view mirror. "Is that a question or a statement?" He is trifling.

"I'm not sure what your deal is, but I didn't request a chauffeur. Your boss said she would send someone to escort me. I think you need to talk to her about the inconvenience."

He grumbled loudly. "I fully intend to speak to my boss."

Chapter 4

Noah

I'm not sure which is funnier: the comment about Madelyn being my boss or the sight of this woman sitting in my back seat, steaming mad with a head full of curlers. Despite the death glare she's giving me, I've got to admit she's adorable in the curlers. I was set to apologize for my behavior, but watching her fiery spirit silenced that notion, and piqued my interest in how mad I could make her. Madelyn asked me to take the long way around the farm to give her more time to finalize the setup, so I had time.

"Why are you doing the blind date photo shoot, anyway?" I asked, fully expecting her to tell me to take a leap.

"I selected the wrong slip of paper out of our family's dare jar."

That answer threw me. I had her pegged for a social media influencer looking for content. "Did you know this was the consequence when you put your hand in the jar?" I'm invested now. I glance back at her and wait for her reply. She looks up, and we lock eyes for a couple of seconds before she looks away. I didn't notice her deep green eyes when I opened the truck door earlier, but that fleeting moment has me wishing she'd stared a little longer.

"My sister took advantage of me at a weak moment, and I know full well she rigged the selection."

It's encouraging to know she didn't volunteer for this experiment. "Why would she go to all this trouble?" My curiosity has gotten the best of me.

"Why does it matter?"

Ok, that's a fair question since we've just met. "I struggle with the concept of two strangers falling in love after dressing up and twirling for a few hours for pictures. It's not a knock-on, Madelyn, but my cynical side isn't convinced it works." I'm shocked I blurted that out. I haven't even shared these feelings with Madelyn.

"I completely agree with you. I argued with my sister about this whole setup, but no one in our family backs out of any dare."

I'd made my mind up the moment she stepped out of the car with her bags and large curlers that she was fully invested in the romantic fantasy, hook, line, and sinker. It's been a long time since anyone's truly surprised me. The ding from a message on my phone interrupts my thoughts.

I stop the truck and read the message. It's my foreman. He needs me to swing by the back pasture to check out a fencing project. "Madelyn needs a little more time to finish setting up, and I've got to check on a project at the back pasture. So, we'll be taking a minor detour." I look in the rear-view mirror, and she gives me an unenthusiastic thumbs up.

I see Dave, my foreman, standing by his truck as we pull up.

He walks over as I open my door and says, "Titus is over at the fence with a deep cut from the wire. I used the first aid kit, but he's going to need stitches."

I turn to tell my passenger to hang tight while I check, but she's already out of the truck, striding toward me.

"How bad is he?" she asks Dave, as he follows her to the fence. It takes me a second to register what she's doing, and I catch up to them.

Dave responds. "We were doing some repairs, and his glove ripped open. The wire caught him on the center of his palm. It's deep."

It takes me a second to realize her intentions. "What do you think you're doing?"

She keeps walking. "I'm a trauma nurse at Regional. I can help."

This is the second time today that she has surprised me. "That's impressive. Thanks for the assist."

She laughs. "I don't remember you asking me to be your assistant. If anything, you can be mine."

It was my turn to laugh. "Yes, ma'am."

She jumps into action, calms Titus down, and stops the bleeding. Dave assures her that he's taking him to the emergency room to get stitches and a tetanus shot. I end up being her assistant, handing her supplies as needed.

As Dave drives Titus away, he tells her to come back anytime.

We hop back into the truck, and I check to see if Madelyn is ready. She says she won't be ready for an hour. I message back, asking what exactly I am supposed to do for another hour. She suggests going to the main house so Scarlett can freshen up and dress for the photo shoot.

I figure I've pretty much lost my whole day because of Madelyn. She owes me big time. "Hey, I'm Noah. I'll run you up to the main house so you can get a warm drink and get ready. It looks like she needs another hour to finish prepping." I look back at her in the rear-view mirror, waiting for a reply. "I'm Scarlett." That's all she said. I don't know why, but the lack of further banter makes me smile.

Chapter 5

Scarlett

I didn't want to be involved, and now I'm running around this farm freezing half to death because I forgot my coat, playing nurse, and best of all, being chauffeured by the farm manager. I don't care about the blind date, but I'd better look stunning in the pictures after all the drama this morning.

I don't know if it's being at the farm, but my mind drifts to the possibility of making a real connection today with a stranger. It's hysterical that someone I haven't met is going to fix me up with who they think could be my soulmate. The notion makes me laugh out loud.

"What's so funny?" Noah asks as we turn down a long driveway lined with white fencing on both sides.

The house sitting at the end of the driveway is incredible. It's a large two-story farmhouse with black shutters and a huge wraparound porch. I also notice it has a tin roof. I've always loved the look of a tin roof and wondered how it would sound lying in bed while it rains. "I was thinking about the whole blind date thing and how crazy it is that a woman I've never met is going to fix me up with my soulmate. Or at least her version of who my soulmate should be."

He chuckles as he parks his truck. "You're brave for following through with it. I couldn't imagine my sister picking out my soulmate."

From his remark, he is single. "Do you know if I am supposed to get ready here and then we go to the barn for the date?" I'd much rather check this place out than do the pictures anyway.

"Yeah, it seems that's the plan." He climbs out and makes his way over to me. He smiles as he opens my door. "I'll actually help carry your bags this time." He has a great smile. He's handsome when grumpy but downright gorgeous when he smiles.

"Thanks." I hand over the bags and hop out of the truck. We make our way up the front stairs, and he holds the door open for me.

"You can use the bathroom to freshen up and prepare for today; it's down the hall on the right. I'll fix some coffee if that's good with you."

I step inside and fall in love with the house immediately. "Coffee would be great. I haven't met Madelyn, but I'm envious of her place."

He nods in agreement. I walk around the living room and zero in quickly on the stone fireplace with a rustic wood mantle holding what looks like family photos. The fireplace is the main draw in the living area, and there's an oversized sectional sofa with some cozy blankets thrown on the back. I could curl up and sit by a fire there all day. The kitchen is across the room, and the area has several windows overlooking a pasture. He looks comfortable standing behind the counter, making coffee. The updates in the old farmhouse are significant, but it still has a vintage vibe.

"Have you worked for Madelyn's family long?"

He looks up as he sets a mug on the counter. "It feels like a lifetime." He chuckles and slides a mug toward me. "Here is your coffee and your choice of creamers." He leans back against the counter, facing me, and sips from his own cup. He seems comfortable. His next question surprises me. "You don't seem like somebody who would need matchmaking, so what's your story?"

It catches me off guard. I stir creamer into my coffee and take a sip too soon. The hot liquid burns all the way down, and tears form quickly. There is zero chance of playing this off.

"You, okay?" He grabs a glass out of the cabinet and fills it from the faucet. I take it and start chugging. It helps ease the burn, but does nothing for my embarrassment.

"Sorry if my question got you all choked up." He looks rather smug.

"Don't flatter yourself. The question caught me off guard. You've seemed annoyed since you arrived at the front gate." I finish my water.

"You're right. This was not on my agenda today. Nowhere close."

I totally relate to that statement, so I answer his question. "I was engaged to my college boyfriend. Two years ago, he broke it off because he fell in love with a coworker. I was devastated, and my sister helped me get through it. She's been on me to start dating again, and this is her way of pushing me off the diving board, into the deep end, I guess." I can't believe I just said all that. I don't even know this guy. My curlers might be too tight on my head.

He sips his coffee and looks at me over the mug, but says nothing.

"I guess I'd better start getting ready before Madelyn sends word for us to head her way. Where is the bathroom I can use?"

He sets his mug down and heads toward me. "I'll show you, it's right down the hall."

He grabs my bags, and I follow. My irritation is momentarily pushed aside as I enjoy the view of his long legs, broad shoulders, and other attributes. He gives off cowboy vibes even without the standard hat or horse. Madelyn should get him to do a photoshoot. He opens the bathroom door and sets my bags on the counter while I hang my wardrobe bag from a closet door hinge. As I turn, he's standing in the doorway.

"I think you're brave and a great sister for going along with this. And for what it's worth, your ex-fiancé is a fool." He turns and closes the door.

Chapter 6

Noah

I've known her for a little over an hour, so I'm not exactly sure why I commented on her ex-fiancé. It's been a long time since anyone has piqued my interest. Madelyn is matching her with a potential mate, so why am I thinking so much about her and wondering how her dark brown hair will look without the curlers? While I can fully appreciate the face of makeup that I'm sure she's applying, I'm attracted to how she is right now, bare face and all.

She was mad at me earlier, and we stared each other down in the truck, but truth be told, I baited her so she would keep looking in my direction. Her green eyes are mesmerizing. My phone rings just as I close the door leading out to the back deck. It's Madelyn.

"Hey sis, are you ready for your guest?" I ask, hoping to put some distance between this woman and me. I find I'm very attracted to her, and I know it's not right, considering she's set to meet someone else.

"Noah, don't freak out, but I've got a huge problem." My sister has stirred up a big mess with this adventure.

"What exactly is going on?" I ask, knowing it won't be good.

"The guy I selected to be Scarlett's blind date just cancelled. He gave me the lame excuse of getting back with his ex."

I'm not shocked by this development. She has a good heart but struggles with details and follow-through. I feel terrible that her bravery is for nothing since the jerk cancelled. "What are you going to do? I think it will crush her when she finds out the guy bailed."

"I am absolutely sick over this and scrambling to get either the second or third choice to head this way for the photo shoot, but it's a long shot."

I hate to think she has to revert to second- or third-string as though this were a darn football game. "I think you need to tell her the truth and let her make the choice to continue or not." The dare may have gotten her here, but it still took courage to follow through.

"I'm freaking out right now, Noah. I promised her sister this would be magical. I know that sounds stupid, but Scarlett went through a bad breakup and hasn't dated since. Her sister wanted this experience to boost her confidence and maybe spark a romantic interest.

"What's your plan if you can't get guy two or three?" Nothing less than a miracle will work right now.

"I'm still going to do her photo shoot. It will just be solo. She deserves to feel as beautiful as she is. I'll need a bit more time, so keep her there, and I'll call you with an update soon."

She hung up. Grrr!!! This is aggravating and uncomfortable, knowing the potential bombshell on the horizon. I turn to walk back inside, and she's standing on the other side of the sliding glass door. I smile and open it.

"So, what's going on?" she asks as I shut the door behind me. "You don't look happy."

"It's a bit of a cluster. I'm going to start a fire and warm it up in here a bit. You want another cup of coffee or tea?" I ask as I get the fire going.

"That cluster remark doesn't sound good, but I for sure wouldn't mind sitting by the fire with some hot tea." She sits on the sofa and grabs one of the blankets off the back.

She looks comfortable on my couch. I know Madelyn might be upset, but I'm going to be honest and tell her what's going on. My gut tells me it's the right thing to do, and if it were me, I'd want to know.

It takes me a few minutes to make our drinks, and after I bring them over and set them on the table, I take a seat in the center of the sofa. She's sitting at the end closest to the fire, leaning against the arm, the blanket draped across her lap and her feet tucked to her side.

She sips casually and looks my way. "So, tell me the bad news."

Her questioning look makes me angry at this guy for bailing on her. "I wasn't super friendly when we met, and we got off on the wrong foot. So. My name is Noah, and Madelyn is my older sister."

Her eyes grow wide with surprise. "Do you live here on the farm?"

"Actually, this farm is mine. I bought it a few years ago, and I've been fixing it up and growing my business. Madelyn asked me if she could use the barn for her photo shoot today." She smiles at me. I could get lost in her eyes and that smile.

"My name is Scarlett, and it's nice to meet you officially, Noah. I think you have an amazing place here, and I am grateful for your hospitality. Please fill me in on this cluster news."

She's direct. I like her more for that. "Madelyn just called to tell me that the guy she matched you with canceled. She's hoping to pair you with another guy that just missed the cut, but it could take some time."

Scarlett sips her tea and laughs. "I appreciate you being honest with me. I have a feeling my sister and your sister's scheming has backfired. I know the intention was good, but I think this is my sign to cut my losses and leave."

She places her feet on the floor and takes the blanket off her lap. I don't want her to leave. She stands up, and before she can say anything, I blurt out, "I'll be your blind date."

Chapter 7

Scarlett

"You'll be my what?" I stare at Noah in confusion.

"Please, sit back down. I have an idea to fix this situation. Let me explain."

I sit, wondering how to escape this disaster. "Our sisters got us tangled up in their scheme. I think the best solution is for me to be your date. It solves the problem of you fulfilling the dare, and then you don't have to worry about them trying to rope you into doing this again."

That might work. I hadn't thought about them trying to schedule another session and having to go through all this again.

"You would do that? Why?" He was put off by the whole idea of this earlier.

"We both know what it's like having a sister that gets you into all kinds of uncomfortable situations. I think this will settle things and make sure there is zero chance of rescheduling."

If I backed out now, Amanda would for sure try to reschedule. "Are you sure you want to do this with me?"

He nods. "Don't take this the wrong way, but I am not a fan of having my picture taken. I want to make sure you don't have to deal with this stress again."

It's strange, but my nerves have calmed at his suggestion of doing the shoot with me instead of some other guy. I don't know if it's the fact that I've spent time with him and he's Madelyn's brother, or because I'm secretly excited to do this with him. I'd never admit that to anyone, especially Amanda, but the idea of putting on the new dress for Noah is thrilling.

"I agree. What will you tell your sister?"

"Don't worry. I'm going to tell her the truth. That it's not fair to make you wait around for another stranger to show up. You agreed, and we're doing the photo shoot together." He stood and stuck out his hand for me to shake. It seems old-school, but it's cute.

I stand up and put my hand in his. His grip is firm, and his hand engulfs my own, the callouses and rough skin far from being a turn off. I liked that he works his land and takes pride in his business and home. My cheeks flush, standing there looking directly into his eyes, my hand still tucked into his.

"I'll let Madelyn know the new plan while you continue to get ready. She can come pick you up while I get ready, and we can meet you at the barn afterwards. Does that work?"

"I can simply ride back with you after I get ready. It will save everyone an extra trip." That seems simple enough.

"No. We've met and know what each other looks like, but we haven't seen each other dressed up, so meeting there will help it feel more like an authentic blind date. I'll see you at the barn."

I'm caught off guard by his romantic gesture. It's been quite a while since anyone has done anything remotely romantic for me. I'm a bit shook.

"Thanks, Noah, for going to all this trouble. It means a lot." I lightly touch his arm as I pass and head back towards the bathroom to get ready.

"My pleasure, Scarlett," he replies with a slow southern drawl. I dare say that a layer of my emotional wall crumbles after that comment. It's funny, but I almost wish Amanda were here so I could share that, because she's repeatedly nagged me about it since my relationship with Jason ended.

Noah gives me a glimmer of hope that I can put myself back out there. It's tiny, but still a glimmer.

I head to the bathroom and hear Noah shut the front door on his way out. My spirits lift in anticipation of doing the shoot, even though we barely know each other. I set my phone on the counter and turn on some background music to energize me. I'll start with my makeup, then my hair. My hair is a mystery, considering how long it's been up in curlers. There isn't a backup plan for the hair, so I'm hoping for the best.

Amanda has been guiding me in the makeup department since my routine has been lagging for a while. She instructed me to use brown shadows and eyeliner, but told me to use a special violet mascara to make my green eyes pop in the pictures. Time to unpack all my makeup, give myself a quick pep talk, and start the arduous path to beauty.

I hadn't been at it very long when someone opened the front door and called out. "Hello Scarlett!" Madelyn's arrived.

"I'm down the hall in the bathroom."

Her feet make quick time down the hall and into the bathroom. "Do you hate me?" she asks with a full face of anxiousness.

"Honestly, it was touch and go for most of the morning. I don't hate you, but I won't be doing this ever again."

She walks over, and I turn as she pulls me into a hug. "Scarlett, please know I am sorry about everything."

I hug her back. "Of course, I forgive you."

She steps back and appears calmer. "How can I help? Your makeup looks amazing, by the way!"

I haven't heard a compliment like that in a long time. "Thanks. I guess Amanda does know a thing or two about makeup. I need to fix my hair and then get dressed. How are we on time?"

"Noah agreed to stay in his office until it's time to meet. I have to help you both with your blindfolds before I start taking pictures. Thanks for agreeing to do the photo shoot with him. I know it isn't what we had planned for today, but I do think the pictures will turn out amazing."

I agree, and my mood lifts as I admire my appearance in the mirror.

Chapter 8

Noah

My sister texts me to apologize for the day being a fiasco and to stay put in my office until she arrives with my blindfold. I reply that I'll do my best to help her salvage this, but the blindfolds are a bit corny. I grabbed clothes and boots to change into as I left so that Scarlett could get ready.

The best part about remodeling the barn and adding my office is that I put in a full bathroom. I knew I'd be spending a ton of time here, and it's easier to get cleaned up here than going back to my house sometimes.

This feels like a real date, almost like being back in high school, when the prettiest girl agreed to go out with you. My nerves are on high, and lord knows it's been a long time since I put this much effort into my looks. I grab my toiletries bag, which includes my razor and cologne. I spend so much time working on the farm that I don't think about those steps, and I hope Scarlett approves.

My outfit will be my best pair of jeans, best pair of cowboy boots, and a dark blue long-sleeved button-up shirt. That was all I could grab on such short notice. I have church clothes, but this doesn't feel like the right time for those. I want to be comfortable and help her feel the same.

I think my sister must have put the fear into everyone working the farm today, because I haven't received any calls or messages since Dave messaged to say Titus was home and resting after being discharged from the emergency room. I'm grateful his injury wasn't worse.

My shower-and-shave doesn't take long, and before I get dressed, I want to call to check in on Scarlett. I message my sister asking for Scarlett's number. She replies with her digits and a happy face emoji. I text her that it's me and ask if I can call. She sends a thumbs-up emoji. I dial her number with a big smile on my face. I'm glad nobody is here right now to witness me embarrassing myself.

She answers on the first ring. "Hi Noah!"

I like hearing her say my name. "Hi Scarlett. How are you?"

"Better than earlier, plus you'll be happy to know that I finally took the curlers out of my hair."

I laugh. "Dang, how will I recognize you?"

Her turn to laugh. "You may not recognize me at all, with my hair and makeup done. It's a big difference from this morning." I could hear hesitation in her voice.

"Scarlett, I'd know you anywhere." That rolled out without thought. It's absolutely true.

"I need to finish dressing and then head your way. See you soon." She hangs up. I will stand by the statement if ever asked. She's unforgettable.

Twenty minutes later, I'm dressed and waiting to hear from my sister that they're on their way. I take one last look at myself and feel good that Scarlett won't be upset with how I cleaned up—my phone dings with the message that they're leaving my place. Madelyn tells me to stay put so I don't see anyone or anything before the reveal. I can't sit down, so I pace around the office.

My mind is swirling with how I initiated this plan. The day could have ended with me doing what I was initially asked to do. Escort her and keep her company until Madelyn is ready. It wasn't my fault that the date backed out.

But if you know me, you know there's zero chance I would leave my sister in a bind and upset. Her business is essential, and I can relate to the pain of getting a business off the ground. The second thing that swayed me was learning about Scarlett and seeing her vulnerability when she discovered the date had been canceled.

And finally, I'm aware of my developing attraction for her and the need to spend more time with her. I know we have many conversations ahead of us, but I want to give this incredible new feeling between us a try. The possibility of having someone in my life is appealing, and I'm hopeful that she will love this place as much as I do.

While this is way out of my comfort zone, I'm excited to make her smile and show her how beautiful she is.

My office door opens. It's Madelyn holding a red blindfold. She looks at me and says, "Wow! You look so handsome. I can't wait to see the magic unfold in my photos. You two are going to be an absolutely stunning couple. On camera, of course." She winks after that last comment, then puts the blindfold on me and walks me out of my office. "Thanks for being the best brother. I love you, Noah."

I squeeze her hand as we walk out the door.

Chapter 9

Scarlett

Madelyn blindfolded me upon our arrival at the barn. She told me she wants everything, including the decoration and set-up, to be a surprise. It's scary to walk into a place you've never set foot in before, blind to the surroundings. I'm forced to put complete trust in her and pray I don't fall. My nerves settle when Madelyn finds one of Noah's coats for me to wear to keep me warm since I forgot mine. The warmth of the coat is top-notch, but the best part for me is smelling Noah's scent. That alone helps calm me.

I couldn't FaceTime Amanda to show her the results, but I did snap a photo to send her. She assured me that I knocked it out of the park. The red dress lives up to the hype and fits like a glove. My curls behave despite the morning's drama. They are cascading beautifully. Since the dress is stunning on its own, I kept the jewelry low-key—a pair of gold dangle earrings and a matching necklace. I'm glad Amanda talked me into wearing my boots. They pair up great with the dress and, even better, keep my feet warm. No one will know that I'm wearing a cozy pair of socks.

Music is playing in the barn, not loud enough to be distracting, more background ambiance. Madelyn guides me to a comfy high-back chair that I assume she uses for her photo shoots, and I imagine families sitting around while she takes holiday pictures. She assures me that it won't take long to get Noah. I hope she's right since my anticipation is high. I feel pretty, and even though he isn't my official date, I hope he thinks so too.

"We're heading your way," Madelyn announces as I hear footsteps approaching from across the barn. My heartbeat picks up when I know Noah is nearby.

"Hi, Scarlett." He says my name with that deep southern drawl I was drawn to earlier, despite my initial irritation.

"Hi, Noah." He and Madelyn are close enough that I pick up on the hint of his cologne. It's the same scent that I've been smelling on the coat I'm wearing.

"Okay, we're close, but don't take off your blindfolds yet. I have to get you both situated and then get behind my camera. I'm going to start with Noah, so Scarlett, just sit tight."

I hear them jostling about, and then Noah laughs at something his sister says. His deep laugh is intoxicating. I think I've gone off the deep end with all this romance talk. I'm blaming it on Valentine's Day coming up.

"I'm finished with Noah," Madelyn says. "Coming your way now."

Madelyn takes my hand and helps me stand. "I'll guide you to your spot near Noah."

I take six steps, sense his presence, and hear his breathing.

Madelyn chatters cheerfully. "I want to thank you both for your patience and willingness to continue despite the hurdles we faced today. This is a chance to put yourself out there and open your heart to finding love again. Love doesn't always arrive on time or by a master plan." Madelyn must have a speech rehearsed for this type of event. I don't know if the love part holds for Noah and me, but the words are sweet and heartwarming.

"I'm going over to my camera, and when I'm ready, I'll count down and tell you to take off your blindfolds. Try not think about the camera. Just focus on the excitement of seeing each other."

We're both silently waiting for her countdown. I hear her walk towards the camera, followed by some shuffling. "Okay, let's roll. Please take your blindfolds off on my count. Three, two, and one."

I take my blindfold off and look up at Noah. He's smiling right at me, and I can't take my eyes off him. He looks even more handsome now, and I didn't think that would be possible.

He steps toward me and lifts both of my hands into his. "Scarlett, you look incredible. I'm completely in awe of your beauty." He squeezes my hands, never taking his eyes off me.

I do feel beautiful. For the first time in a long time. "Noah, you are gorgeous, and I feel lucky to be here with you right now."

Noah releases my hands and asks if he can hug me.

"I'd like that very much."

When he pulls me close and holds me, it feels like home. I never thought I could fall for anyone like this, but it feels right. He whispers in my ear. "Scarlett, you smell incredible, and I don't want to let you go." I assume he whispered because Madelyn was nearby. I like that he wanted to say that to only me. I like the thought that this wasn't a show or a pity date.

"Noah, I don't want you to let me go. I actually want you to kiss me." I couldn't believe I said that out loud. He pulls back a little so he can look at me. He's beaming, and I smile back at him. The next thing I feel is his hands cupping the sides of my face. I love the feel of his hands and the gentle way he's holding me. He tilts his head and places his lips on mine. It's warm, sweet, and promising. I put my hands around his waist and hold him tight.

The next hour flies by as Madelyn talks us through some candid shots. The barn is decorated like a winter wonderland, filled with red Valentine's decor. Just enough to balance out the rustic barn.

"And that's a wrap," she finally says. "The photos are spectacular, and you two definitely brought the heat. Wow!"

My cheeks grow hot. Noah holds my hand and whispers in my ear. "Don't you dare be embarrassed about what you felt. I feel it too, Scarlett." He kisses my cheek and squeezes my hand again.

Madelyn catches us both off guard. "I have a confession to make, but I need to bring someone in first."

What is she talking about? We look at each other, and Noah appears just as confused as I am.

We hear footsteps, and then I see Amanda walking toward us. I thought she had a migraine. She waves at me, walks over, and hugs me. "Letty, you look sensational. I love the glow you have right now." She hugs me tighter.

Madelyn and Amanda share a grin before Madelyn says, "I hope you both understand what I'm about to tell you. Amanda and I have been talking for a few months about this blind date photo shoot, and during our conversations, we discovered that you two might be perfect for each other. We both knew neither of us would ever agree to do it, so we set our plan in motion. It wasn't ideal, but getting you two together was the plan all along. There wasn't another date that was canceled."

Madelyn and Amanda watch us after the explanation.

I'm speechless that they went to all this trouble. I glance at Noah, and he simply shakes his head in disbelief. "I don't agree with the way you two went about this, but I have to admit you succeeded." Noah turns to me, waiting for my reply.

I am not at all shocked that Amanda had her hand in this scheme. I usually tell her to mind her own business, but today turned out far better than I could have imagined. "I'm not a fan of how you two set things up either, but I'm happy with the outcome. I forgive you both."

Noah lifts me off my feet and twirls me around as Amanda and Madelyn laugh. "Scarlett, I'm thrilled you picked that slip of paper," he says as he sets me back on my feet.

I look into his eyes and softly touch his cheek. "Me too."

About R.K. Fultz

R.K. discovered her love of storytelling early, sneaking chapters of her mom's romance novels and quietly building entire worlds in her head. Years later, a life changing writing retreat gave her the courage to finally put those stories on the page. She now writes contemporary romance and romantic thrillers that are emotionally grounded and explore trauma, resilience, and the unexpected connections that help us heal. When she isn't writing, R.K. enjoys traveling, taking long walks outdoors, and discovering new music. R.K. lives in Virginia and is a proud mom to two amazing sons.

Connect:

- Instagram.com/r_k_fultz

by Myria Wild

Chapter 1: Fluffy Cows

Carrie

There he was, pulling into my parking spot. Again. I grumbled and drove past as he stepped out and shut the door of his beat-up black Sierra truck. He looked my way, but I pretended not to notice him and leaned on the gas pedal. Surely, he'd seen me park in the same spot right up front twice a month on Saturdays for the past twenty years, but he'd still taken it anyway.

After finding another place to park a few rows away from the auction house entrance, I slammed my truck into park, grabbed my purse, and rushed out. I would have been here early like always, but when I tried to leave the house, I found my daughter's gelding cantering down the driveway for the third time this week. He was smart enough to stay away from the road, but he still liked to play like he was a reckless idiot. It took me thirty minutes of shaking a bucket full of alfalfa cubes to lure that spotted monster back to the barn so I could lock him up again.

My breath puffed in the early February air as I strode to the back of the line waiting at the auction house door. My mood darkened as I counted all the people ahead of me. I liked to be at the front of the line. Always. Not in the middle. Not in the back.

At the very front.

Melanie—the owner of the newest plant nursery in our little town of Hart Oaks, Michigan—stood at the front of the line. She was coming up on the one-year anniversary of the nursery's opening, and she'd been in the area just a little longer than that. Long waves of perfect dark hair cascaded down her shoulders, not a single strand of gray showing, even though I knew she was only a few years younger than me. As she waited for the cashier window to open, she chatted with none other than the man who'd stolen my parking spot.

Wes Walker.

Something about him had always bugged me, and even more so this afternoon. The growing slashes of silver in his short beard, the way the locks of his thick, dark hair spilled out over the collar of his black Carhartt jacket. That damn grin whenever he caught me staring at him.

The cashier window snapped open, and the line started moving as people registered for their bidder numbers and headed inside. By the time I registered and collected my number—33—the livestock holding areas were filled with throngs of people. I didn't always need to buy a new horse, cow, or whatever other random animal might catch my eye, but I came anyway. Sometimes, it was the animals that drew me, and sometimes it was the search for deals on new tack or farm equipment. But more than that, the twice-monthly auctions were my personal ritual—and the ritual of so many others here. It was my break from the farm, my chance to get out and enjoy a change of scenery.

The older I got, however, the less I enjoyed being around people. They could leave me alone with my dogs, my cats, and my horses, and let me keep my peace.

"Carrie!"

I turned at the sound of my name and found the best human friend I'd ever had running at me.

"Sabs!" I didn't try to stop the genuine smile that warmed my face.

We hadn't seen each other in at least a month, so I hugged her tight before linking my arm with hers.

"Tell me we're sitting together?" I asked, hopeful.

"Of course! Besides, Rob's not with me today." I caught the light blush that rose to her cheeks even as she looked away, trying and failing to hide it.

"Y'all are still in love?" I asked, incredulous. "You've been together five years already."

"Stop." Sabrina chided me. "It's only been a few months, as you're well aware."

I poked her in the ribs through her coat, causing her to jolt away before swatting my hand.

Pulling her back, I kept teasing. "Whatever. When's the wedding?"

Sabrina pursed her lips and narrowed her eyes, then lightly slapped me with her bidder number.

We headed for the auction house's small cafe to grab coffee, an essential part of our ritual that I was more excited to keep up with now that she was joining me again. There was a short line, but just ahead of us, Melanie retrieved her burger and Coke. She sat down at a table near the windows and scrolled on her phone as she ate.

We had just over an hour before the auction would begin, giving us plenty of time to catch up and view the livestock together.

Sabrina stiffened beside me, then nudged me with her elbow. "Is that Wes?"

I resisted the urge to glare daggers at her, mentally begging her to let it go.

"Yes. And?" I whispered back. "He's here all the time, just like me. And just like you used to be. Has that love potion wiped out your memory?"

Sabs stuck out her tongue. "Yeah, but he's never ahead of you in any line."

That got under my skin, and I grimaced. "Apparently, old dogs can learn new tricks. He even stole my parking spot."

"Your spot? I guess Hell must have frozen over, because that never happens." She frowned and did a double-take. "Old dog? Umm... you know he's our age, Carrie. I don't know about you, but I refuse to call myself old. Not yet."

Now it was my turn to lightly smack her shoulder with my bidder number. "You know what I mean. Enough of that."

She tilted her head and eyed me with suspicion. "What's got you all prickly?"

"Nothing," I ground out between clenched teeth, wishing she'd find something else to needle me about. "So, how did you peel yourself away from Rob? Did that require surgery?"

She pinched my cheek and gave me a toothy smile. "Ease up, you old hag! Rob has been summoned to deer camp by his friends. They warned that if he wasn't there on time like he is every other year, they'd file a missing persons report."

"Men." I rolled my eyes, then put on my best smile as I reached the front of the line.

"Just a coffee for me," I said, then looked at Sabs. "And..."

"Same."

"Two coffees." I paid, and we quickly accepted our drinks and walked out of the cafe. On the way, I spotted Wes sitting with Melanie. The two smiled and laughed over their meal, and I scowled as I watched them from my periphery.

I tried to ignore the twinge of annoyance. Why should I care who Wes was dating now?

It wasn't an answer I was willing to dig into. Not now, not ever.

Sabrina and I headed to the livestock holding area to mosey through the wide hallways and peek at the animals. A pen full of healthy Hereford cattle eyed us as we passed, and we stopped at the next pen to try to coax the mini Highlands forward for pets. A white calf with black spots and fluffy black ears stepped up to us and nibbled at my hand, then dipped its head for scratches between the ears. That spot was typically itchy for most cows and horses, and the mini shook his head up and down in appreciation, stretching forward so I could scratch more.

"I've always wanted a mini," I mumbled, keeping my touch gentle as I rubbed the cow's soft ears.

"What's stopping you? Or who's stopping you? That's a better question," Sabrina observed. "You don't have a man telling you 'no', all your kids are grown and out of the house, and you live alone."

A chill swept over me, and I shivered. "That's the problem. I already have enough animals counting on me and just enough sense to know that there's only one of me to love all of them."

I gave the spotted mini's head one more good rub, then withdrew my hand and sipped my coffee as I stared at its big, pretty face drooping with long, shaggy hair.

"Oh, he likes you," a man said from behind me.

I turned slowly and forced a polite smile. It tightened when I came face to face with Wes.

"Hey, Wes!" Sabrina smiled too, but hers was genuine.

It seemed like everyone was happy to see Wes but me.

"Hi, Sabrina." He beamed at us, his perfect, straight teeth gleaming white. Those blue eyes glittered from beneath his dark brown Stetson as they turned on me. "Caroline."

"Hi, Wes." I tried to sound warm like Sabrina had, but it fell flat.

I couldn't keep the contempt from my voice. He either didn't notice or pretended not to. "So, are you in the market for some fluffy cows?"

Forced to bite back a chuckle at his unexpected use of the term, my face softened in spite of my feelings. I shook my head. "I was just telling Sabrina that I really shouldn't take on any more animals."

"Are you sure?" He shifted on his feet and pushed his thumbs into the pockets of his jeans. "I'll cut you a good deal on that one."

I shot a fleeting glance toward the pen, then back at him. "Wait... They're yours?"

He nodded, and his dimples showed. There was a tickle of nostalgia in me, and I started to remember why just about every woman our age had a crush on him at some point—and why I'd fallen for him back in high school.

Wes tipped his head to the calf still leaning against the gate and staring at us. “That’s the one you like? I’ll even haul him for you. No charge.”

It was kind of him to offer and kinder than I'd expected him to be toward me, but it didn't change the reality of my situation, so I shook my head. "No, thank you. I really can’t."

"Oh. Okay." He shifted on his feet again. "If you change your mind, you're always welcome to visit me at the ranch."

Sabrina damn near vibrated beside me, and I hoped she could hold her tongue at least until we were out of Wes's earshot.

"Thanks, Wes," I said, trying to be nonchalant. I couldn't afford to take the offer seriously. Everyone knew how he was with women. "I'll keep that in mind. Have a good day."

I sipped my coffee, gave him one last glance over the lid of my cup, then linked my arm in Sabrina's again, and we walked away.

Chapter 2: The Unhappy Appy

Wes

I wanted to tell Caroline that I'd give her the cow for free if she really wanted it, but that might have seemed desperate. Was I desperate?

Maybe a little.

So instead I only muttered, "I don't want her to leave, but I love to watch her—"

The mini cow mooed and bumped his head against the gate.

"Yeah, you're probably right, little buddy." I leaned against the gate and rubbed his head for a minute. When I looked again, Caroline and Sabrina had disappeared. "You might be my ticket to redemption, floof ball."

I withdrew my hand and walked away to wander the aisles, consciously heading in the opposite direction from Caroline and Sabrina. She wouldn't fall for my trademark charm, but maybe I was rusty. Or maybe that charm was too weathered now, a faded remnant of its once youthful glory. The years were slipping by faster than I could have fathomed, and all my sharp edges were dulling as time passed. I'd already been facing the facts for a few years now, so it wasn't a new revelation, but I was still surprised when my smile couldn't instantly melt a woman. Even that one.

Wandering the aisles between the pens, I glanced over the cows, goats, and pigs, but studied the horses more closely. I was always on the lookout for good trail horses, as some of mine were retired due to age or injury. My ranch was one of the few that still offered year-round trail riding and ranch resort experiences, and it required a lot of upkeep to remain financially viable. There were a few grade Quarter Horses and a Standardbred in the holding pens that caught my eye, so I wrote down their tag numbers before heading toward the auction ring.

The small arena was surrounded by tiered seating on three sides. On the opposite side of the ring, an auctioneer's booth was centered on the ring's wall and flanked by passageways. Each animal or group of animals was brought through one entrance and, after bidding ended, left through the other. This system kept the flow of livestock moving quickly and efficiently.

I took a seat in the center of the third row, directly in front of the arena, facing the auctioneer's booth and set down my water bottle and notebook, then pulled out my phone to read an ebook while waiting for the auction to begin. This was my favorite spot, right at the front of all the action and eye level with the auctioneer. People slowly filled in around me as I dove deeper into my thriller novel. The author, P. A. Duncan, lived in Virginia and was a former FAA employee. She knew how to write a helluva story, and I'd been hooked on her work ever since I read War of Deception. These stories were such a far cry from my own world that they provided the perfect escape from my not-so-perfect life. At least when I read about Mai and Alexei saving the world, I could feel part of something powerful, something bigger than the mundane hum of daily life. And something more hopeful than the ache of my loneliness, and the jagged thirst that couldn't be quenched by water alone.

In my periphery, I watched Caroline and Sabrina walk in, styrofoam to-go cups in hand as they climbed the steps and sat almost directly behind me.

"He got loose again?" Sabrina asked.

Caroline sighed. "I swear that Appaloosa can't be contained. He always finds a way to unlock the stall door or get out of the paddocks."

Sabrina grumbled, "And why can't Tori come take care of him?"

"She's..." Caroline began, but then her words trailed off. "I don't know."

"Just get rid of him, Carrie." Sabrina gestured toward the auctioneer's box. "Hell, bring him here and make a little money."

Caroline didn't respond immediately, and her silence was telling. "I would never bring Cochise here. I love that horse more than I hate him."

"Maybe he needs a muzzle. Hey, Wes," Sabrina called down to me.

I turned to look up at them. Caroline frowned, and her gaze flitted away as she brought her coffee up for a sip. Sabrina nudged her conspicuously, grinning wildly.

I inclined my head. "How can I help, ladies?"

"Fine, Sabs," Caroline grumbled at her friend, before her pretty, almond-shaped hazel eyes fixed on me. "I've got an Appaloosa that won't stay where I put him. He's always escaping, and I... Well, I don't know what to do with him."

"Sounds like your Appy isn't too happy," I ventured, putting on my best grin for her, but she wasn't amused by my rhyme. "How old is he?"

She thought about it for a minute, counting on her fingers. "He must be sixteen now."

"Is he sound?"

Caroline nodded.

"What kind of schedule do you have him on for exercise?"

She winced. "Well... I don't really have time for that. I barely get to ride for myself anymore."

"It sounds like he wants attention," I observed, trying to keep my tone as gentle as possible. She was the last person on the planet I'd scold for anything.

"So, take him out for a ride?" Sabrina waved a hand in the air.

Sabrina's blond hair, blue eyes, tan complexion, and light freckles made most of the men in town giddy, but I had let go of any crush I'd had on her back in high school. Once I'd met Caroline, I had no interest in her best friend.

"That would be a good start," I agreed.

Caroline closed her eyes and rubbed her temple with her free hand. "I can't imagine adding yet another thing to my weekly to-do list right now. Not even with the holidays over, and I'm practically alone on the farm now."

"And Tori can't come ride him once a week?" Sabrina pressed the question again, though a little differently this time. "You have five kids, but you can't get any of them to help?"

Ouch. I winced on Caroline's behalf. If anyone knew what it was like to feel abandoned by their grown children, I did. Except, I probably deserved it. Caroline, on the other hand, did not.

"Sabs, please!" Caroline said softly, her voice pleading, clearly embarrassed. "Stop. They're adults. I can't make them do anything."

Sabrina bit her lip, sighed, then put an arm around Caroline's shoulders and hugged her.

I couldn't cool the jealousy that burned in my chest, but I smiled through it anyway. "If the unhappy Appy needs a job, I might be able to use him."

She turned those pretty eyes on me again, but they were filled with suspicion and distrust. "That's the second offer in one night, Wes. Is there something you want from me?"

My friendly expression slipped away despite my efforts to hold it, and my ears burned. I only shook my head. "Not a thing, Caroline."

I turned forward again, blood boiling as I sipped from my water bottle. That's what I get for trying to help. The part of me that wanted to see her, to talk to her, even to hold her again, turned cold just as the auction started.

Chapter 3: Crying on the Catwalks

Carrie

That didn't feel as good as I might have thought it would. In fact, it kind of hurt to watch Wes's ears turn red and his charming smile fall away. But the words were out now, and there was no taking them back. It shouldn't have mattered how he felt, but it realized too late that I cared more than I thought I would.

"Dang, girl," Sabrina muttered near my ear. "You sure know how to hit 'em where it hurts."

"That man couldn't care less about me," I whispered back, fuming at the accusation despite knowing it was true. And obviously, he was trying to be extra nice to me. But it wouldn't do anyone any good to admit any of those things.

"Really?" she asked, incredulous. "You're kidding, right?"

Her blue eyes were locked on me, and the heat rose in my cheeks, but I couldn't bring myself to meet her eyes.

"Good afternoon, everyone," the auctioneer said over the PA system, and I thanked the heavens for the interruption. "We're going to start the day the same way we always do—with tack and equipment."

"It's time to get some good deals," I said, forcing a smile as I finally glanced at my friend.

She looked skeptical but nodded and gave me a side hug. I was grateful for the hugs, which were one of the rare instances of human touch I could get these days. Being an independent widow with five grown kids who'd all gone their own ways made for a lonely life. I couldn't help but think I must have done something wrong since none of my children wanted to take over the farm, but that made me all the more stubborn about keeping the place going. John and I had worked so hard to build our dream. Could I really build that dream without him?

That question had plagued me ever since John's passing, and four years later, I still didn't have an answer.

A tear slipped down my cheek before I even registered the stinging in my eyes. I wished I could have a drink, but I couldn't even do that. There was no one else to handle the farm so I could let loose. Even my weekly trip to the auction came with a world of worry weighing on my shoulders.

We spent most of the rest of the tack portion of the auction in silence. I grabbed a new winter blanket for Cochise and a wool seat cover for his trail saddle. It was still early in the winter season and would only get colder. As much as I hated to admit it, Wes was right. The gelding was bored and lonely. While the other horses were content to be left to their own devices for weeks or months at a time, Cochise wasn't. And frankly, neither was I. Since when had I become the type of person who pushed people away at every opportunity?

The livestock portion of the auction began with Hereford cattle, then Angus, and so on. Then came the mini Highland cows. My favorite calf—the white one with black spots, floofy black ears, and a soft black snout—ran into the arena as nervous as all the others. His eyes were so wide that their whites showed, and even the cattle farmer in me was softened by the little guy. He had no control over his fate, and I felt helpless watching his nervous trots and tiny gallops through the ring alongside the herd.

I sprang to my feet with my purse in hand and darted away, weaving past all the people seated between me and the stairs, then trotted down them and headed for the door.

"Carrie? Carrie!" Sabrina called after me, but I didn't slow down.

What was wrong with me? These days, I cried all the time. Nothing helped, and everything hurt. Worse yet, it was embarrassing.

I burst through the door and out into the livestock area, the colder air aching in my lungs. Tears stung my eyes, and a lump welled in my throat as I sped toward the back of the barn. Tears streamed down my face, and my vision blurred, but I still managed to make my way to the narrow stairs leading up to the network of catwalks stretching high above the holding pens.

This was where I'd spent my time at the auction when I was younger, at least when I wasn't helping the adults. John and I had quietly strolled these catwalks together as friends when we were children and then when we dated as teenagers. Every now and then, as adulthood set in, we found ourselves back up here for a little slice of quiet and nostalgia. But now it was just me up here, save for a handful of kids who scattered away when they spotted me.

After I found a dark corner beyond the reach of the heaters, I leaned over the railing to let my tears fall. It wasn't long before Sabrina climbed the stairs and joined me. We watched in silence as another group of cattle was herded from the pens toward the auction, passing the mini Highlanders along the way as they exited the auction ring. Whoever had bought Wes's fluffy cows would pick them up after checking out, but I took comfort in knowing minis were usually kept as pets. Usually. I had to hold out hope.

Maybe I still wasn't that much of a cattle farmer, even after all these years.

"Do you want to talk about it?" Sabrina asked, her gaze still fixed on the animals below.

At least I could appreciate that she didn't put her hand on mine or rub my back like other friends might have tried to do. When I was upset, the last thing I wanted was to be touched by anyone.

I swallowed, fighting the lump in my throat. "What's there to talk about?"

"You could tell me why you bolted? What's going on inside that head of yours? Or how my best friend could be anything less than kind to her neighbors?"

A bitter laugh escaped me before I could restrain myself. "My neighbors? Besides two or three people, yourself included, who was there for me after John?"

I had to bite my lip to keep from sobbing, but a fresh wave of tears streamed down my face.

"Wes is your neighbor, too. He was John's best friend. He's always been ready to help. If you'd ever let him. He really was there for you, but he honored your wishes by waiting for you to ask for help."

I chewed my lip and let out a shuddering breath. "I hate crying in front of people. I just feel like I'm at a breaking point."

She moved a little closer and leaned her head against mine. "I'm sorry you're still grieving, honey. I hate imagining what you've been going through all these years, and I wish I could take some of that pain from you for myself. But I can't, Carrie. All I can do is be here for you. Can you let your friends lend a hand?"

She handed me a tissue from her purse, and I dabbed at my face with it. "Yes, I think I'll have to. And you're right. As always."

Sabs pulled out another tissue. "Let's clean you up and head back in. I'll be right there with you."

I didn't want to go back, but I was tired of running every time I got triggered by something. If I didn't change that, I'd spend the rest of my life running away every time things got hard. "And I guess you're right about Wes, too. Does it look like I've been crying?"

Sabrina shrugged, and the corners of her mouth tugged into a wry grin. "Don't worry about it. You're allowed to have feelings, and if anyone has a problem with it, they can go pound sand."

Chapter 4: Right in the Shin

Wes

I couldn't help but feel bad for Caroline as I watched her race for the door and disappear into the livestock area. I glimpsed her head bobbing beyond the door as she strode toward the holding area, and I kept my gaze pinned on her until I couldn't see her anymore. Leaning forward, I tapped one of the auction assistants on the shoulder and asked him to pass a message to the auctioneer, then sat back down again.

My eyes were on the auction, but my mind was chasing Caroline through the dusty halls and wrapping her up in a hug she probably needed. Maybe. Running a hand down my face, I took a couple of deep, slow breaths and channeled my focus. Caroline and I hadn't been friends since we broke up back in high school, and as much as I would have loved to reconcile with her, she'd never given me the chance. Something strange lingered in the air and settled in my heart as I watched a handful of Angus cows herded in for bidding. I saw her here almost every time, so why was I getting all flustered now?

Just as I'd gathered the courage to go out and check in on Caroline and Sabrina, I spotted them walking in together. I forced myself not to stare, not to push her with my smile. Instead, I pretended like I didn't notice. They halted, standing close together on the stairs, until I couldn't resist anymore. I glanced up despite my best efforts.

The pair stared at the row of seating just behind me, so I looked, too. Their spot had been filled, and now there were slim pickings. Except for the spaces next to me. I waved at them, then moved the saddle and the other tack I'd purchased to the floor at my feet. Patting the bench, I gestured them over.

Caroline frowned, but she didn't hesitate very long. She was in front of Sabrina, so she couldn't turn around, and it would be awkward to make her friend squeeze in around her.

She would be sitting directly next to me, and there wasn't much space to spread out. In a few short strides, she maneuvered around the legs of the people sitting between me and the stairs, then sat down next to me, bringing an air of tension with her.

"Thanks, Wes," she said, leaning close to talk over the auctioneer's clear, sharp voice booming out over the PA system.

The way she said my name sent a tickle down my spine and warmed my chest. "Of course. I would've saved your spot if I knew you were coming back."

She gave me a smile, a tired smile, but it was better than nothing. Her eyes were red, and her eyeliner rubbed away.

"Are you all right?" I leaned in so she could hear me and caught the scent of peaches from her hair. Soft, sweet, and reminiscent of a warm summer day.

She swallowed, gaze dropping to the dusty toes of her boots. "Yeah. I mean... Yes. Of course I am."

I nodded and returned my attention to the ring. Others might push, but I knew better. People changed in some ways, but in other ways, they didn't change at all. There was no forcing her to talk if she didn't want to, so I let her be and focused on the auction, comforted by knowing she was right beside me for now.

A few heads of Dexter cows finished out the cattle portion of the auction, and then they brought in the horses, the biggest reason for my attendance each week. The first was a black Standardbred gelding. His ears were a little nervous, flicking back and forth as he was ridden around the small, oval-shaped ring in front of the auctioneer's booth. He moved quickly as the teen girl on his back tapped her heels to his sides, and he chuffed hard as he trotted and turned, trotted and turned, over and over again.

"No papers here, folks, but this twelve-year-old gelding has been a kid's 4-H horse for the past eight years, and now that the kid has moved on, he's looking for a new home," the auctioneer babbled quickly. "I'm told he's an easy keeper and all-around good mover. That's right, folks. This one does it all! He wins in the ring, is bombproof in parades, and swift-footed on the trails. Let's start the bidding at five thousand."

The auctioneer slammed his gavel and started his rapid-fire chant, but there were no takers.

"What's wrong with him?" Caroline asked, her warm breath tickling my ear.

I studied his legs, his eyes, the tension in his ears. "Nothing that I can see. But you know how hay is right now."

She groaned. "Ugh. I hate that you reminded me."

"What about four thousand, folks?" the auctioneer said, stopping his chanting to encourage potential buyers. "Come on, this guy is kid-safe, husband-safe, even grandma-safe! And did we mention he's only twelve? He has plenty of years left in him."

The teen slowed the Standardbred to a lazy walk, letting him lower his head to sniff the gates and the ground, further demonstrating how calm he was in loud, chaotic environments as the auctioneer's clear, sharp chanting resumed over the speakers.

"But if he's an easy keeper and kid safe," Caroline ventured, and I turned to watch her bite her lower lip. Pretty black eyelashes coated in mascara fluttered as she studied the horse.

"Why don't you buy him, then?" I grinned and nudged her gently with my shoulder.

She sucked in a breath. "I know I'm too soft-hearted because I'm considering it. But I don't have time for the couple of horses I do have."

I shifted and leaned closer. "Are they your horses?"

She shrugged. "Technically speaking, yes. But they're all actually the kids' horses."

"You don't have your own horse?"

"No. My gelding, Popeye, passed a couple of years ago..." Her words trailed off. She swallowed hard and blinked back the sudden tears glistening in her eyes.

My heart ached to see her pain.

"It was shortly after John passed, and..." She cocked her head suddenly and turned to face me. "Honestly, I don't think I've ridden once since the last time John and I went out."

That bottom lip quivered, and I made a split-second gamble, daring myself to do something—anything—to make her feel better.

I held out my hand, keeping it low, an offer for a moment of comfort.

Though I'd been sure she'd slap my hand away or cuss at me, she didn't. She lifted her hand, hesitated briefly, then rested it in mine. I gave her a gentle squeeze, then released, letting her know I was here for her. I expected her to leave it at that, but she squeezed my hand in return and shuffled an inch closer until our shoulders and thighs were touching.

"Five hundred people!" The auctioneer's astonishment at the lack of bidding on the horse was clear in his wide eyes and exasperated voice.

I jolted in my seat, hand tensing briefly before I remembered I held Caroline's. How had the bid dropped to five hundred?

The auctioneer conferred with the owner at the side of the ring, a woman who looked like she'd bit into a lemon.

"It should be criminal to let him go for so little," the auctioneer said. "Wait! There, finally! I've got five hundred!"

The auctioneer's chant continued, and I looked to where he was pointing to find the first bidder. A big man in saggy old blue jeans, a red Carhartt coat, and a brown Stetson held up his bidder number. A cut horsetail hung from a white handle that jutted from his back pocket. It was heavy-handed and macabre.

I clenched my jaw.

"Is that..." Caroline started, but she didn't finish the question.

But she didn't have to. I knew what she meant to say. "Yes. That's Walt. The meat buyer."

The processing of horses for meat wasn't legal in the US, but meat men attended every auction and bought horse flesh to ship to Canada or Mexico. That part wasn't illegal. I wouldn't argue culture and food, but I personally couldn't stand the thought of eating horse meat, and apparently, Caroline was of the same mind.

"He's not really going to send that good horse to meat, is he?" Her eyes brimmed with tears again as she glanced between the Standardbred and Walt.

I expelled a frustrated breath. "He doesn't ride."

"Are you sure? Maybe he has a kid—"

"He's only here for one reason, Caroline." I gently squeezed her hand, suddenly shocked to realize she still hadn't taken it away yet. "I'm sorry."

She squeezed me back, but then flexed her fingers and withdrew her hand from mine. "Thank you, Wes, for... Well, for being so kind and all, but I can't watch this anymore."

Her voice shook, her body shivered alongside mine. Now that I thought about it, she hadn't usually stayed for the horses over the past few years. She almost always came, and she was usually first in line, but she never stayed for the whole thing.

"I've got five hundred going once, going twice... Come on, people. This is the perfect horse and your last chance to bring him home!"

Caroline bent forward to grab her purse as she muttered something to Sabrina.

"Damn it." I sighed, unrolled my bidder number, and held it up, waggling it toward the nearest ring assistant. I shouted, "Six hundred!"

"Wes!" Caroline stilled, purse in her lap. "What are you doing? I thought you didn't want him."

I opened my mouth, but no answer came. What could I say that wouldn't be weird, pathetic, or worse—scare her away?

"There's my favorite equine enthusiast," the auctioneer teased, saving me from having to speak. Then he chanted the six hundred to seven hundred and pointed to Walt.

Walt nodded.

I wanted to kick him. Right in the shin.

The auctioneer chanted seven hundred to eight hundred as he pointed at Walt, then he swung his gavel to point it at me.

Without a second's hesitation, I nodded firmly. I was sure I had Walt's measure, which was what the horse was worth to him across either border. If the horse in question had been one of the draft horses or draft crosses I'd actually come to look for, then I'd really be in trouble.

It wasn't that Standardbreds weren't great horses, too. It was simply that I already had enough light saddle horses. I needed some bigger horses for the heavier customers who often came for trail riding or my Ranch Life experiences. One of my greatest ambitions was to offer more people the opportunity to fall in love with equestrian life, which meant maintaining a broad-ranging herd of rideable horses.

"We have eight hundred! Do we have nine?"

Walt didn't nod. He turned and looked at me, and I stared back, subtly tapping my bidder number against my leg.

Then he nodded again, and I went from wanting to kick him in the shin to wanting to meet him in the parking lot.

"We have nine hundred, folks, and it's still only a fraction of what this good-looking horse is worth!" Then he chanted nine hundred to one thousand and pointed to me, as no one else was bidding but me and Walt.

I set my jaw and nodded again, undeterred.

"One thousand, folks!" And the auction chanted to eleven before turning to Walt.

Walt shook his head firmly and held his bidder number rolled up in his hand.

"One thousand, going once... going twice... and sold!" The auctioneer slammed his gavel and pointed it at me once more. "Show me that bidder number again, Wes."

"Thirteen, Bob," I yelled, holding the paper up for him.

He grinned back at me and winked as the assistant sitting next to him marked it down. The Standardbred was ridden out of the ring and disappeared back into the livestock area. I'd have the horse held here for a couple of hours after the auction so I could run back and get my horse trailer. I had three of them, and which one I brought depended on how many horses I bought by the end.

"Wes? Did you really want that horse?" Caroline asked, resting her hand lightly on my shoulder. I swear I could feel the warmth of it even through my coat.

I turned and put on my signature broad smile.

Her bottom lip quivered. "Tell me it isn't my fault."

I'd have given anything in that moment to touch her face, pull her close, chase away every worry. "Your fault? Do you hear yourself?"

I hadn't meant to sound scolding, but judging by the way she winced, I guess I had anyway.

"Of course not," I hurried to reassure her, pressing my hand to the one still on my shoulder. "I run a horse ranch. And I always need new horses."

"Seriously, Wes?" Sabrina said, one eyebrow arched. She and I had remained friends throughout high school and into adulthood, though we'd never been—and never would be—as close as she was with Caroline. I'd always asked Sabrina to speak to Caroline on my behalf, but she'd only dressed me down and refused vehemently.

I shrugged and held out my hands, palms up. "What was I supposed to do? Let some kid's 4-H horse get ground up for dog food?"

Caroline shook her head and sniffled. "I know, and I'm glad he'll get another chance at life. But you didn't have to bid on a horse you didn't want just because I felt uncomfortable."

Was I that transparent?

I stuffed my hands in my pockets and stared down at my boots for a few seconds. Without looking up at her, and hoping against all hope, I had to shoot my shot. "Well, let me get him settled in and evaluate him, then... maybe you'll tell me you'll consider stopping by for a ride someday, or at least to come see him."

The buzz of conversation filled the spaces around us as everyone waited for the next horse to be brought in, and my hope withered faster than spring sprouts hit by a late frost.

Chapter 5: The Pain

Carrie

Sabrina grabbed the sleeve of my coat and answered before I could. "Of course! I'll drive her over. I don't think she's ever been out to see your place, have you, Carrie?"

I glared, thankful I stood between her and Wes so he couldn't see my face. "No. I haven't seen it yet."

"Just text me some good days," she said to Wes. "And I'll coordinate with Carrie to see what works best for her. Okay?"

Wes's cheeks flushed, but he nodded, and his smile was genuine. "Of course. I'd love to show you the farm when you have time. And I'll make sure the Standardbred I just bought is ready in case you feel up to riding."

He rubbed the back of his neck with one hand, and his face turned a deeper shade of red.

I wanted to laugh at the ridiculousness of the entire day. I was still a complete mess, and my best friend and my ex-boyfriend from high school were bending over every which way to try to ease my pain a little.

Instead of surrendering to the urge to laugh and cry at the same time, I sucked in a deep breath and steadied myself. "I don't know if I'll be ready to ride any time soon, but I appreciate the offer."

He looked hurt, and I became painfully aware that my response sounded like a complete rejection. I hurried to add, "But I'll be glad to finally see your place and see that horse happy there with you."

His expression turned surprised, and a slight grin brightened his face again. "I look forward to it."

What was I doing? I'd sworn I hated Wes all these years since high school, but here I was, holding his hand for comfort, playing nice, and committing to seeing him out at his ranch.

"I'm a little tired, though, so I think I'm going to go pay for my things and head out." I grabbed the tack I'd bought and settled my purse strap over my shoulder as I stood. "Thank you, Wes."

"Save my spot," Sabrina told Wes. "I'll be back after I walk Carrie out to her truck."

She walked out ahead of me and waited in silence as I paid, but set to jabbering as soon as we stepped out into the parking lot.

"Oh my God, Carrie! Are you and Wes a... a thing again?"

I stopped in my tracks and glared at her. "A 'thing'! Now, why in the hell would you say something like that?"

"Holding hands?" She waggled her eyebrows. "And the fact that he just bought you a horse."

I scowled. "He didn't buy me a horse. It's his horse, for his ranch."

"Yeah. Uh-huh. And the hand holding?"

My neck and ears burned with embarrassment. "I don't know. He offered, and..." I shrugged. "It just felt right in the moment. It doesn't mean anything, right? We're not kids anymore."

I started walking again, squeezing the horse blanket and tack under one arm while I fished through my purse for my keys.

"You're right," Sabrina said, her voice sullen now. "I wasn't trying to—"

"I know, Sabs," I cut her off, then sighed heavily as I unlocked my truck. She opened the door for me, and I loaded my things in silence. "You're the best friend anyone could ask for. Don't worry about it, and don't overthink it. You always do right by me."

I hugged her tightly, my eyes stinging with the threat of tears again, but this time I resisted.

"So, you're not mad about me offering to take you to Wes's place?" she asked, pulling back to study my face.

I sighed and chewed my lip. "No. I guess not. As long as you're with me, it'll be fine. It's probably even good for me. I'll admit, I've been pretty cooped up lately."

"Lately? You mean over the last four years?"

"Well, yes. But—"

She raised a hand to cut me off, then patted my shoulder gently. "I know. I'm not saying you didn't need time to mourn, or that your grieving should be confined to some time-defined box. But I don't believe that hiding away from the rest of the world helps you. And I know you can remember back when you liked Wes and, more importantly, all the years that he was John's best friend."

I couldn't deny any of that, regardless of how hard I'd tried to forget. When John and I started dating in high school, Wes wasn't bothered. But as things got serious, he grew cold and distant. Despite being the best man at our wedding, we saw him less and less as we settled into married life—at least until Tori was born and he asked to be her godfather. The return of John's best friend into his life had reinvigorated him, bringing back the type of friend that a spouse couldn't be. Things went on like that for years. There were slow times when we didn't see him much, and then there were months when he and John would see each other constantly. Our families became close, going to the same holiday parties and community events, and spending barbecues together.

"There's a hole left in me, in our family, in the hearts of each of our childr en..." I swallowed against the lump forming in my throat and squeezed my eyes against the unwelcome threat of tears. "I haven't had time to think about how John's passing has affected Wes, too."

She nodded sympathetically and rubbed my shoulders with her hands. "It's okay. No one expects you to. All of it, well, it's just too much for one person. Just know that you still have friends out here in the county."

"Wes was my husband's friend before he was mine," I observed.

She studied my face. "Whatever happened between you two back in high school was kid stuff. It's not a big deal, and it doesn't matter. Let it go, honey."

I thought over her words as I drove the dark, quiet roads back to my farm. She was right, as usual. What happened between Wes and me back in high school was just kid stuff. It didn't mean anything. And I could stand to be a little kinder to my late husband's best friend. What could be the harm in that?

Chapter 6: Get My Hopes Up

Wes

Almost two weeks passed before I got a call. Thirteen days of a rollercoaster of hoping, forcing myself to accept reality, and then daring to hope again. When I saw Caroline with Sabrina at the auction again over the weekend, she only waved at me and didn't sit near me or get close enough to talk. I didn't want to intrude or risk being seen as a creep, so I gave her space and left her alone.

I was exercising the new Standardbred, Murray, in my indoor arena one evening when my cell phone buzzed in my pocket. I halted him near the center of the ring, dismounted, and sat on the mounting block before checking the screen. Murray's ears pricked forward, and his nostrils flared as he inspected my phone, but I didn't make a big deal out of it so that he wouldn't either.

I swallowed hard when I saw it was Sabrina's name on the caller ID.

"Hello?" I answered.

"Hey, Wes!" Her tone was bubbling with excitement.

"How are you doing?"

"Great! I actually wanted to see if the invite still stands."

"What invite?" I knew exactly what she was referring to, but I didn't want to sound too eager.

She scoffed. "Boy, don't play with me."

"Boy? I'm all man."

"Ew. Gross."

"Hey!" I protested. "That's not very nice!"

Sabrina laughed. "Well, that's what you get. Now, shut up and listen. I finally got Carrie to agree to some dates."

My pulse quickened, and I stopped laughing. "Dates?"

"Not 'date' dates. 'Days' dates," she clarified. "Basically, any Thursday afternoon or Saturday morning."

Tomorrow was Saturday. "So, tomorrow morning?"

"If you're free," she said. It was more like a question than a statement.

"Let me check my bookings." I pulled the phone away from my ear and turned on the speaker while I navigated to my calendar. I wasn't messing with her. I had to make sure no one had scheduled rides, lessons, or any other appointments that would pull me away from a visit.

The calendar showed I was clear, so I blocked off the morning while I answered her. "Perfect. I'm free all morning tomorrow. What time will you be here?"

"She said she'd like to come early, around eight, if that's okay."

"Yes, that's great. I'll get everything ready!" My mind raced, and Murray rubbed his head roughly against my shoulder.

She went silent for a moment. "Um, like what? What do you need to get ready?"

I tilted my head back and forth as I thought. "Well, uh, does she like coffee?"

"Yes, with cream and sugar."

"What about breakfast?"

"She prefers egg bites and cheese danishes. Why all the questions? We're coming to see the farm, not—"

"Sabrina. Could you just see if we can have a light breakfast here at my place? My lounge is pretty nice, and it's heated. I'd love to just have a few things out that she likes."

"Then I want pancakes."

I sighed. "I'm not making pancakes."

"Come on!"

"No. Just some coffee and easy, small things I can buy in town and bring back."

"Jeez. You're really going all out. You know, we could bring something—"

"I'm trying to make a good impression. You know how I feel. How I've felt all these years."

"I... I know, Wes." Her tone turned somber.

"No one ever spoke up for me to her, so now, my actions have to speak for me."

She sniffled. "I'm sorry I couldn't do that for you."

I shrugged despite knowing she couldn't see me. "I was mad about it when I was a kid, but I know now that no one could have done what I was hoping for. That's not how it works."

"Well, I'll always put in a good word for you when I can. I'm rooting for you, and I know John would want her to be happy—for you both to be happy. We all know you're a good guy, and she deserves something more than... well, whatever this limbo is that she's been living in."

I stabbed my toe into the dirt as Murray's eyes closed, his breathing slow and calm. He was falling asleep while I wrestled with all my unspoken feelings. "I don't want to get my hopes up, Sabrina. And I know I'm not 'the best' guy around. There's plenty of better men in every way who'd love to make her smile again."

Sabrina sighed. "Stop it. John wouldn't want her to be alone, and if she'll give your dumb ass a chance, then you're the only one John would trust to do right by her."

"Even after what happened—"

"Back in high school? How many times do I have to tell both of you to let it go?!" She cursed, but the word was muffled.

"Both of us?"

"Oh. Shoot." She groaned. "Um. Forget I said that."

"You've got intel, Sabrina, and I need it. Now!"

"No! I said nothing. Don't try to distract me." She was resolute, and whatever she knew she'd keep locked up tighter than Fort Knox. "Let that kid stuff go and get on with your life. Haven't you had enough petty drama?"

My face grew hot, and I couldn't pinpoint exactly why I felt embarrassed by the way she said it. "I hate drama. What are you talking about?"

"Don't get defensive. I'm talking about Kathy."

Just the mention of my ex-wife's name soured my mood exponentially. "Okay. You've had your fun picking on me—"

"I'm not picking on you. I'm just saying that it's time to grow up. It's time to—"

"What do you want for breakfast?"

"No, Wes. This is important. Learn your lessons and—"

"Okay. Thanks for calling, Sabrina. I'll see you at eight a.m. sharp." I ended the call in the middle of her tirade and switched my phone to silent.

Murray bobbed his head lightly and opened his eyes as I stood again.

"Let's call it a day, boy." I patted his neck, then led him out of the arena so I could untack him, give him a good groom, and settle him in his stall for the night.

After feeding all the animals and closing up the barn, I jogged through the icy darkness and made a beeline for the house. It was big, and now that Kathy and the kids were gone, it was empty. If it wasn't for my dogs, I'd feel too alone to stay here. I spent the next hour tidying up, making sure everything was perfect. It was pretty easy for one man to keep himself and his dogs.

A pang of loneliness hit me out of nowhere as I looked around the open rooms, silent beneath the grand, vaulted ceilings. Everything here was haunted by the memories of the people I loved most. Kathy may have left me and started her life over with someone new, but I still loved the mother of my children. I missed those damn kids, too. Four of them, all grown now, and two of them didn't speak to me anymore.

My phone buzzed, breaking the spell before I could consider reaching for a bottle of something dark to drown my regrets.

It was Sabrina. I opened the screen and tapped on the message. She'd sent a picture of herself sitting with Caroline. They both smiled and waved at the camera. The text below it read, "See you tomorrow!"

I shook off the ghosts, turned on the stereo system, and connected the Bluetooth. AC/DC's Back in Black album blasted through the house as I vacuumed, mopped, and dusted instead of rotting on the couch with a fifth of whiskey in hand.

Chapter 7: Coffee and Danishes

Carrie

By the time seven a.m. rolled around, I had already fed the animals, showered, and dressed. I also put a little extra effort into styling my graying hair, pulling it into a low, messy bun with a few strands left artfully loose. Then, I did something I hadn't done in so long that I couldn't even remember the last time I'd done it: I put on makeup.

Not a lot. Just a little eyeliner, mascara, and a nude lipstick. And when I took a good look at myself in the mirror, I was shocked. I looked so much... younger, even with just that little bit. Vibrant. Sharp.

Alive.

Maybe I'd been moving a little slowly through life since John's passing. Okay, I was moving like molasses. I hadn't wanted anything in this life but to be with him. Sure, we'd had our ups and downs like anyone else, but our love was real.

It was true. And when he passed, I didn't want to move on with life. If it wasn't for my kids...

I shuddered to think about it, knowing what had beckoned to me from the darkest depths of my grief.

But I hadn't ended the pain and joined him in the afterlife, and I was proud that I'd stayed, not just for the kids but to take care of everything he and I had built together.

As I put away my makeup, I paused with my hand on the tube of lipstick and caught the style name printed on the label: Worth It.

That reminded me of something John used to tell me. Do it because you're worth it.

The memory stung as I fought against the realization that I hadn't been doing more than the bare minimum to take care of myself. I had used my grief as an excuse to sink into a dark, lonesome abyss of depression and self-neglect. The hollows above my clavicle bones were sunken, and my hips looked a little sharp. Eating regular meals was harder now that I had to cook for one. When the kids were younger, John and I had imagined how we'd thrive as young empty-nesters. We never imagined something like this, and we hadn't prepared for it. So I had to go it alone, without the person I'd devoted myself to growing old with.

My phone buzzed, and I jumped, then exhaled and picked it up. The screen lit up with a text message from Sabrina.

Sabrina: Are you ready? I don't want to be late.

Ready? I glanced in the upper right corner of my screen to find that it was already quarter to eight.

"Damn it," I muttered as I took one last swipe at my lashes with the mascara before running out the door.

"Everything okay?" Sabrina asked as I jumped in her Pathfinder. She pressed a lead foot on the gas pedal, and I was thankful the roads weren't too slick today despite the fresh blanket of snow that fell overnight.

"Of course. Why wouldn't it be?" I clicked my seatbelt and settled in for the ride, one hand on the pocket of the door handle to steady myself as she whipped out of my driveway and headed south on the main drag.

"Because you're never late for anything." She glanced between me and the road.

I shrugged. "Oh. Well, I was a little slow getting ready this morning. Sorry."

She huffed out a breath. "I wouldn't normally be bothered, but it would be rude to be late. I know Wes will be there waiting for us."

I shrugged, watched the road wind west ahead of us, away from town. "I guess that's valid."

We finally turned north off the main drag onto one of the backroads. It looked like so many other rural Michigan backroads in agricultural areas: forest and fields flashed outside my window, and the shoulders of the road were often bordered by trees, deep field ditches, barbed wire, or electric fencing. Sabrina turned one more time onto a dirt drive and crawled the car over a small hill flanked by thick forest. When we crested the hill, a vision of wondrous, winter splendor spread out before us.

The forest encircled a shallow valley filled with beautiful, symmetrical black-fenced pastures, where blanketed horses enjoyed their breakfast hay. A few trotted and cantered playfully toward the fence to greet us, flicking up specks of powdery snow behind them. A grand house in log-cabin style was centered in the valley and silhouetted against round, tree-covered hills.

Farm, house, barns, and mountains all sported a fresh, sparkling white blanket of snow. Barns flanked the main house: a pole barn that looked like a garage on the left and a set of three horse barns to the right. The largest barn clearly housed the indoor arena I'd heard talk of. Surveying the beautiful but cold landscape, I recalled hearing how well-insulated and warm it was in the winter. The other two barns were smaller, single-floor structures with stall doors that led to individual paddocks.

It was a long driveway, but sure enough, Wes was leaning against the door of his truck and waiting to greet us as we pulled up in front of the main barn. He was bundled in his Carhartt with a simple black wool scarf. His cheeks were red with cold, and I glanced at my watch. It was 8:18.

Guilt pricked my conscience for being late, and this time, I didn't try to fend it off. I deserved to feel guilty. It was only twenty degrees outside, and that was before the windchill.

"I'm sorry we're late," I said, jumping out of Sabrina's car before she could put it in park. "It took a little longer to feed all the animals this morning."

"Not a problem." He smiled, and it looked so genuine that I relaxed a little. "Let's head inside. It's freezing out here."

With Wes and Sabrina leading the way, we walked in through the main entrance, then into the barn's main lounge.

Wes met my gaze as he held open a door for us. "Did Sabrina tell you I'd have coffee ready?"

"She did," I said as I poked her in the back.

We walked to the counter near the kitchenette at the back of the lounge, passing a few small round tables set aesthetically with chairs, tablecloths, and centerpieces, and a square of comfy-looking couches around a long, reclaimed barnwood coffee table. Two boxes of coffee from the local coffee shop sat beside a large white box of pastries and two covered dishes.

"This is a lot." I peeked into the pastry box, and I could hardly stop myself from salivating when I spotted the danishes.

Wes shrugged off my observation, but a dimple formed in one cheek. "First impressions are important, and I want the farm to make a good impression on you."

I tipped my head back the way we came. "The view coming up the drive does all the work in that respect, but this is great too. Is that coffee?" I pointed to the carafes.

"Yes." He grabbed a stack of to-go cups, slipped one free, and handed it to me. Then he pointed to a bowl of extras. "I've also got cream and sugar."

"The danishes look delicious," I said as I poured myself a cup of coffee

"Please." He gestured to a stack of ceramic plates and napkins, then lifted the lids on each covered dish. "I also made bacon and cheese egg bites. And pancakes."

"Pancakes? Wes, you're the best!" Sabrina grabbed one of the ceramic plates and took three of the pancakes, then slathered them in butter and maple syrup before taking a seat at one of the low round tables.

I grinned as I added egg bites and a raspberry Danish to my plate. "Wow. This is great, Wes. Thanks!"

I sat next to Sabrina, and soon Wes joined us with his own plate and cup of coffee. He only had a few egg bites.

"Where'd you get the pancakes?" Sabrina asked. "I swear they're the lightest, fluffiest pancakes I've ever had!"

"I made them," Wes said between bites. "I made the egg bites too."

I stopped chewing and stared at him. "Really? These are delicious! Did you make them last night?"

He smiled over the lid of his coffee, failing at nonchalance. "This morning, actually. I wake up early anyway, so I thought I'd make everything fresh before running into town for the coffee and Danishes."

It was a lot of extra effort, and I couldn't help but worry that I was somehow inconveniencing him. The idea rooted itself in my mind, and I couldn't shake it. "That's so much work. You really shouldn't have."

"Don't worry at all. It's my pleasure to be a good host," Wes said, blowing off my clear concern.

I took the hint and let it go. "Well, thank you. This is a nice change."

He tilted his head. "Nice change from what?"

"I usually don't eat until lunch, and then..." I let the words trail off as I thought about it. The answer wasn't a socially acceptable one. I didn't eat much, as evidenced by my sunken skin and protruding hip bones. I didn't even want to imagine what my spine might look like if I bent over. "I guess I'm a bit of a grazer."

Sabrina and Wes nodded, but neither looked me in the eye. I knew they didn't believe me. They could see the truth when they looked at me. I fought to keep my hands from trembling as I mentally scolded myself for making it awkward.

The silence was uncomfortable for several seconds before a buzzing sound broke it.

Chapter 8: John Would Be Proud of You

Wes

We all instinctively reached for our pockets and slipped out our cell phones. Neither of the women had brought purses, meaning their phones were in their jackets, like mine was.

My screen was dark, and so was Caroline's.

"Rob?" Sabrina answered. "What? Oh my God... Slow down..." Her eyes widened, then her gaze flitted between Caroline and me. "No, of course. I'll be there right away."

She hung up the phone, slipped it back into her pocket, and pulled out her keys as she bolted up from her seat. "I'm sorry, guys. Rob was in an accident."

"Oh, no!" Caroline said, pushing her seat back.

"Is he okay?" I asked, rising with them.

Sabrina nodded. "Actually, yes, he seems to be okay. But his car is being towed, and he's refusing the ambulance ride to the hospital. They want to evaluate him for a concussion."

"Let's go," Caroline said.

I dug in my pockets for my keys. "I can drive—"

"No, please." Sabrina held her hands up. "Both of you, just stay here. Neither of you has met Rob yet, and this is not the time for introductions. I have to go." She set her gaze on me. "Can you drive Carrie home?"

"Yes." I strode forward to hold open the door for Sabrina. "Don't worry about it. Just call if you need anything."

"Call me when you can," Caroline called after her friend.

Sabrina waved over her shoulder but said nothing before jumping into her SUV and speeding down the driveway.

Caroline and I stood at the window and watched Sabrina until she disappeared over the hill.

"Do you want to go home?" I asked the question I'd been avoiding for several painfully long minutes.

She didn't answer right away, her gaze drinking in the scenery of the farm as she sipped her coffee. "I don't see why. Unless you want me to go. Do you—"

"No!" I answered a little too quickly. "I mean, no sense in heading home out away, in case Sabrina calls later and needs us to come to town."

"That's a fair point." She headed back to our table and sat down at her plate. Her hazel eyes stared up at me, and she smiled softly. "Let's enjoy this lovely breakfast you put together."

I let myself relax a little and sat down to join her. "You're right. I'm sure if it was worse, Sabrina would have asked us to follow her."

"That's right," Caroline agreed. "So, tell me about your place here. And," she stood to bring the carafe of coffee from the counter to the table, "I'm sorry I never came out here with John to see it."

I can't deny that it still stung, even after all these years. All the barbecues were held at the Bennett Farm, or any of our other mutual friends' places. But the Bennets never attended the ones hosted by Kathy and me.

"Why didn't you?" I dared to ask.

Her gaze dropped to her plate, and she shifted in her seat. "I had a lot of anger for a while."

"Anger? About what?" I asked, but I was sure I already knew what she referred to.

"About what happened between us." She looked anywhere but at me.

My leg started bouncing under the table. "Back in high school? Before... you and John?"

She nodded, but still didn't look up. A lock of hair slipped out of her bun, caressing her cheek.

I clasped my hands in my lap and studied her face, silently pleading for her to meet my eyes. "I'm sorry, Caroline. Looking back, I know now how much I must have hurt you." I couldn't remember ever having apologized before, but there was no time better than the present. "I'm sorry, and I hope I can earn your forg—"

"Please, Wes." She held up a hand to stop me from continuing. "Sabrina was right. That was kid stuff, and it was years ago. But I appreciate the apology anyway. I held onto my anger about it for far too long, and it feels good to start letting it go."

"Sabrina? That's funny," I said, then paused to sip my coffee. "She said something like that to me, too."

She locked eyes with me, her gaze clear and hard. "It broke me back then, when you cheated on me with Kim Harrison."

"I kissed her," I clarified. I still remember how horrible I felt afterward. "We were at a party at someone's house. I can't even remember who's house it was. Their parents were out of town, of course, and somebody brought booze." I shook my head. "One drink too many, and I gave in to the first girl who flirted with me.

"You're right," she said, nodding slowly. "It was just a kiss. But when you're that age, it's the same thing as cheating, isn't it?"

Heat crept up my neck, and I unzipped my jacket. "No, it's not right. It was cheating then, and it would be cheating now, too."

She nodded, solemn, but her eyes softened a little. "After that, I couldn't imagine trusting anyone again. Until I fell in love with John. Now, after all we've been through, all the growing up we've all done since then, all that stuff from high school feels petty."

I huffed out a sigh. "It does. But I'm still sorry—"

She held up a hand to stop me. "Remember? You've already apologized, and it's not necessary. But I do feel a little bad about something entirely different. And tell me if it's too sensitive of a topic for me to ask about. What happened with you and Kathy?"

I clenched my jaw and stared at my coffee cup, rubbing my thumbs along the sides of it. "I assume you heard we got divorced?"

"Yes. About three years ago, right?"

I nodded. "Almost a year after John died. I was depressed after he passed, and my grief took me to some pretty dark places."

Her gaze was neutral and unflinching. No sign of remorse, compassion, or understanding crossed her face.

It didn't matter if she believed me or felt sorry. I didn't need her pity, but I'd been working on myself too much to just leave it at that.

After refreshing my coffee, I spilled my guts. "I'll admit that at first, I felt abandoned by her But I realized too late that I'd abandoned her. Not just in my grief, but every day in little ways that mattered." My face and ears burned with shame as I recalled everything Kathy had told me during and after the divorce. "She had handled too much on her own, and I was checked out. So, yes, I drank away my grief after John's passing. But it was only the final straw on the camel's back."

"The timing doesn't really seem fair," Caroline said.

I scoffed. "No, it doesn't seem fair, but the way I behaved in my marriage for twelve years wasn't fair to her either. Or to our kids." I leaned forward on the table, clasping my hands in front of me to keep them from shaking. I hadn't talked about these things with anyone but my therapist, but it felt good to say them aloud to someone out here in the real world. Maybe it was stupid of me, but I felt like I could trust her. "She was out in Montana visiting her sister when she met the man she left me for."

She shook her head and blinked rapidly. "Wait. Kathy cheated on you?"

My leg bounced wildly under the table now. "No. It was after she'd already filed for divorce. And he... Well, he gave her back the hope she'd lost while she was married to me. He was waiting for her, ready to leap in with both feet as soon as the ink dried on our divorce decree."

Caroline's eyes were still and wide as she stared at me. "Is that where she is now?"

"Yes. She's making bread from scratch, dyeing homespun wool, and living the life she always dreamed of out on a big ranch in the mountains with a man who worships the ground she walks on."

"Does it hurt?" Her voice was soft, but it still stung.

"Of course it hurts." I didn't even hesitate.

"If you could get her back—"

"I wouldn't," I interrupted Caroline's train of thought. I knew exactly where she was going, and it was a dead end road. I exhaled a ragged breath and ran a hand through my hair. "Honestly, I'm happy for her. I had my chance, and I screwed it up. I'll never do anything to interfere with her happiness again. She deserves this guy. He can treat her like a queen and give her everything she wants in life."

"I had no idea all this had happened," she said, shaking her head. "But it sounds like you're in a good place, and I'm happy for you."

I laughed bitterly. "Oh, me? No, Caroline. I'm not in a good place. But I am in therapy." I raised my cup to throw back the last dregs of my coffee. "But Kathy is in a good place, and the kids went with her. They backed her, and I don't blame them. I didn't ask for a war with my family, but never fighting for our marriage made them hate me for the way it hurt their mom. It took a lot of reflection and counseling, but I understand their reasoning, and I can clearly see now where I went wrong. All I can do is accept responsibility, and leave the door open in case they want to come back some day."

She chewed her lip, drank her coffee, and eyed me carefully before asking, "If you could go back in time to ten years ago, what would you do differently?"

The question surprised me. It was something I'd run through in my mind a thousand times, but I didn't think anyone would ever ask me and expect a real answer. "I would have done more around the house and spent more time with her and the kids. I'd stop drinking cold turkey, and I'd never even look at another woman again."

She arched one dark eyebrow. "Are you still drinking?"

I ran a hand through my hair and looked away. "Well, I quit a few months after the divorce was finalized. But I started up again after about a year. It's been a long road to getting it under control."

She nodded, then placed her warm palms over my tightly clasped hands. "We can't go back in time, but I know John would be proud of you for getting this far, and for working so hard to see the truth. He wanted you to have a good life."

"I know," I say, but my voice was hoarse, and I had to fight the lump in my throat. I wanted to say that I wished John was here to see me and his wife reconciling, and to see me sober someday, but if I said anything else, I'd break down in front of her. So instead, I clamped my mouth shut and pretended my heart wasn't shattered into a thousand jagged pieces.

We sat in silence for several minutes while we finished our breakfast. Once we were done eating, I packed the leftovers neatly and put them in the nearly empty lounge fridge.

"A little more coffee?" I asked, holding up a carafe.

"Yes, please." She took off the lid to her cup and held it forward. I filled it slowly until she signaled for me to stop.

I couldn't believe I was pouring Caroline's coffee. It would've seemed like a small thing to anyone else, but only two weeks ago, I'd thought she'd never speak to me again unless she was forced to. But here she was, in my lounge, sharing breakfast with me, listening to the sad state of my life, and letting me refill her cup.

"Well, thank you for listening to all that. If there's anything I can do for you—"

"Same," she interrupted, her gaze flicking up to meet mine. "We only have to ask each other, right?"

"That's right." I nodded toward the door, and we headed outside.

Chapter 9: The Scent of a Horse

Carrie

Wes started his tour by showing me the two smaller barns. One barn was for boarders and the other for quarantine. Separate sections of the barn were set aside for quarantining new or potentially sick horses. Some of the stalls led out to private paddocks, and some of them were triple the size of others, likely for mares in foal. Everything was neat and clean, and the blend of luxury English and rustic American architecture was surprisingly beautiful.

I whistled as I appreciated the glow of winter flooding in through the skylights. "Who designed the barns?"

"Kathy found the builder, and she picked out everything for these smaller barns. Then she directed me to make all the decisions for the indoor arena and that whole building."

"She has excellent taste," I said, running my hands along the smooth lines and solid wood supports.

"She sure does," he agreed, but there was an edge of bitterness in his voice, and I felt guilty that I might have been callous before.

I needed to change the subject so he wouldn't remain in the dark abyss of all his regrets. "How is the Standardbred? Did you really end up keeping him?"

"Of course I kept him," Wes said, then bumped his elbow lightly against my arm. "He's a good horse. Already desensitized, easy keeper, everything the old owners said he was and more. I don't know if he should simply sit here and be a trail horse."

"Why's that? I thought you said he's perfect?"

"That's just it. He's perfect, and he's still pretty young too. He's got a lot of life left in him, and so much potential."

"Is there anything you think he prefers to do?"

"That's the million-dollar question, Caroline. I'm not quite sure what he enjoys. He's so easy going that he hasn't pushed back on anything yet."

"Can we go see him?" I had been nervous about seeing the horse for a reason I could only guess at. I wondered if maybe I saw him, petted him, and got too close, I'd want to go for a ride. But it felt wrong to want to ride again. Without John.

"Yes. I'm glad you asked." He grinned broadly. "I was hoping you'd want to."

We made our way to the main barn that housed the indoor arena. One side of the barn, near the front, was where the lounge had been built, along with the empty manager's apartment on the second floor. Two sides were lined with stalls on the main floor, with hay storage areas above, and viewing areas on two sides of the second floor. Stairways led from the lounge and office to the other floors, and a small passageway led to a viewing area with bleachers between the lounge area and the main arena. The remaining side of the building was left without additions, allowing easy access to the arena for vehicles and heavy equipment.

"Wes, this is crazy. This isn't just a barn with an indoor arena. This is a full-on event facility. What were you planning to use all this for?"

He leaned against a gate and stared out over the arena, his eyes seeing things that weren't there. "I did have a lot of plans."

Then it hit me. Of course he'd had plans for this incredible facility that he had custom built. But somewhere between his drinking, his foolishness, and not being the best husband and father he could have been, his plans had faded and worn before turning to dust.

I couldn't help but challenge him, just as I would have challenged John. "What are your plans now?"

He cocked his head sideways and stared at me. "Plans? I don't have any plans now." Then he stared back out at the empty arena again. "Not since John's passing and my divorce."

"This is too beautiful to let it just sit like this." Then another thought struck me. "How on earth are you keeping this all running? It must cost a fortune to maintain this place."

"I wanted to run it as a business, but... well, you know. When it comes to money, I got lucky. My grandfather did very well, and he left each of us grandkids a pretty nice inheritance. I have enough to get me through another five years or so."

"How much did you give to Kathy?"

"As much as she let me. I would have given it all to her if I could have bought her forgiveness. All in all, I gave her about half, and she put it into special savings accounts for the kids. Her new husband reassured me that he had more than enough to take care of her, and they didn't need anything from me. She told me to use the rest of my inheritance to make our old dreams about this place come true."

My heart sank. "But you didn't."

He let out a bitter chuckle. "It's been a long time since I've heard you grill someone."

I bumped his shoulder with mine and stayed close to him. He was warm, and a whiff of his spice-filled cologne drifted my way. "Oh, Wes. This isn't me grilling you. Not yet anyway. We're just getting started."

"Great," he said sarcastically. He turned and nodded his head for me to follow. "Murray's waiting for us."

He led me down the halls, and in one of the big, roomy stalls with private paddock access, Murray was half asleep. Remnants of morning hay and grain littered the straw bedding, and he looked healthy. Even in the dim light, the gelding's coat had a shine that had been missing before. His eyes opened when Wes entered the stall, but he didn't jump or shy away. He stood still and allowed Wes to halter him, and then followed calmly when Wes led him out.

Wes put the horse in cross ties and brought out a grooming box cleaner than any I'd ever seen before.

"Dang, Wes. Do you ever use this thing? Or is it brand new?"

"A little of both. I wanted him to have his own kit, but I don't have many horses left here to groom anyway. It's easy to keep things clean. Help me groom him?" He tossed me a rubber curry, and I barely caught it.

"I see how it is. Lure me out here with food and coffee, then put me to work."

"You figured me out!" He laughed and winked at me.

Something stirred in me, a sensation I hadn't experienced in decades. Something about his old charm, those perfect dimples, and his smile stirred up all the old feelings I thought had disappeared after John and I had fallen in love.

I tried to brush it off. Maybe it was just that we hadn't ever really gotten closure until recently, and that's why the feelings had lingered so long—and why I felt more confused than ever right now. How could I still feel anything for him? He wasn't even cute. Right?

The questions jumbled in my mind as I gently curried Murray, and didn't stop when I switched to the hard brush. My mind settled before I'd made my way to the soft brush to finish. Grooming a horse was an active meditation, soothing and repetitive, but satisfying too. I could see my progress as I worked, and whenever I found a horse's itchy spot, I got to watch them lean into it and toss their heads up, flopping their lips in the silliest way.

I laughed when I found Murray's itchy spot on his chest and scratched with my nails. He stretched his neck out, bobbed his long head, ears flopping, and puckered his lips as I hit a spot he couldn't reach on his own.

"You found it!" Wes said, his laughter joining mine.

He watched me, delight in his eyes, as I scratched until Murray's itch was gone. I hugged the horse around the neck, and burrowed my face into his soft, winter coat. The smell of horse filled me with nostalgia. So many memories assaulted me as I breathed it in, and I didn't know whether to laugh or cry.

Memories flooded me, from nearly every summer night of my girlhood and early adulthood that had been spent on the back of a horse. Riding in the springtime when I was six months pregnant with Tori. The heartbreak I'd felt while stroking the neck my favorite horse, Blue, as he succumbed to old age. A honeymoon spent riding the beaches of Oahu. And then the hardest memory slammed into me, and my breath caught in my throat.

The smell brought back the last time John and I had gone riding, only days before he died. His smile beaming color to my world, the way he held my hand as we rode side by side, the warmth of the mid-morning summer sunshine on my face.

A hand touched my shoulder. "Are you okay?"

I looked up to Wes and sniffled. "I'm fine. Why?"

He took off one glove and gently rubbed a thumb over my cheek and held it up for me to see. "You're crying."

I was crying. Again. My hands trembled, and I fought to force a smile. "It's nothing. I'm just..."

The lump in my throat seemed to come out of nowhere, and I couldn't finish my sentence. My knees bucked, but Wes caught me before I fell.

"Hey, hey," he said, his voice low and soothing. "It's okay. You're safe. You can tell me."

"I can't... breathe!." I said through the choking sobs that wracked my chest. Tears blurred my vision, and I wanted to curl up in the dirt and cry until I couldn't anymore.

Wes lowered me down onto the floor and sat me against the wall. "Slow breaths. In through the nose, out through the mouth."

I tried to do as he asked, but I was too far gone. I stumbled away, vaguely aware of Wes putting Murray back in his stall and locking it up. He followed me as I walked back toward the lounge, unsteady on my jelly legs and barely able to see.

A blast of warm air hit me as I pushed open the door to the lounge and walked inside. I dropped onto the couch, and buried my face in a pillow.

Wes's footsteps followed me in, and I didn't bother looking up when I felt him cover me with a blanket.

"Talk to me, Carrie," he said, even though he hadn't called me that since high school.

I shook my head, my body still trembling, teeth chattering. Though I hadn't been cold, my body still reacted as if I was, and I couldn't get a hold of myself.

"You're okay," Wes said, kneeling on the floor next to the couch. He leaned close, took my hand in his, and stroked his thumbs over my knuckles.

"I-I'm sorry," I managed to say. I wished I could calm down and shove all my feelings back to being just under the surface like I usually did.

He rubbed my hands. "It's okay to cry, Caroline. You're safe here with me. And... I think I know why you're upset. I miss him too."

This was why I had avoided Wes so much more since John passed. It wasn't really because of what happened when we were kids or my views on how he'd lived before his divorce. It was because he had lost John, too. Like it or not, he'd been among the people closest to John, and he'd lost his best friend at the same time I'd lost my husband, and my kids had lost their father.

And, somehow, it hurt more to be reminded that I wasn't the only one who was still grieving. Tears filled his eyes as he stared back at me.

"No." I lifted my head and locked eyes with Wes. "I'm sorry I haven't seen you or even asked how you were doing. You've been going through this too, alone and—"

He clenched his jaw, then leaned forward and wrapped me in a hug. I twisted on the couch and returned his embrace. We held each other as we let the tears fall, our breaths stolen by soul-shaking sobs, and we cried together until our wells of sorrow were dry.

Chapter 10: Trust Me

Wes

I didn't know how much time had passed before the sound of a car approaching woke me from my grief-induced haze.

"Caroline," I said softly, rubbing my thumb over the back of her hand. "Wake up. Someone's coming."

I'd fallen half asleep while seated on the floor and leaning against her. I became suddenly aware of our closeness, so I shook myself awake and stood up. When I had righted myself and adjusted my clothing, I glanced over to find her staring up at me. Her face was calm and still, but I could almost see the thoughts whirling behind her hazel eyes. I didn't have time to ask.

The car that had pulled up to the barn quieted as the engine turned off, and then a door slammed, followed by boots crunching through the snow and gravel.

I grabbed the throw blanket lying on the back of the couch and unfolded it before handing it to Caroline. Then, I made a beeline for the kitchenette behind the counter. The visitor opened the door just as I put the kettle on for tea.

"Why isn't anyone answering their phone?"

I turned to find Sabrina taking off her scarf and hat. "You called?"

She glared at me. "Both of you. Like a hundred times."

"Shoot." I fished through my coat pockets until I found my phone. Sure enough, the screen showed she'd called me at least a dozen times. "I always have my ringer silenced in the barn. Sorry about that."

Caroline was already sitting up, her face pale and groggy as she pulled her phone from her pocket. "I had mine on silent, too."

I couldn't believe what had happened. It felt hazy, like a dream, and I wondered if she was feeling the same way.

"How's Rob?" I asked Sabrina, leaning over the counter separating me from the rest of the lounge.

She huffed a breath and rubbed her temples. "Thankfully, he's fine. It was only a fender bender. He's a little shaken up, but he doesn't have a concussion or any other injuries."

"And his car?" Caroline asked as she flipped on her ringer and stuffed her phone back in her pocket.

Sabrina waved a hand dismissively through the air. "It'll probably be in the body shop for a few days. It needs work, but hey, it could have been worse."

"I'm glad it wasn't." I clasped my hands together and let my gaze fall to the countertop. "Want some tea?"

"Actually, that sounds great." Sabrina dropped down on the couch opposite of Caroline's and leaned backward. "This morning was way too stressful. What did I miss here?"

"I got the grand tour of the barns," Caroline said, and I didn't miss the tired lull in her voice. "And I got to help groom Murray."

Sabrina leaned against the arm of the couch and propped her chin on her hand. "Who's Murray?"

"The Standardbred I bought for her," I interrupted, finally lifting my gaze to grin at them.

Caroline glared at me, but it was playful this time, and there wasn't any hint of malice or real annoyance. "I did not agree to that."

"That's okay. I'll just hold onto him until you're ready." I gave her a playful wink, but knew I needed to be careful. Too much might make her uncomfortable, but too little teasing would tip off Sabrina that things hadn't been as simple as Caroline had explained. Neither of us would want to suffer her hard questions and discover any answers we weren't ready for.

It had somehow felt otherworldly to hold her hands, to grieve with her. I'd been alone for so long, and I'd grieved alone too. There were nights I'd considered drinking myself into oblivion to end the pain, but I'd somehow held onto life. Somehow, I always felt like John was still here with me, telling me not to quit on life like I'd quit so many other things. I couldn't have known how much I'd missed the touch of another human, even platonically. Whatever we shared before Sabrina arrived had sparked a strange sense of healing within me.

My only hope was that it had started to heal something in Caroline too.

The kettle whistled, and I set out new to-go cups, dropped in tea bags at each woman's request, and took chamomile and honey for myself. While the tea steeped, I cleaned up the few dishes from breakfast and listened to them talk about Rob and the car.

"So, are we going to ride, or what?" Sabrina asked.

I put the final plate in the drying rack, then shook my head as I dried my hands. "I don't know if that's a good—"

"Yes," Caroline said, her voice firm. "Let's do it. Do you have three horses for us, Wes?"

I was surprised at Caroline's answer after her meltdown while grooming Murray, but I didn't dare let it show. "Sure. I've got seven here, and they're all dead broke."

We enjoyed our tea on the way to the arena, then left our cups near one side of the railing to cool while we retrieved our horses. After grabbing saddles and bridles from the tack room, we got out each of the horses and put them in cross ties to groom and saddle up. Murray was already groomed, so Caroline led him to the arena ahead of me and Sabrina.

"Is she okay?" Sabrina asked as she brushed Sammie, the buckskin Quarter Horse I'd given her.

"Yeah," I said, considering how much I should tell her. "She had a moment while grooming Murray, so I put him away and took her back to the lounge so she could calm down."

Sabrina paused and looked me directly in the eyes. "A moment?"

I swallowed, giving myself time to word it carefully. "She seemed sad."

It was all technically true. It wasn't the whole truth, but I wouldn't breathe a word of the whole truth unless I had explicit permission from Caroline. She and I might actually become friends after this, and closer friends than I'd ever had aside from John himself, so I wouldn't do anything that might ruin that future friendship before it had a chance to blossom. I played it all back in my head and kept my mouth shut tight as I finished grooming Lottie, my Friesian mare. Had I imagined the closeness I felt with her as we grieved together? And the easy moments after we'd been roused from our restful but drowsy haze...

I shook it off and saddled Lottie. It was definitely all in my head. While I wasn't the same horn-ball kid I'd been before I married Kathy, I still got comfortable easily with women, and Caroline wasn't like that. She was my best friend's widow, not some potential girlfriend.

Some part of me still felt deeply for her with emotions I didn't have the words for. They mingled and landed somewhere between love, desire, and curiosity. She was a beautiful woman, even if she was underfed. I wasn't one for skinny women, but her beauty wasn't just in her appearance. It was in her smile, her brains, her business, and the way she'd always treated my kids and ex-wife so well. Even when she didn't like me very much, she had still treated my family like gold.

Caroline was a good woman, and whatever I felt for her was on me alone and would stay trapped in my imagination where it belonged.

I finished tacking up Lottie just before Sabrina finished with Sammie. We led them out together, and I swear, every time I looked at that woman, she was staring at me with her eyes narrowed suspiciously.

"What's wrong?" I asked before we entered the arena.

Sabrina shook her head. "I'm not sure yet. But trust me, I'll let you know as soon as I figure it out."

"Great." I didn't try to mask the sarcasm in my voice. Sabrina was one of the few people left that I could call "friend" even if we weren't as close as she and Caroline were. She was also the most annoying friend I had left.

Caroline stood near the mounting block with Murray's reins held loose in one hand while she petted his neck with the other. The horse was so calm that he was on the verge of falling asleep. His head nodded, eyelids drooped, and one hind leg was bent and relaxed. She spoke too softly for me to hear what she was saying.

I didn't want to crowd her, so I stopped a fair distance away and waited until she turned to look at me. There was a gentle smile on her face now, and I breathed a little easier. Maybe she wouldn't break down crying this time.

"You still want to ride?" I asked. She nodded, so I passed the reins over Lottie's neck and left her standing behind me as I went to Caroline. "Want me to hold him?"

"Please," she said, then stepped onto the mounting block.

Anyone could have seen how nervous she was, her body trembling and her eyes wide. I knew that this first ride had to be perfect, or she might never ride again.

Chapter 11: No One Wants to Feel Like a Burden

Carrie

I couldn't stop myself from shaking as I climbed the mounting block. It was one thing to get close and breathe in that old familiar scent, only for it to remind me too much of the last time I rode with John. But it was another thing altogether to ride. Could I really back out now, after everything that had happened today?

No. I couldn't.

I wasn't sure why hugging Murray had brought it all back. It wasn't like I didn't have horses and their uniquely horsey smell back at my farm. But as I thought about it, I realized that I didn't spend much time getting close to them. I'd hired people to help with the farm, and they helped with the horses, too. I never needed to brush them, tack them up, or spend time bonding with them anymore.

Wes cued Murray to side-step closer to the mounting block until he was positioned perfectly for me.

I grasped the saddle horn in one hand, and the cantle in the other. Then I hesitated.

There I was, prepared to step into the stirrup and swing my leg over, but I froze in place. A million thoughts raced through my head, too fast even for me to catch. Here and there, visions of John and the kids and I riding as a family flashed through my mind.

"It's okay," Wes said, stepping into the small space between the horse and the mounting block. "I won't let you fall."

My heart twinged at his words, and my face grew hot. I tried to brush it off, embarrassed that I was blushing. Why should those words affect me so much? They're what any friend should say to another.

But I couldn't deny that it felt different coming from Wes than it would have coming from Sabrina. It reminded me of when we were kids. The gentle attention he showed me back then and how smitten he'd been had made me feel special and cared for.

I knew that my children loved me, but they were all out living their own lives, working, traveling, chasing their dreams, and falling in and out of love. These days, they were all so busy that holidays were the only times I was guaranteed to see them, even though everyone but Shane still lived in state. So, maybe I was a little lonely despite my bi-weekly visits to the auction and quick trips to the grocery store to cook for one. Did being lonely make it so easy for a few simple words to break through the armor I thought I'd built around me?

The mental distraction relaxed me a little, so I stepped into the stirrup with perfect form and carefully swung my leg over. I sat comfortably, pushed my heels down, and felt the familiar rush of excitement sweeping through me. There was nothing else quite like being in the saddle, on top of a powerful, thousand-pound creature. Riding had never been about power for me, but about the bond a horse and rider could share. Even for just one ride, a relationship could be developed, desires communicated between both parties, and understandings reached in order to achieve the day's goals. In my opinion, as informed by my beloved late husband, the best riders lived in a state of constant gratitude and never took the companionship and work of horses for granted.

"How are you feeling?" Wes asked as he handed me the reins.

"Actually, good. So far." I exhaled a steady breath and leaned forward to pat Murray's neck. "I feel... excited, I think."

"I wish we could go out on the real trails, but it's really cold today, so I hope you won't be disappointed if we stay in here today." He gestured around the indoor arena.

"That's probably for the best anyway." I laid the knotted reins in my left hand and dropped the right to my side. "I think I need a few warmups before I'm ready for the big world outside."

"That's a great point, Caroline."

I tried not to notice how he'd gone back to calling me Caroline even though he'd slipped and called me Carrie earlier. John, Sabrina, and my closest friends all called me Carrie. I wondered if that meant he still didn't feel close enough to me to use my nickname despite that intensely vulnerable moment we'd shared in the lounge together. It wasn't a point worth overthinking, I decided and reined the horse away to head for the edge of the arena. Sabrina trotted her horse up to mine and we rode side by side, glancing back to watch as Wes mounted his Friesian. The black horse's mane and tail were thick, perfectly combed, and had a glossy shine that showed the time and care Wes gave his horse.

"What happened while I was gone?" Sabrina asked, speaking quietly enough that only I could hear her.

My stomach flipped, but I held a neutral expression. "Nothing. Why?"

"Oh, yeah? Then what's this weird energy between you two?"

"Weird energy?" I scoffed and shook my head, hoping it would be convincing enough. "What are you talking about?"

"Stop. Promise you'll tell me later?" Her voice had fallen to a whisper as Wes caught up to us at a canter.

"Nothing to tell," I murmured before greeting Wes. "And here he is."

I expected him to ask what we were talking about, but he swept right past our mutterings as if he hadn't noticed. "How are you feeling so far?"

I nodded. "Good. Murray hasn't threatened to throw me or run away with me yet, so I'm pretty thankful for that."

He stared at me, expression serious. "You don't think you could handle a misbehaving horse?"

"I'd be pretty surprised if she couldn't," Sabrina said.

Thinking about it for a moment, I considered the implication of my own words. "I think it's hard to be a confident equestrian if it's your first ride in at least four years."

"That's fair," Wes agreed.

Sabrina shook her head. "I know why you stopped riding, but I can't imagine taking that long of a break from it."

Before I could think too hard about it, Wes clicked his tongue and cued Lottie into a slow, smooth trot.

"Have you been training in dressage?" I asked, intrigued by the horse's disciplined movements.

"I have." Wes smiled like he was trying to hold it back, highlighting his dimples. "When I quit drinking, I needed something else to keep my head and my body busy, so I started driving down to Caledonia once a week, and that's how I met Lottie. Thankfully, she was already started in dressage, so it's just been me catching up to her level so we can grow together."

"Do you compete?" Sabrina asked, sounding as bewildered as I was. "I can't imagine your lessons or your young, dressage-trained Friesian were cheap."

He laughed. "No, they were not cheap, but I don't compete yet. I want to. In fact, I've wanted to for a long time now. My trainer has been bugging me to start for the past year now, but..."

He never finished his sentence, instead giving some imperceptible cue to Lottie. She transitioned into a canter, and I watched, fascinated, as he practiced flying lead changes at the canter and transitioned to a collected trot before practicing their passage and half-pass.

"Did you know?" I asked Sabrina.

She shook her head. "I had no idea. And now I feel bad for not knowing something so important about one of my friends."

I opened my mouth before I could think better of it. "I don’t think it’s you. Sometimes, we hide away pieces of ourselves, especially from the people we love. No one wants to feel like they're burdening their friends."

She stopped her horse, and my cheeks burned as I realized my admission. Murray tried to stop with the other horse, but I urged him on, hoping for some escape from a conversation I'd avoided for years.

"What aren't you telling me, Carrie?"

Chapter 12: Entirely Alone

Wes

I tightened my legs against Lottie's sides, urging her into a canter so I could catch up to Caroline and Sabrina.

Sabrina had pulled her horse to a stop, but Caroline kept going. "What aren't you telling me, Carrie?"

"Nothing, Sabs—" Caroline started, but Sabrina cut her off.

Sabrina trotted her horse toward Caroline's. "I'm serious. I've known something has been off about you ever since John died, but I thought you just needed time and space to grieve."

Caroline finally pulled Murray to a stop and spun him around. "Grieving isn't this one-and-done thing!"

There was a fire in her voice that stunned both me and Sabrina. I halted Lottie just short of them.

"I know that," Sabrina said sympathetically, but there was an edge to her voice. "I've had to grieve too. You aren't the only one who's lost someone. It's part of us all getting older."

I winced at her words, but she wasn't lying.

"What am I supposed to do?" Caroline asked, her voice rising and her face burning red. "Just forget about all that I've lost? Move on like it never happened?"

Sabrina let out a frustrated sigh. "Of course not. But nobody benefits from you being miserable. Is that the only way you can honor John's memory?"

"Oh, give me a break." Caroline scoffed. "What would you know about honoring John? I'm the one who bore his children and built a life with him. There was so much more he wanted to do in life, and so much more we were supposed to do together. We never planned for me to have to do it all on my own!"

Tears trickled down Caroline's face as she leaned forward over the pommel of her saddle, angry eyes glaring daggers at her best friend.

Sabrina's jaw dropped at the outburst. "No one said you had to do it on your own!"

"And who's going to do it with me? You? You have your own life, Sabrina. And my kids have their own too." She lifted a hand to her mouth and choked on a sob. "I'm all alone in this world now, and it's too much for one person."

Her voice softened, breaking over her words. She leaned down over the pommel, buried her face in Murray's mane, and covered her head with her arms.

My heart broke as I watched her melt. I shot Sabrina a glare and urged Lottie forward, but she looked just as shocked as I'd been earlier this morning. I completed a side-pass with Lottie to move up next to Caroline, then rubbed one hand on her back. "Hey, it's okay. We're your friends. You aren't alone."

Sabrina joined me, riding up on Caroline's other side and reaching over to stroke her hair. "I'm sorry, Carrie. I didn't mean to snap." Her voice trembled, and her eyes filled with tears. "You're my best friend, and I love you. I'm just so worried about you. I want you to see you doing better, to see you really smile again. You deserve to be happy."

"She's right," I added, slowly rubbing my hand up and down her back. Her bony spine was hard under my fingers, and it only worried me more.

Caroline lifted her head and looked at Sabrina, then at me. "Do I really? If John can't be here and happy, how could I possibly be happy without him?"

The pain in her eyes only drove the knife deeper into my heart. "Do you believe in the afterlife?"

She sniffled and blinked. "Well, yes."

I nodded. "And if he can see you from beyond, then how do you think he'd feel about seeing you like this? What if all your pain and holding on keeps him from a peaceful rest while he waits for you?"

Realization sparked in her eyes, and tears streamed down her face. Her bottom lip trembled, and she squeezed her eyes shut. "Please stop. Don't say that. I'd never hurt John."

Sabrina tipped her head, eyes glistening as she studied her friend. "He only ever wanted to see you happy. Seeing you like this would break his heart."

"I... can't... breathe," Caroline rasped, face turning pale.

Without a second's hesitation, I slid down from my saddle and caught her in my arms just as she started to lean dangerously. Murray, calm and attentive, stood quietly and turned his head to watch me. Caroline's chest heaved as she hyperventilated. I carried her to the edge of the arena and pushed through the gate to the bleachers while Sabrina gathered all the horses' reins.

"Easy," I said as I set Caroline down on the first row of seating. "Do you want to sit here for a minute or go to the lounge?"

"I just need to catch my breath," she said through her tears.

"Okay." I started rubbing her back again, then paused. "Is this okay? Does it help, or should I stop?"

"It helps," she said. "But I'd rather you not right now."

I stuffed my hands in my coat pocket and sat beside her. "Do you really feel alone?"

"Entirely." She wiped the tears from her face, then dropped her head into her hands. "I don't know what I'm doing or why I'm even doing it."

Sabrina arrived with all the horses and tied them loosely to the railing. She reached us in time to hear it, and she responded before I could. "Remember that first trip you planned to the Kentucky Horse Park? It was supposed to be your first big trip together since you had kids. What happened?"

Caroline sniffled. "Right before we were supposed to leave, the weather forecast turned bad. It would have rained the entire time."

I remembered hearing this story from John, and I was curious to hear it from her perspective.

"And what did John do?" Sabrina asked.

She swiped under her eyes. "Well, I was ready to give up and just cancel it. I didn't want to spend our one vacation being miserable in the rain for a week. But he told me we were going anyway." Caroline shook her head, her gaze lifting to meet Sabrina's. "I was so mad at him, but I was too tired to keep fighting with him about it."

I did a double-take, shocked to hear a detail John hadn't included. "You two fought about it?"

"We did. He insisted that we'd lose our deposit and we should just go and make the best for it. Little did I know, he'd already moved our reservations to the following year." A smile curled Caroline's lips and her eyes grew misty as she remembered. "John said we had to go get camping supplies, but took me to the airport instead. Imagine my shock when he pulled into long-term parking and told me to come inside with him for a 'quick errand'. Then he pulled my suitcase—that he had packed—out of the trunk, then handed me my passport. I had no clue until we checked in that he'd secretly booked us a vacation to Puerto Rico."

Sabrina beamed at her. "And you spent a week riding together on sunny beaches."

I shook my head, grinning. "I think he only fought with you to keep you on your toes."

Caroline nodded. "John spent most of our flight apologizing for the ruse. But honestly, he never yelled at me. He just seemed stubborn."

Catching her gaze, I added, "Even when you didn't think he did, he heard you. And he did everything within his power to make you happy."

Her eyes darkened again, and Sabrina and I exchanged worried glances. "Maybe that's why it feels so wrong to be happy if he's not here. I want to do all the things he wanted to do."

Sabrina clasped her hands together and held them under her chin. "You're running your farm the best you can and keeping it in the family, just like you and John planned. Right?"

"Like I said, Sabs," she sniffled, "We planned to run it together before passing it on to the kids."

Silence fell around us as Sabrina sat on the other side of Caroline. Sabrina was divorced and only had one kid, Farah, who was a senior in high school and an honor student. They lived in a cute little house on the outskirts of Hart Oaks, but Farah had no current interest in inheriting it. Her plan was to study abroad, travel the world, and become an archaeologist specializing in Imperial Roman colonies. No one expected her to stick around or even to come back once she left.

And my kids? Well, I was lucky to hear from them at all. Who would inherit my farm? I didn't want any of them to have it, but it wasn't because of their justified anger toward me. I knew they'd simply sell it and split the profits, and every dream I'd worked so hard to build would evaporate and be forgotten, as if it had never existed.

As if I had never existed.

I swallowed hard as it hit me. Finally, I thought I might have uncovered the real secret behind Caroline's pain, loneliness, and despair.

"You're afraid that if you let yourself be happy, it'll feel like you're letting John go?" I asked

She paused, rubbed her eyes, but didn't answer.

Sabrina picked up on my realization. "And that if you don't take care of the farm, even if you're suffering by yourself, then it'll feel like all his work was for nothing and his life will be forgotten?"

Caroline sucked in a shuddering breath, and a fresh flood of tears poured down her face.

"Oh, honey," Sabrina said as she slipped between the rails and sat on the other side of Caroline. "Is that what you're feeling?"

She only nodded, swiping at her tears, choking on her chest-racking sobs.

Sabrina shook her head softly. "But you have to know that it isn't true. Don't you?"

"It's logical." Caroline sniffled, her hands swiping in a futile war to clear her face. "But grief isn't logical."

I rested my elbows on my knees and leaned forward so I could be closer and speak softly to her. I pushed my hand forward, close enough that she could reach out and take it if she wanted. "Forget what's logical. What does your heart tell you?"

Chapter 13: The Warmth of Another

Carrie

I stared at Wes as I considered the question. "What does my heart tell me?"

He nodded.

"It's a fair question," Sabrina added, encouraging me.

I hated that they were both staring at me, but I didn't feel like bolting either. As much as I'd avoided the topic up to this point, I was too tired to keep running away from it.

"I'm forgetting the sound of his voice," I admitted, wincing as the grief manifested into physical pain that ached through my chest and my stomach, pounding in my head. "The way his eyes sparkled when he looked at me, and his smile. It's all starting to fade. I have to listen to his voicemails and look at pictures on my phone so I don't forget him."

I waited in case either of my friends wanted to say something, but only silence greeted me. Feeling a little stronger somehow, I continued. "All the times we danced on the porch or in the fields, the way he'd sweep me off my feet—literally! It's all getting fuzzy now, and I don't want to forget. I loved that man. And I still love him."

"You'll always love him," Sabrina said, leaning forward like Wes had.

Wes tapped the toes of his boots on the dusty floor. "No one could ever doubt that you love him Everyone who's ever met the two of you knows just how deeply you loved each other."

Sabrina squeezed my hand. "But you can't live like some martyr, bearing the weight of all this pain like your personal cross for the rest of your life."

I scoffed. "Um, isn't that exactly what I'm supposed to do as a widow?"

Sabrina shrugged as I settled my gaze on her. "You can. If you want pity and sympathy everywhere you go. If that's how you want everyone to remember you. Not to mention your children."

My heart pounded in my chest. "What about my children?"

She rubbed a thumb over my fingers, her eyes softening. "What are they going to remember about their mother? That she was strong, resilient, and always there for them? Or that when their father died, their mother died too? I've talked to your kids."

I wished that she'd stop, but I couldn't speak the words. If I opened my mouth or took too deep of a breath, I'd start to choke on my sobs again.

"It pissed me off when I thought they'd basically abandoned you, so I hunted them all down and gave them an earful. But I didn't hear what I'd expected." She leaned closer and pushed the hair back from my face. "They miss their mother, Carrie. They miss the woman who would laugh, sing, dance, and bring them together for dinner on Sundays. They're not only mourning their father, but they're already mourning you too."

Her words hit me like a bag of bricks, weighing down on me until I felt like I couldn't breathe anymore.

"No one expects or wants you to just move on," Wes said. "But no one wants to see you grieve yourself to death either. And John would lose his mind if he saw what you were doing to yourself."

"He would understand how—"

"No, he would not." Wes interrupted. There was no give in his voice, no margin for argument in his words.

Sabrina gave a firm nod in agreement. "John would feed you steak, croissants, and cheesecake until he couldn't see your bones anymore—and then some! That man lived for you. You do more damage to his memory by forgetting what he wanted and killing yourself slowly."

Fire flooded my veins. "And what did he really want? Do you really think you know that answer better than I do?"

"We all do," Wes said, defending Sabrina. "More than anything else in the world, he wanted you to be happy."

"That's right." Sabrina rested a gentle hand on my shoulder.

Wes laid a firm hand on my other shoulder. "He loved your smile and the way you laughed. How your face lit up when he'd surprise you with dancing or dinner. The way you used to blow the loose strands of hair out of your face when you were stacking hay bales."

My ears perked up, especially at that, and it took a moment for me to remember that Wes used to deliver our square bales.

"To John," Wes continued, "you were the sun and the moon and all the stars in the great beyond. He poured blood, sweat, tears, and soul into building a life that would make you feel truly alive. Carrie, everything he built was for you. Everything you wanted, he spent his life getting it for you."

"I know that!" I snapped, my grief sharpening into anger. "Can't you see? That's why I can't get over it. That's why I thought about ending it all and joining him. What's this life without him?"

That sucked the breath out of everyone, and I looked up again to find both Wes and Sabrina staring at me wide-eyed and slack-jawed. Even I was stunned at my admission. I'd never told anyone and thought I'd take that knowledge to my grave. But this was validation. I'd always known that no one would understand the pain I'd been suffering.

Finally, Sabrina spoke, standing as she did so. "Carrie, no one can tell you what to think, how to feel, or whether your life is worth living. Not me and Wes, not your kids, not the rest of your family who loves you and loves having you around. You have to decide it for yourself."

I stood with her, ready to defend myself, but she held up a hand to stop me and shook her head.

"Gimme a hug," she said as she pulled me into her embrace. "I love you, honey. You're my best friend, and I want you to be happy again. We all do. No matter what, please call those kids and schedule a Sunday dinner like you used to. I just..." She let her words trail off and looked away. "I'm going to head home and let Wes drive you back. Okay?"

All I could do was nod. My admission had hurt her, that pain was visible in her wet eyes and in the exhaustion written in the deepening lines on her face.

She let me go, then slipped through the gate and back into the arena, untied her horse, and led him out.

"If you leave him in the crossties—" Wes started.

"Damn it, Wes, I can take care of my own horse!" She flipped him the bird without looking back, but I knew it wasn't malicious. It was just the way those two communicated.

Wes was too somber to smile this time.

The cool, still air was thick with tension between us, and I was left wondering if he felt the same way Sabrina did.

"She's right, you know?" He stood and leaned against the railing, then reached forward to stroke Lottie's face.

I stood and followed him, then reached for Murray, who lowered his head so I could scratch an itchy spot in his forelock. "She always is. Do you want to beat me up too?"

Wes huffed a sigh. "Nobody is beating you up. We care about you. We want the same things for you that John wanted. And we want to honor him too, maybe just as much as you do. Maybe more."

I swallowed against the lump in my throat. "More? How could you possibly want to honor him more than I do?"

"Because he wouldn't want any of us—especially you—to kill ourselves in his memory. He'd want us to squeeze as much joy as possible out of every minute we can. He'd want us to dive into the deep end whenever we could, and like his brother Cole said in his eulogy, John wanted a wake, not a funeral. He wanted a party, a celebration of life, not just for himself, but for every person who loved him."

I couldn't deny the truth of it. Cole knew his brother best, and that was exactly my husband's philosophy. And Wes knew it too.

"But you are your own person, Carrie. No one can tell you how to live or how to honor your husband's memory. Just don't pretend to those of us who knew him that killing yourself is honoring him. Starving yourself, hiding away, and punishing yourself every day, living in self-induced misery and darkness won't bring him back or win you any points in heaven." He sighed and dropped his hands, then walked through the gate and took the reins of both horses. "I think we should call it a day. It's been less happy than I wanted it to be for you, and I'm sorry for that."

I wanted to tell him not to apologize, but he started walking away before I could force the words to come out.

He didn't look back when he said, "Besides, we have to get ready. If there's one thing neither of us wants to miss, it's a Saturday night at the auction."

Wes led the horses out, and I lingered, leaning against the railing and resting my chin on my arms as I stared at the grand, empty arena. I tried to parse everything that had been said today, both of my breakdowns, and all the ways my friends had tried to provide comfort and wisdom.

It was too much to figure out all at once, but I could feel the truth in my bones as I let the silence linger. Birds fluttered in the rafters overhead, breaking the quiet, and I watched as two of them flew to a shared nest. The sparrows fluffed their feathers and settled in together, their eyes closing as they nestled warm against each other.

I'd been missing closeness since John died. I missed the warmth of another by my side and the strength it gave me to push through the harder parts of life.

Now, I was forced to face what life had become for me in my lonely despair, and what I wanted my future to look like.

Chapter 14: When We Were Young

Wes

After a few minutes, Caroline joined me in untacking the horses and then feeding the rest of the animals scattered between the three barns and the pastures. We also fed my small herd of mini Highlanders, and I was surprised that she didn't notice the mini spotted one she'd fallen in love with at the auction a few weeks ago. To be fair, he wasn't the only spotted one, and I had gathered quite a large herd of the adorable bovines.

More time had passed than either of us realized, so we agreed to go to the auction together. I brought her up to the house—extra thankful I'd spent the night cleaning it instead of drinking—and let her freshen up. Apparently, her Carhartt pockets were packed with her wallet, phone, and a little makeup. She was an attractive woman without, and I hadn't minded how she'd fallen out of using it after John had passed.

I was a fool a hundred times over, but never fool enough to tell a woman what to do with her appearance.

We left my place, and she called one of the two hands on her farm and asked them to manage feeding the animals for the evening without her. It was a short conversation, devoid of emotion, though I could hear a little worry in the man's voice before he relented when she insisted she was fine. Once that was settled, we headed straight to the auction, arriving early.

"Park there," she said, pointing to a spot right at the front.

"You have a preference?"

She stared at me in silence as I pulled my truck in and parked. I looked over at her before killing the engine. "What?"

Caroline shook her head and let out a light chuckle.

"Seriously," I pressed. "What?"

"It doesn't matter." She glanced at her phone's screen to check the time. "I guess we have twenty minutes before it opens."

"Are you okay with waiting?" I asked. "Or do you want to head into town and get something to eat before it starts?"

She cocked an eyebrow. "And lose this spot? I don't think so."

We both burst into unexpected laughter, and our arms touched over the armrest. I swore I could feel the warmth of her through our thick coats, and that raucous laughter softened as we stared at each other.

I dropped my gaze and pulled my arm away an inch, not wanting to crowd her.

"It's been a hell of a day, hasn't it?" I lifted my ball cap and ran a hand through my thick, short hair.

"It has," she said, leaning her seat back a little and crossing her arms behind her head. She checked her phone again, nibbling on her bottom lip.

Desire pulsed in my veins, and I had to push it down. “Waiting for a call?”

She glanced up, surprised. “Oh, no. I was just surprised I haven’t heard about Tori’s Appy jumping the fences again today.”

I laughed. "That reminds me. I can take him for a while if you want."

"I think that's a good idea." She set her phone aside and dropped her hand on the console between us. "I know you'll take good care of him."

Silence settled between us, but it wasn't tense or awkward. It felt comfortable. Safe.

Only two minutes passed before she broke it. "Could you put on some music?"

"Sure." I turned the ignition forward into the accessories position. "Radio or... Is there something you want to hear?"

"Surprise me," she said, giving me a side-eyed look paired with a tired smirk.

"That's way too much room for me to ruin the day with." I laughed and thought about it for a minute before queuing up a song to play over Bluetooth.

"Oh, I love this song!" She bobbed her head as the music opened with a fast tempo and the minor notes striking out over an electric. "Somewhere With You by..."

"Kenny Chesney," I finished for her. "I'm glad you like it."

Caroline sang along, never missing a word or a beat, and I watched her, unable to hide my smile. Her hazel eyes lit up with joy despite the regret and grief expressed in the lyrics. There had to be some special memory attached to this song for her.

And for a moment, I wished that I had been part of whatever that memory was.

No matter how I'd fought it all these years since high school—especially while she was with John—and even now, more than thirty years later, I still longed for her. I longed for all the love we never got to share because we were just kids when we dated, and then she found the one great love of her life, my best friend. I'd never fully relinquished all my longing for her, and as I watched glimpses of that sweet, carefree girl bubble back to the surface again, I knew I never would.

The song ended, and she turned down the radio, tears glimmering in her eyes. "God, that felt good."

"I can tell. I love to see you living like that. Smiling like that."

She waved a hand dismissively and snorted. "Stop. I was just singing in the car."

I turned up my palm and stretched it her way, an offer she could accept or reject without expectation on my part.

Surprising me again, she took it loosely.

The sparks arced through my veins as her soft palm lay against mine. I swallowed hard and gently stroked the back of her hand with my thumb. "No. You were letting yourself be you again. And it was a sight I'll remember for a long time."

With my free hand, I found one of my playlists, hit shuffle, and turned up the volume again. "Let's leave this newer stuff to the kids and enjoy something we liked when we were young."

As soon as the guitar opened the song, she laughed her eyes lighting up. "Your Love!"

"The Outfield" I sang along, putting special emphasis on the line about how he likes his girls a little bit older.

“Hey!” She swatted at my arm, but she laughed, and smiled more brightly than I'd seen in years.

I melted inside, even as she joined me in singing every lyric, dancing in our seats and exaggerating all the notes. We ended the song laughing until we were in tears. Happy tears, this time.

Brooks and Dunn came up next. Within two seconds of the song starting, she was trying to figure it out. "Something about a broken heart, right?"

"Working On My Next Broken Heart." I nodded, grinning at just how perfect of a song it was right now.

"Oh! People are starting to line up." She pulled her hand from mine and shoved her phone in her coat pocket, then checked her hair and makeup in the mirror.

I barely restrained myself from a discontented sigh, especially with the sudden emptiness of my hand. The spot hers had occupied against my palm was already growing cold. I could have sat here all night with her, singing along to old songs, watching her smile, and listening to her laugh.

But I knew how important the auction was to her, so I turned the key back and slid it out of the ignition.

"Wait." Caroline rested her fingers over my hand.

I glanced up, meeting her eyes and praying she wasn't going to say something that would break my heart just as I was starting to feel us both coming back to life again.

Chapter 15: An Unexpected Moment

Carrie

I'd been avoiding the question simmering in the back of my mind all night, but I couldn't hold it in anymore. I felt like I'd been through all the emotions a person could ever feel all in one day: excitement, grief, contentedness, heartbreak, joy, worry, and sweet, wholesome fun.

But there was something else, too. Something about the way Wes's ears turned red when I took his hand, and the unexpected tingle that rolled through me, butterflies roaring into flight in my stomach as we sat with our fingers interlaced. Was there something here, or was I exhausted and delusional?

"I'm sorry to be so forward, and this might sound weird, Wes, but I just have to ask. Do you... like me?"

"Of course I like you," he said, nonchalant as if he didn't understand what I really meant.

I shook my head slowly, keeping my eyes locked on his.

"You mean..."

As nervous as I was for the answer, I tipped my head in confirmation. I needed to know.

He gripped the steering wheel with his free hand and directed his gaze ahead briefly. After an huff, he turned his gaze back to me and spoke. "Listen, Caroline. I'm your friend, first and foremost."

My heart sank, and the sound of his rejection stung more than I thought it would. My gaze fell to the armrest between us, but he reached over and tipped my chin up.

"But I..." His Adam's apple bobbed in his throat. "I do feel more for you than that."

My heart pounded in my chest, but I kept my lips sealed and let him finish.

"I thought I'd let you go years ago, obviously, but spending even just a little time with you... Well, it's made me feel a lot of things I never thought I'd feel again. Not since we were in highschool during those three short months we were together."

The memory stabbed at my heart. "You're mine—"

"And I'm yours," he finished the cutesy mantra we used to say nearly every day for three short months all those years ago.

I resisted the urge to bite my lip, holding back the flurry of questions that threatened to fall out of my mouth all at once.

"So... what does this mean?"

He took my hand in his, but before he could answer, a knock on his truck window startled us.

We both looked up to see who had interrupted our rare moment of vulnerability. It was Melanie, the owner of the new nursery.

Bundled up in a coat, scarf, and gloves, she smiled and waved.

"I forgot." My face burned with heat, my stomach turning. I grabbed the door handle, but he stopped me.

"Forgot what?" He asked, looking flushed.

"I saw you two sitting together a few weeks ago. I didn't realize..." I swallowed the lump forming in my throat and opened my door. Of course he had someone else waiting on him, but here he was, holding hands with me. It was just like him to mess around with one woman after he'd promised himself to another. "It doesn't matter."

After jumping out, I strode toward the door of the auction house to get in line. When I reached it, I looked back to see Wes standing next to his truck while he talked with Melanie. He glanced my way, eyes pleading, but my heart was already hardening.

Thankfully, I didn't have any tears left in me today. I could simply go back to being the cranky woman I'd been before he'd wormed his way back into my life. The clerk's window opened, and this time I was only the third person in line so I got in quickly. It was back to business for me, back to the little rituals that kept my ghostly vessel wandering through this empty world.

Back to being alone.

I hadn't eaten anything since breakfast in the lounge of Wes's main barn, and I'd been looking forward to sharing dinner with him in the cafe. But now? I couldn't even think about food. The smell of it turned my stomach so I simply ordered my usual coffee.

Once I had my hot cup in hand, I headed for the livestock holding area and climbed to the catwalks. I sipped my coffee and leaned over the railing, watching as the members of my community trickled in and viewed the animals that would be up for bidding tonight. The coffee was bitter, the air was bitter, the chill was bitter, despite the heaters blasting into the enclosed space.

Or maybe it was just me who was bitter. But if anyone blamed me, they weren't any friend of mine.

A couple of tween boys ran up the narrow stairs to the catwalk, froze in surprise, then slipped around me to run down the catwalks, laughing when they caught up with girls who looked to be a little older than them. I sat down in a narrow corner on the catwalk, settling myself against the railing, then set my coffee down and pulled my phone from my pocket.

I wanted to text Sabrina, but when I turned on my screen, I found messages from her already waiting for me. I scrolled to the first of my unread messages from her and replied to each.

Sorry I had to run. I didn't mean to abandon you.

You didn't. It's fine. I know how frustrating I can be.

How was your day? Other than the end, of course.

It was good. I actually enjoyed the little bit of riding I got to do.

Hey. What's going on? Are you at the auction?

Yes, I'm here. Are you?

Can you call me?

What's going on?

What happened between you and Wes?

I leaned my head back until it thumped against the dusty wooden boards of the railing and sighed heavily. Pressing the side button, I turned off the screen and flipped the switch to turn it on silent mode before slipping it back into my pocket. The last thing I wanted to do was talk about how badly I'd messed up by thinking there might be some spark worth tending between Wes and I. He was just an attractive guy I knew—one I had history with—and I was lonely. It would be easy for anyone in my position to confuse his closeness with something more.

His blue eyes still stared at me behind my eyelids, his charming grin warming me even as anger flared through me.

Think of the devil, and he'll appear.

"Can I sit with you?"

I opened my eyes and glared up at Wes. His hands were stuffed in his coat pockets, and his ball cap tipped low over his face.

"Do you have to?"

He sat next to me anyway and leaned back against the railing, but he didn't speak right away.

"I've got enough on my plate," I said, my voice barely above a whisper. "I can't handle your drama."

"I don't have any drama. Just—"

"Don't say it. I know you. You give your love to too many, too easily. You haven't changed at all." Guilt stabbed at me for saying it like that, but I felt justified.

"Like who?" he asked, his tone defensive.

"Melanie."

He groaned. "You can't be serious."

"Why not?" I challenged, turning my head to lock eyes with him.

Wes stared at me like I'd grown a third eye. "Because she's my cousin. By blood!"

My face grew hot, and I covered my mouth before sputtering with laughter. He shook his head, but his bitter chuckle turned to laughter.

When we finally settled, he held out his hand, palm up.

I stared at it, still tense from my misplaced anger and embarrassment, but knew I shouldn't be mad at him. Before I could think about it anymore, I settled my hand in his.

"We used to play up here as kids," he said, holding my hand loosely. His skin was warm and smooth, and his fingers strong.

"I remember. John and I came up here all the time when we started dating."

He nodded. "And that's about the time I stopped coming up here."

I squeezed his hand. "I'm sorry."

"Don't say that. You don't mean it."

I bit my lip. "So, what are we?"

"Whatever you want. Like I said back in the truck. I'm your friend first, and I'll always be your friend no matter what happens."

"But..." I encouraged him to finish his thoughts.

"But if you want to see where this could go, then I'd love to cook dinner for you, take you on trail rides, and give you the mini cow I paid an auction fee to keep."

My muscles froze, and I studied Wes's face, searching for any hint that he might be joking. "You kept him?! The cute little spotted one?"

"I did," he nodded, and he smiled at me. "I couldn't let him go once I saw how much you liked him. I still can't believe you didn't see him when we fed the cows earlier."

I did a double take. "He was there? I can't believe you bought me a horse and a cow already. What's next?"

"Whatever you want." He winked, but I didn't let him charm me out of a challenge.

I offered a mischievous grin. "What if I asked you to fulfill your potential?"

He tipped his head, smile faltering a little. "Excuse me?"

"That indoor arena shouldn't be so empty. Your ranch shouldn't be a ghost town. It should be a bustling, premier equestrian center. And you should be competing in dressage."

He looked shocked, his typical charming smile faltering as he studied me with those pale blue eyes.

"Is that too much?" I squeezed his hand.

Wes shook his head. "I forgot what you're like when you have a man to boss around."

“Hey!” I poked him through his coat with my free hand. "I don't boss anyone around. I just expect the best."

"I have a feeling I'm in for a lot of work," he said, but then he pulled up my hand to his lips and kissed the back of it.

A warm tingle spread over my skin where he'd kissed me, and a heat I hadn't felt in years stirred within me. "There's still time to back out."

"Not a chance." He kissed my hand again, then used his free hand to gently stroke my face.

I leaned forward, inviting him to take my dare, but I didn't have to wait long.

Wes lightly brushed his lips against mine, and when I didn't pull away, he kissed me more firmly. I ran the fingers of my free hand through his hair, pushing his hat back. The tickle of my fingernails against his scalp must have done something for him, because he pulled me close and kissed me harder, and I gave him the same energy back. He tasted like mint and smelled like fresh sawdust mixed with a spritz of spiced cologne. His warmth drew me in, and the firm but gentle passion with which he kissed me was intoxicating.

This unexpected moment, kissing Wes in the dusty, cobweb-ridden catwalks of the auction house brought me back to my youth, and I felt like a teenager again. Then another thought broke me from the spell.

I pulled away from his kiss and stared into his eyes. "Wait. Is this... okay? What would John think?

"Oh my God!"

We both jumped, startled, and looked up to find Sabrina staring at us. She stood slack-jawed in her shock, but her eyes twinkled with mischief. "Do your parents know you're up here?"

"Don't tell on us," Wes deadpanned, but he didn't let me go. I loved that.

I felt safe in his arms, comforted in our parallel lives and shared loss, and it all culminated in this: a second chance at life after loss, a second chance for a love we never got to explore. I couldn't believe I hadn't realized it sooner, especially when we'd held each other sobbing in his lounge earlier that very morning.

"Ha! Well, I'm glad you both finally see the light." Sabrina winked.

"What?" I asked, hyper-aware of Wes's gentle touch as he rubbed his thumb over my hand. "Are you saying you knew this would happen?"

She tossed her hair over her shoulder. "Of course I did. I was getting so frustrated at how long it took to get you two alone together."

"You—" I started, but Wes cut me off.

"Honestly, I can't be mad at you this time."

I shook my head as if I was disappointed in her, but I couldn't hide my smile.

"And John? I think he'd be happy for both of you. In fact, I don't think there's anybody he'd trust more to care for either of you."

"You really believe that?" Wes asked. He still held onto me, but I could feel a nervous tension growing in him.

Sabrina nodded. "I really do. You both want to honor him. The life he lived and the people he loved. And honoring him together? That's got to be an exponential amount of good. He's looking down right now and smiling at us."

I thought about it, listened through my memories for his voice and wisdom to come back to me. "I know you're right." I locked eyes with Wes. "She's right. My grief for John will never completely be gone, but it doesn't have to drown me. Living for his memory can be healing instead. As for us?" I pointed at Wes. "I think I'm ready to see where this could go. At least if you want to."

He stared into my eyes and grinned, then nodded solemnly. "I really do."

"Well, lovebirds," Sabrina said, nodding to different points around the catwalks where teens and tweens were staring at us and giggling. "You've got an audience, so I think we should go have dinner before the auction starts. Hey, would this count as your first date?"

"Dinner at the auction hardly counts as a date." Wes brushed off his pants as he stood.

"But it's Valentine's Day!" Sabrina argued. "You have to!"

"It's Valentine's Day?" Wes and I asked in chorus.

Sabrina laughed and ignored our question. “Hurry up, you calendar-challenged people. I'll bet twenty dollars that Carrie hasn't eaten since breakfast this morning, and she’ll wither away if we don’t peer pressure her into eating."

"Shut up, Sabs," I said as Wes pulled me to my feet.

"But am I wrong?" Sabrina laughed as she padded down the stairs, leading the way to the cafe while Wes and I walked behind her, our fingers interlaced.

About Myria Wild

Myria Wild writes emotionally grounded, character-driven romance about second chances, long roads back to love, and the quiet bravery it takes to let someone see you again. Her stories blend tenderness with passion, weaving together small-town roots, overcoming past heartbreak, and building steadfast, resilient love.

When she's not writing, Myria lives a full, slightly chaotic life with her family, a faithful coffeemaker, and far too many story ideas waiting their turn. She believes love stories don't have to be extreme to be powerful. Sometimes the quiet acts of love speak the loudest.

Connect:

- Instagram.com/myriawild

- Facebook.com/myriawild

Apple Blossom Benediction

by Nan Sampson

Prologue

Arthur Pennewell

Arthur Pennewell sat at his desk, chin in his hand, staring out at the slanting rays of the February midday sun sparkling on the snow-covered town of Westermere, Massachusetts. In ten minutes, he'd need to leave for Hathorne House, the crown jewel in the town's rich Historical Registry. Westermere treasured all of its past, but Hathorne House was special.

More importantly, though, tonight was Valentine's Day Eve, and as his wife Claire used to say, 'the game is afoot'.

He let his gaze drift to the photo of Claire on the corner of his desk, as he often did. "It's got to be tonight, sweetheart. I'm getting too old for this." He stretched out a hand, now covered in age spots, and touched the glass over the picture. "I want to be there with you, not here alone."

If the image could have spoken, he'd have heard a woman's voice say, "Nonsense, Arthur. Stop being maudlin."

She'd always been a practical woman. He smiled. "I've got a good feeling about tonight."

"You always say that," came the response in his head.

"I know, but this year feels different. The couple I've chosen tonight have names that seem to echo the past. Granted, they're a little older than Mercy and Josiah were, but when I met with each of the young people yesterday, I sensed they're each searching for a real connection. Not just...what is it the young folks say these days? Not just a hook up, but a desire for something deeper, more meaningful. The kind of love you and I have."

He imagined Claire smiling at him in that indulgent way. "You're a hopeless romantic, dear."

"Still. And always." He leaned back in his leather swivel chair, feeling suddenly dwarfed by the furniture. He seemed to shrink a little more each day. His doctor said he was in remarkable health for an eighty-year-old, and he was grateful for that, but time kept racing along, and he didn't know how much longer he had to put the spirits of Mercy Hathorne and Josiah Thayer to rest.

With a sigh and an ooph, he pushed himself to his feet, put on his warm wool overcoat and hat, and tied his scarf around his neck, like Claire would have told him.

Tonight would be the 40th anniversary of his fundraiser for Hathorne House, a colonial-era home originally built in 1678 by Daniel Winslow and passed down eventually to Ephraim Hathorne. The 40th year that Arthur had introduced two hand-selected blind date participants to the wonders of a property that was almost as near and dear to the community of Westermere as it was to Arthur himself. And forty years of Arthur trying to solve the riddle of Mercy Hathorne, daughter of Ephraim, and her lover, Josiah Thayer's disappearance on Valentine's Day Eve, 265 years ago.

Tonight, Arthur prayed, would be the night. Mercy and Josiah would find in this couple sympathetic ears and hopeful hearts, and they would divulge their long-buried secret. Then, the mysterious crying in the cellar, the shadow figures on the stairs, and the sense of restlessness and longing Arthur felt every time he spent the night in the house would end, and Mercy and Josiah would finally find their long-overdue peace.

Tugging on gloves, Arthur braved the bracing February wind, climbed into his car, and started the drive out to the old orchard home one more time.

Chapter 1

Verity

"Vee, don't make me drag you to the car. We need to leave."

Verity Dickenson trundled her wheelie overnight bag over the threshold of her townhouse and out onto the salt-strewn sidewalk. "You would, too. I'm coming. Although I can't believe you're going to drop me off and leave me without a vehicle to escape in."

"And that's why. Because you'd chew off your own foot when faced with the possibility of spending the evening with a man. I have no choice but to trap you there."

Verity tossed her suitcase in the back of her best friend Dana's VW Golf. "I can't believe I let you talk me into this, Dee." She climbed into the passenger seat and warmed her hands over the air vents. "Only desperate people go on blind dates. I—"

"Look up desperate in the dictionary, honey, you'll find your picture." Dee softened the blow by patting Verity on the leg. "Vee, you've got to get back out there. I know you're still hurting, but you can't just stop living life. You haven't been on a date in 17 months. Not since—"

"Don't." Verity didn't want to talk about Brad. Or think about Brad. Or hear anyone mention Brad. The man she'd thought was the love of her life had turned out to be a hot-tempered, jealous, self-centered prick, and she was grateful to be rid of him.

Dana paused at a stoplight—the *only* stoplight in the small town of Westermere—and glanced over at Verity. "Sorry. But honey, you're my best friend. You deserve happiness. Or the next best thing. Like a fun romantic evening, all expenses paid."

"Yeah, paid by you. I know how much it costs to apply to this fundraiser. I also know you're not made of money. It should be you going, not me."

"I am in a happy, committed relationship. You are...the CEO of the Westermere's Lonely Hearts Club. Look, Vee, you don't have to marry this guy. You don't even have to date him after this. But I have it on good authority he's good-looking, and after a gourmet meal prepared by a real chef, and a couple bottles of wine, you might at the very least get laid."

The light turned green even as Verity's cheeks turned red, and Dana swung onto Apple Orchard Road. Ten minutes later, they were beyond the borders of the town, and the country fields, broken into now meaningless parcels by stone walls, wore a winter's worth of crusted snow. "Besides. You love antiques, old dead poets, and even as kids, you loved going to Hathorne House on school trips."

Verity grunted and stared out the window.

Soon apple trees appeared, dotting the landscape, and another ten minutes brought them to the long gravel drive that would take them to Hathorne House.

Verity felt her stomach flutter. Which was stupid. There was nothing to be nervous about. She was going to have dinner with some random dude with whom she had nothing in common, drink a glass of wine, then get up tomorrow and go home. That was it. There would be no romance. There would be no swapping spit on the bearskin rug by the fire. And there certainly wouldn't be a need to test whether the springs squeaked during strenuous activity on an antique brass and iron bed.

Another thought skittered through her head, one she quickly squashed. There would also be no ghostly presences, the phantom scent of apple blossoms, or the faint sounds of a woman crying. Because there were no such things as ghosts, no matter what Dana had claimed she'd seen on their 5th-grade trip to Hathorne House. That was all just fodder for the tourist trade.

Still, her pulse sped up as Dana pulled up into the small parking lot in front of the carefully preserved and maintained saltbox home, with its steep gables and enormous central chimney. Painted a pale blue, in the sunlight, it was a cheerful place, surrounded by the orchard on the west and a stand of old-growth forest on the east.

Today, though, it looked forlorn; more gray than blue, the lawn a sea of snow, and the orchard skeletal under a leaden New England sky.

Didn't help that in an hour, the sun would set.

Verity turned to Dana as they climbed out of the car. "The place has electricity and central heating now, right?"

"Tonight's all about reliving the past, remember? I'm sure there are lights and such, but for the evening's festivities, it's all supposed to be candlelight and crackling fires."

"Great. Dark and cold. How special."

Dana marched over to her and took her by the shoulders. "Vee. Verity. Bubeleh. Please. Try to get into the spirit of the thing. Do you know how expensive this place is to book if you wanted to just stay here for the weekend? Mr. Pennewell said they even provide period-accurate costumes for the participants. Why do you think he asked you all those questions about your clothing sizes? It's a really exclusive experience. If nothing else, at least enjoy the food and the luxurious bed linens."

When Verity scowled, Dana responded with a groan. "You know, you used to be a lot more fun than this."

That one hit home. Verity had been fun once upon a time. Then she'd let Brad suck all the joy out of her. "You're right." She glanced at the house, which had been beautifully restored. And she'd always loved colonial architecture and 18th-century poetry. She'd even considered getting her degree in Early American Literature back in the day, until her parents' medical bills necessitated a cheaper, faster route to a steady income, and she'd become a certified accountant instead.

Dee squeezed her shoulders. "Good. Then you'll try to have fun. And every time you find yourself rolling your eyes, or going, "Oh gawd," think of me doing this." And she smacked the back of Verity's head with her thickly mittened hand.

"Wow. Way to offer support." But Verity grinned when she said it.

"That's what best friends are for. To smack you upside the head when you need it." Dana glanced at the house just as the front door opened.

An elderly man stood framed in the entryway, fluffy white hair blowing a bit in the chilly breeze, and a bright cherub's smile on his pink-cheeked face.

"There's Mr. Pennewell now. Go on in. And please, for the love of *me*, have a good time. I'll be here to pick you up at one tomorrow."

Verity groaned. "Fine. I'll have fun. Just be here at 1 PM on the dot, okay?"

"With bells on."

As Dana slid back into her car, Verity faced the elfish little man beaming at her and tried a smile, an expression foreign to her face lately. With a deep breath, she strode forward and stuck out her hand. "Mr. Pennewell, nice to see you again."

"Yes, yes. Please, won't you come in? It's rather chilly today. I've got a pot of tea for us while we wait for Mr. Merrick to arrive. He should be along any minute."

Before she knew it, Pennewell had ushered her inside the house, and the "experience" had begun.

Chapter 2

Zach

Zach Merrick sat in the idling Ford F-150 wondering how he'd let Hobb talk him into this. He replayed the conversation in his head for at least the 50th time. Maybe it had been all the beer he'd consumed. Or the temptation of the plate of poutine Hobb Nolan had bribed him with.

"It'll be fun," Hobb had said. "You love colonial houses. You're a professor of Early American History, and that house is full of it."

"Was. Was a professor. Now I live with my parents and work for my father picking up building supplies at Home Depot."

Hobb waved his hand. "Just a temporary stop on the road to something better. You'll get another teaching gig soon." He leaned back in the booth and spun his cola glass in circles on the wooden table's shiny polyurethane coating. "Remember the old legend? The story they told us at summer camp? That Josiah Thayer seduced Mercy Hathorne while Old Temperance was visiting relatives, and the two ran away to Boston to save Mercy from the shame?"

Oh God, here we go again. "And I'm telling you that's a load of bunk. I spent the whole next term that year scanning online records, and there is no evidence that a Josiah Thayer ever lived in Boston." He grumbled. "Of course, online records are notoriously limited, and I never had the funds or the access to the archives in Boston."

"Spare me the lecture. I mean, maybe the two went somewhere else. What's his name said he saw them riding off down the Boston road—"

"You mean Benjamin Fitch? I think he lied to spare himself the infamy of being affianced to a scandalous woman. Plus, there was no "Boston road" out of Westermere."

Hobb pushed the remnants of the poutine closer to Zach. The move wasn't lost on him. "Does that mean you ascribe to the 'they committed suicide by drowning themselves in the river' theory?"

Zach felt himself getting sucked in again, even as he realized the trap his best friend was setting. "If you were in love with a pretty girl, and you wanted to marry her, would you suggest going to the river, at night, in February, and taking a permanent swim?"

"Well, no, but options were probably more limited then."

Zach shook his head. "It was February. All existing records that I could get my hands on, which I'll admit were few, indicate that the wedding between Mercy and Benjamin Fitch wasn't supposed to take place until spring. Mercy and Josiah had months to figure out an alternative solution. One that didn't include killing themselves or freezing to death."

Hobb was wearing that familiar smile. The self-satisfied smirk he used when he knew he was close to signing a deal for his architectural firm. "Then tell me, O Learned One. What do *you* think happened?"

Zach shrugged. "There's no evidence to say, one way or another. But I guess a part of me hopes they got away somehow." Someone deserved a happy ending, even if it wasn't Zachariah Merrick.

He finished one beer and took a swig of the next, the one he hadn't noticed the waitress set down in front of him.

Damn it, Hobb had outmaneuvered him. Again. "Do I have to do this thing?"

"Come on, man, it'll be fun. Look at it as a way to get your hands on the real historical records. Like you said, online archives are limited, and face it, my friend, you love this stuff. It's gotta be better than watching old TV reruns on the sofa with your dad. And who knows, maybe you'll like this girl."

"It's never about me not liking them. They don't like me."

"Says you. I think you just need to get out of the basement. Therefore, yes, you do have to do this thing. I already paid the money, it's for a good cause, and you need to get your mojo back, personally and professionally. Plus, you've been obsessed with that house for years." He pointed his fork at Zach. "You white folk need to preserve what's left of your history before some idiot developer paves it over for another fast food joint and a strip mall."

"And pays you a bunch of money to design it."

Hobb, which was short for the Wampanoag name Hobbamock, gave him a slow smile. "Me like white man's wampum."

That had been two days ago. Yesterday morning, Zach had met with old Mr. Pennewell, a man Zach's grandfather had known and who'd been an attorney in town for longer than anyone could remember. The lawyer had an absolute fixation on Hathorne House, more so even than Zach.

Over the last twenty years, Pennewell and the Historical Society had done a magnificent job restoring the place. The old Crowell Orchard had played a big part in the history of Westermere, and ordinarily, Zach would have jumped at this opportunity. Just not when it meant some awkward blind date with a woman who probably didn't know the difference between a saltbox house and a Cape Cod.

Now, Zach sat outside Hathorne House in the parking lot in his father's truck, while the ghost of a winter sun set behind the trees, and his heater blasted air hot enough to make his skin feel tight. Why was he this afraid? It was just dinner with some woman. They'd make stupid small talk over a meal and maybe have a glass of wine later. Then, he and this girl he'd never met, and would never see again, would go up to their separate rooms and tomorrow part company after sharing grumpy good mornings over bad catering coffee and a plastic-wrapped banana nut muffin.

His nerves couldn't have anything to do with his track record with women. He'd never been much of a lothario, even before he'd lost his job. Before he'd been forced to move home. Now, since everyone in town knew everyone else's business, he'd pretty much been branded a loser.

He heaved a sigh and watched as the front door opened, and Old Man Pennewell appeared framed in the entryway.

"It'll be fun," Hobb had said. If it was so fun, how come Hobb wasn't here instead of Zach?

Pulling his winter parka closed and slinging his overnight duffle over his shoulder, Zach climbed out of the truck and hustled toward the open door before the older man froze solid. The sooner Zach went in, he thought, the sooner it would be over.

Chapter 3

Verity

Verity had only just divested herself of her outerwear, which a young woman named Meghan from the Historical Society had whisked away along with her overnight wheelie, and accepted a cup of tea from Arthur Pennewell when they both heard the crunch of another vehicle in the parking lot outside. Pennewell went to the window to peer out, then turned back to her, rubbing his hands together.

"Excellent. That will be Mr. Merrick, right on time."

She wanted to step further into the home, maybe sit down. She felt unaccountably nervous, and her teacup rattled in her saucer as she stood there on the braided rug in front of the door, shivering now without her coat.

The letter from Pennewell's office, announcing that she had been chosen as one of the two participants for this year's fundraising event, had requested that guests wear casual and warm attire, so she'd chosen a pair of black dress pants and a red cashmere sweater. Stylish and seasonal—it was Valentine's Day Eve, after all—but nothing too fancy, and the sweater would keep her warm. Or, she'd thought it would. The hall, as Pennewell had called the room she found herself in, had a distinct chill to it.

But instead of inviting her to have a seat before the fire in the enormous fireplace, Pennewell had insisted she remain standing here until her "date" arrived. Something about a house tradition. So she waited, trying not to slosh tea and embarrass herself.

And waited.

And waited.

Good Lord, what was Merrick doing out there?

After what seemed like ten minutes, but was probably only two, Pennewell flung open the door to admit a rangy, blond-haired man, wearing a heavy parka over a collared shirt and a pair of black jeans. The guy looked almost as uncomfortable as Verity felt. Like his collar chafed, and his shoes were too tight.

He had to duck to get under the lintel, and while older homes did have shorter doorways, Verity figured that put his height at something over six feet.

Thank goodness for that. Verity herself was 5'8", and had spent her adult life trying to find men to date who didn't object to her height.

Stop it. You are not dating this man. You're just having dinner with him.

Although...he was attractive. And when he'd finished being greeted by Pennewell and glanced her way, he had a lovely, if hesitant, smile and lively, intelligent eyes.

Pennewell stood between them, beaming. "Ms. Dickenson, may I introduce Mr. Zachariah Merrick. Mr. Merrick, this is Ms. Verity Dickenson."

She suddenly felt unsure of what to do. The awkwardness, combined with the old-world feeling of the place, had her wanting to curtsy, which was silly. They both stood there, staring at one another, until Merrick stuck out his hand with an embarrassed laugh, and she clasped it.

"Pleased to meet you, Ms. Dickenson."

"And you, Mr. Merrick."

At the formality and ridiculousness, they both laughed again. He had a nice laugh, one that crinkled the corners of his sea-glass green eyes.

Pennewell clapped his hands together. "Excellent. Mr. Merrick, if you would, please leave your bag by the door. Someone will take it up to your room."

Merrick complied, and Pennewell beamed. "Now, before I give you a brief tour of the house, there is a tradition we follow on these nights. We introduce you both to the home. I'm sure you've heard some of the history of Hathorne House, and its original occupants, but the house itself is a bit of a character in our story, and she's a grand old dame. Those of us who care for her like to make sure she knows who we are welcoming under her roof. Please, if you could, both introduce yourselves using your full names as you cross into the center of the hall."

Verity glanced at Merrick, who gave a little shrug, then turned to face the room with the crackling fire. "Um, I'm, um, Verity Rose Dickenson, but most people call me Vee." She looked back at Pennewell. "Is that okay?"

"Just fine, thank you. And you, Mr. Merrick?"

"Okay." He took a long step forward, gaze taking in the room with an almost wistful expression. "I'm Zachariah Adams Merrick, known as Zach to my friends." He sent Verity a smile. "Which I hope we'll become."

Well, damn. She hadn't expected that. He hadn't looked any more pleased to be here than she had when he'd walked through the door.

Although maybe he thought saying nice things would pay off later, a strategy he couldn't know was doomed to failure. She smiled in response and turned back to Pennewell.

The older man, who looked like a stiff breeze would blow him over, almost vibrated with delight. "Now, let me show you around. Are you familiar at all with the history of the house?"

Verity nodded, as did Zach. "We came here on school trips growing up. I think I remember the basics." Plus, she'd looked it up online the night before, not wanting to appear ignorant. "Temperance Hathorne, the widow of a wealthy Boston sea captain, lived here with her granddaughter, Mercy Hathorne."

"Indeed. Temperance's family, an offshoot of the Cabots, settled here in 1678 and built this house and planted the orchard. Temperance inherited the property and continued in her role as the orchard's steward until her death several weeks after the disappearance of her granddaughter in 1761. At her passing, her new grandson-in-law, Benjamin Fitch, who married Mercy's younger half-sister Felicity, took over."

He gestured around him. "This room is called the hall, and would be the place where the household would have spent most of their time. Here was the cooking hearth, where they would make their meals, chairs by the window where they would sit and sew during the daylight hours, and read by candlelight in the evening. Temperance believed idle hands made for the devil's work, thus keeping usefully busy was a hallmark of her life's work. Mercy would often read poetry to her grandmother, as well as Bible verses. Psalms, in particular, as Temperance found great wisdom there."

Verity raised her eyebrows. "I didn't think girls were taught to read."

"That is not necessarily true. In later years, girls often weren't afforded that luxury, but in New England, especially in middle-class households, girls were in charge of the larder and needed to be able to perform the accounting, keep ledgers, and other tasks requiring literacy. Also, it was important to be able to read the Bible."

"Women kept the books?"

"In this house, yes. Temperance was a shrewd businesswoman. She had to be, especially after her husband died and she moved home from Boston. Her father only had daughters, and she was the last living child of old Ezekiel. It was up to her to make the orchard succeed."

Zach raised a finger. "Well, technically, she could have remarried. Wasn't Temperance still young when Captain Hathorne died?"

"Well, by modern standards, yes. She was 39. I suppose she could have found a man who might have offered if for no other reason than the property, but she was closing in on the end of her childbearing years. Not to mention, she was a formidable woman. From her journals and letters to friends she left behind in Boston, she had very strong notions about what she wanted in life and the will to achieve those things. Her match with Hathorne, while approved of by her father, was primarily a love match, and she apparently had no desire to marry for any other reason."

Pennewell turned to Verity. "You and Temperance would have found common ground. You're an accountant, aren't you, Ms. Dickenson?"

Verity nodded, then waited for Zach to make some crack about it being a boring profession. But his face betrayed nothing but mild interest. Okay, more points for him.

Pennewell gestured to a door behind them. "Through there is what they would have called a kitchen, but was more a preparation room, and was connected to the buttery, where they would have stored perishables like dairy products and preserves. We now use it for storage of other things, like extra toilet paper and such." He smiled. "I'd show it to you, but the caterers have just arrived and will be preparing your dinner. I think it's probably wise to leave them be."

Zach chuckled. "Yep. Never disturb a cook in the kitchen. My mom ran us boys out of the house when she wanted to make something fancy for dinner, no exceptions. Took me years to learn to cook for myself."

"Then I should take lessons from you, Mr. Merrick. Since Claire...since I've been on my own, I find frozen dinners have become my friend. I'm utterly hopeless in the kitchen."

Verity didn't miss the catch in the older man's voice and felt a pang of sadness for him. Her father had been much the same way after her mother died.

Pennewell recovered quickly. "Next up is the parlor." He opened another closed door to the left of the front door. "Often doors were kept closed, as rooms were easier to keep warm that way." He made a sweeping gesture, indicating for his guests to precede him. "This way, please."

Chapter 4

Zach

Zach allowed Verity to go through the door ahead of him, although not just out of the politeness Ma Merrick had instilled in all her boys. Whatever else could be said about Verity, she had a hell of a shapely posterior.

He had to admit, Verity was not the sort of woman he'd expected to meet. He'd figured his date would either be some vapid thing that was caught up in the romance of a night in a haunted historical home, or a woman looking to play dress-up before a meaningless one-night stand.

Verity appeared to be neither. She had an edge, no doubt, but she also had intelligence. And while she didn't fit the conventional Barbie doll mold many men found attractive, he liked her dark, curly bob and expressive hazel eyes.

Plus, she had a killer smile. Not that she displayed it much, but a couple of times he'd caught her smiling, especially when Pennewell talked about Temperance. Not as hard-assed as she wanted people to think.

Lost in his thoughts, and with his eyes on Verity, he almost brained himself going through the doorway into the parlor, forgetting to stoop as he passed under the low lintel.

He heard a faint, stifled laugh.

"Mr. Merrick!" Pennewell hurried over to him. "Oh, dear, I'm afraid that's going to leave a lump. I'll just run to the kitchen and get an ice pack. Ms. Dickenson, could you please help Mr. Merrick to a chair?"

Zach tried to push Verity away, but she dragged him briskly and firmly to an upholstered wingback. "You gotta watch that, or you'll be whacking your head all night."

He gently probed his forehead, hurting more from her laughter than from the bump. "As long as it keeps you amused, I guess."

She took a step back. "I beg your pardon?"

"You laughed. I assume you thought it was funny." Damn it, he shouldn't have said that. Maybe he should just leave now.

A stony expression quickly replaced the sudden hurt on her face. "I did no such thing."

"But I heard a woman laugh. A little snicker."

"Well, it wasn't me."

Now his forehead was starting to ache, and he could feel the flesh swelling. "I…I'm sorry. I swear I heard it."

"And you just assumed it had to be me. Lovely."

"Well, you are the only woman here." He squeezed his eyes shut, wishing he'd thought to bring along some pain relievers. "I really am sorry. Although, to be fair to myself, I'm pretty used to women laughing at me. I've always been a klutz. Spilling wine on my date's dress at Homecoming freshman year kind of set the tone for the rest of my dating life."

Her expression thawed, and she approached again to dab gently at his forehead with a tissue she pulled out of her pants pocket. "You're bleeding. And I'm sorry I went straight to Bitch Level 11. It's been a helluva year."

He winced as she ministered to him. "No, you had a right to be pissed."

"Let's just forget it happened."

He was willing. Mostly. "But I swear I heard a woman laugh."

A funny look crossed her face. "Probably one of the caterers. Or the young docent who took our coats when we arrived."

"Probably." He took a moment to examine the simple yet comfortable room they found themselves in. Not all the pieces were period. The chairs were modernized approximations of the kinds of chairs present in wealthy homes of the period, but not likely ones Temperance would have had. The chairs sat in front of a pair of windows that faced the front of the house, a mirror to the two in the hall—saltbox houses were nothing if not symmetrical, at least from the front. A small, highly polished, spindle-legged side table lay between them, on which sat a small silver snuffbox, something Temperance Hathorne would likely not have tolerated, and an antique book of poems he judged was from the early 19th century. He flipped open the cover and noted with a satisfied nod that the copyright was 1801.

Set dressing, he thought. The snuffbox hailed from the right period, and there was a chance it could have belonged to Temperance's husband, but the book was far too late. A real historian would note the anachronisms, but for the purposes of the exclusive bed & breakfast customers or for social event bookings that paid to keep the historical site going, it was good enough.

Verity, perched in the other chair, followed his gaze. When he picked up the book, he noticed how she brightened. "That's Samuel Johnson's The Vanity of Human Wishes, isn't it?"

He nodded. "It is. Not original to the house, of course, it's a later edition."

"But something Mercy might have read, right? That was published in 1749."

His eyebrows rose, as did his respect. "It was. Did you study history?"

She chuckled, the sound nothing like the faint laugh he'd heard before. A register lower than that earlier noise, and more earthy. "No. Not history. But I know poetry, particularly 18th and early 19th century poetry."

"A lyrical accountant. I should probably bring my tax forms to you, then it would be a far more interesting conversation. And maybe even less painful."

She bristled for just a moment before sighing. "Probably not. Not a lot of room to discuss the use of iambic pentameter in Byron's Don Juan when going through your shoebox full of medical deductions."

That made him laugh. "Now I'm definitely hiring you. But only if you let me wax rhapsodic about Georgian porticos and Federal fanlight windows between examining my W2s."

A smile lit her eyes and gave her dimples beneath apple-pink cheeks. "That actually sounds great. I'll finally have a client I don't mind seeing."

Pennewell hurried in from the hall. "Oh my, it's already swelling. My apologies, I should have warned you about the low doorways." He handed the ice pack he carried to Verity. "If you would do the honors, young lady, I'll go upstairs and fetch the bottle of acetaminophen from the bathroom." Pennewell dithered for a moment. "Unless you feel like you need to leave. I did warn you, in order to create the most immersive experience possible, there will be no one here tonight but yourselves. I hate to say this, but if there is a chance of a medical emergency, it would be best to leave now."

Pennewell stood watching them, fretfully wringing his hands.

Zach shook his head. "No need for that."

The older man relaxed. "Oh. Oh good. Now, as I was saying, while there is electricity and modern plumbing, for the optimal experience, we recommend you use the old-fashioned oil lamps, candles, and fireplaces for your creature comforts. You can, of course, get a cell phone signal in an emergency–well, most of the time–but as I mentioned, the night has been designed to completely recreate the Colonial lifestyle."

Zach should have been all stoic and said, no, I'm fine, don't bother with the pain pills, but his head did hurt, and he didn't want to ruin the night by feeling like crap.

"Thanks. I'm sure the pain meds will fix me right up. Really. It's just a little bump."

Pennewell fluttered out again, and Verity approached hesitantly. "Would it be better if you put the ice pack on yourself? I don't want to hurt you more. I'm afraid I suck at all the domestic stuff."

"It's okay. I'm a grown man, I can manage." He tried not to wince as he applied the ice pack to his forehead. Leaning back in his chair, he closed his eyes for a moment. "What made you apply to this thing, anyway? Are you interested in helping preserve the house?" Please don't let her say she was into ghost-hunting.

She paused long enough that he opened his eyes to look at her.

"Honestly? I didn't. My best friend submitted an application for me without telling me."

He sat up straight. "You're kidding me. Me too. I mean, my friend Hobb told me he was doing it, but said I didn't have a choice if I won. And since I owe him..."

"Put your ice pack back on." She pulled her feet up under her, sitting cross-legged. "Apparently, both our best friends think we're losers." She shook her head with a snort.

Well, Zach thought, he was a loser. He'd been unemployed now for almost a year and living in his parents' basement apartment. "It's funny. When we were in high school, I always thought it would be Hobbs who'd struggle to succeed. He was kind of a stoner back in the day. And now..."

She leaned forward. "Since you know I'm a boring accountant, turn about it fair play. What do you do?"

He groaned. "I used to be a history professor at a university in Illinois. Now...now I'm an unemployed history professor in Westermere."

"Ah. Yeah, I have a couple of clients who lost their teaching positions. Tough market out there. Sorry about that."

His forehead felt frozen now, but the ache had lessened. He dropped the ice pack into his lap.

Where the heck was Pennewell? He'd been gone an awfully long time just to fetch a couple of painkillers.

The light coming through the windows had grown faint, the horizon pale in the gloaming, and shadows had begun to gather in the corner of the parlor.

Getting up, he lit all the candles from a spill he found in a container on the hearth and closed the interior shutters on the windows before responding to Verity's expression of sympathy. "I really shouldn't complain too much. As you said, a lot of teachers are struggling, and at least I have my folks to lean on. It's galling, but I'm grateful. Which explains why Hobb thinks I'm a loser. How about you? Why did your bestie feel the need to arrange this weird blind date?"

She remained quiet for a moment, and he sensed her guard go up and that prickly edge return. When she spoke, her cadence was slow and halting, as though choosing her words carefully. "Dee thinks I need to jump back in the pool. Or get back on the horse. Or whatever cheesy metaphor you want to use. I've been unattached for a while, and the guy I was with before..." She trailed off, and Zach saw her jaw tighten. When she met his gaze, she might have been shooting ice bolts from her eyes. "Let's just say the only things he liked about me were the things he made me change."

Ouch. "Sounds like you're well rid—"

A sudden gust of frigid air swept through the room. Candles guttered, the fire snapped and popped in the hearth, and an eerie moan seemed to emanate from the walls.

Then, in the blink of an eye, it was gone.

Chapter 5

Verity

Verity shot to her feet as Zach jumped up and raced over to the fireplace, checking for errant sparks. While he inspected the braided rug, Verity relit the two candles that had gone out.

Before they could resume their seats or their conversation, Pennewell hurried back in. "Ah, I see you're tucking yourselves in nicely. Temperatures are dropping out there. I know the forecast said something about a little snow, but I hadn't expected the sudden cold front." As he spoke, he checked the shutters Zach had fastened. "Well done, Mr. Merrick, well done." He pulled a couple of capsules from his pocket and handed them to Zach. "Here now, I couldn't find the acetaminophen, but there is a bottle of ibuprofen in the upstairs bathroom. I hope that's all right."

Zach looked embarrassed but took the pills. That bonk on the head had to have been humiliating.

But not as humiliating as the way Verity had jumped from her chair at the gust and moan of a simple breeze. It was an old house, after all. Yet that moan had sounded eerie–and feminine. Wind did not normally sound feminine.

She adjusted her sweater, lifted her chin. "Do you usually get such strong drafts in here, Mr. Pennewell?"

He cast her a confused look. "Drafts? Oh, I dare say, no. Never had a draft in here in my recollection. Well, not since the renovation to the clapboard siding in '95." He chuckled. "The one in 1995, that is, not 1895." When they didn't laugh, he said, "Sorry, a little historian joke."

"But just a second ago, there was..." She glanced at Zach, who raised his eyebrows at her as if in warning. Maybe she should let it go. It was probably rude to imply that the house leaked like a sieve.

Pennewell looked at her inquiringly, then at Zach, and when Verity didn't continue, he said, "Does your head hurt much, Mr. Merrick?"

"It's fine, really."

"Oh, good. Very good." He clasped his aged, slender hands together. "Now, we're running a bit late, and I'm not supposed to drive after dark, which means I must let the two of you explore the rest of the house after dinner, which should be served at the table in the hall in just under an hour. The catering staff will stay until 8 pm to make sure you have everything you need and then will come back tomorrow morning to serve you a lovely, albeit modern breakfast."

He crossed to the fireplace and expertly placed another log on the merrily crackling blaze. "Do either of you know how to bank a fire?"

Verity piped up at the same time Zach did. "Yes."

Zach gave her an impressed look. "Girl Scouts?"

"High school beer parties in Absolom's Grove."

Pennewell nodded and smiled benignly. "Then you'll do splendidly."

"Wait," Verity said, "there's no central heating?"

"There is, of course. But for these special events, we want to try to keep the experience as close to what would have been experienced by the original inhabitants as possible. Oh, that reminds me. The clothes!"

Verity nearly groaned. She'd forgotten that part.

"Yes, yes, we've arranged for a variety of period clothing items to be provided to both of you. Now, of course, you don't have to wear them. But many participants over the years have said it really added to their enjoyment of the evening to dress in clothes similar to those worn by Mercy and Mercy's friend Josiah."

Pennewell seemed to sense their hesitation. "As I said, it is an option, not a requirement. If you decide to indulge, the selections will be up in your rooms. Miss Verity, you'll be in Mercy's room. It's to the left of the stairs as you go up. Master Zachariah, you'll be in Mistress Temperance's room, just across the hall. You'll notice the hallway has been somewhat foreshortened to make space for a small but modern bathroom. An unfortunate anachronism, but a necessary one."

He rubbed his hands together. "Do you have any questions before I leave you to your evening?"

Verity shook her head. No heating? She could only hope that there were many large, thick blankets on the bed. Or maybe she'd just bring a pillow and a blanket down and sleep in front of the fire. Morning couldn't come fast enough.

From the corner of her eye, she saw Zach glance at her, then said, "No, sir, I think we'll be just fine."

"Good, good. I hope you have a lovely evening. Wine will be served at dinner, of course, and our own apple cider—that's hard cider. Crowell Orchards were famous for their fine cider—for breakfast. Oh, good heavens! I almost forgot." He reached into the pocket of his trousers and pulled out an old skeleton key. "This is the key to the cellar. Your evening comes with a voucher for two bottles of excellent wine, which we've left along with a treat on the tasting table. Just follow the signs."

He glanced around, the way her father now did, using objects to help remind him of things. "I think that's everything? There are plaques all through the house, providing extra history, and you'll find in the bookshelf over there some compilations of Mercy and Temperance's letters and journals. There is even a volume on the history of the house itself, the various renovations over the centuries, researched and written by our very own Karl Berger. That might be of particular interest to you, Master Zachariah, given your interest in historical architecture."

That was the second time Pennewell had used Zach's full name. And that old colonial title, master. She wondered just how much time the aged attorney spent in the real world versus how much he lived in the past.

There was no accounting for some people's obsessions. Pennewell's was this house. Brad's had been a rather repugnant form of pornography. She'd take historical homes over that any day.

She heard footsteps and the door to the room called the hall opened. The young docent, who had taken Verity's coat earlier, poked her head in. "Time you should be leaving, Mr. Pennewell. It'll be full dark soon, and the snow is really starting to come down."

Pennewell glanced at his watch and nodded. "Thank you very much, Meghan. I was just finishing up."

With a fond smile at the older man, the young woman disappeared, and Pennewell took first Verity's hand, then Zach's. "I truly hope you have an amazing Valentine's Day Eve. This house is a very special place. May you experience all it has to offer, and may tomorrow's dawn bring light onto darkness."

He said it with such solemnity, such earnestness, that Verity curtailed a sarcastic response. "Thank you, Mr. Pennewell. I'm sure we'll have a lovely evening."

Zach nodded and squeezed the older man's hands. "We'll take good care of her tonight, Mr. Pennewell." He apparently referred to the house.

Pennewell's eyes teared up. "I know you will. I have a good feeling about you two. You'll take good care of them all."

He brushed at his cheeks, unabashed at his tears. "Claire would be calling me a silly old fool right now. Time for me to go. I'll see you tomorrow before you leave. And if you have any unusual experiences, feel free to leave some notes in the visitor's book." He winked. "Some people have reported odd incidents when they spend the night here, you know."

Zach's laugh sounded forced. "Right. The Weeping Widow."

Verity knew the tales, too. Hogwash, all of them, but you couldn't grow up in Westermere without hearing them. "And the scent of apple blossoms."

Pennewell's good cheer had returned. "You scoff, but there are more things in heaven and earth, Horatio, as the Bard said. And now, I must be off. Good night!"

And with that, Pennewell took his leave and hurried out into the blustery evening.

Verity turned to Zach with a wry look. "If you see the shadow of the Weeping Widow tonight on your way to the bathroom, tell her not to moan, okay? I'm a light sleeper."

He laughed, but something in his eyes told her he was at least half a believer. Well, that was fine. He could believe anything he wanted. It didn't matter because after tonight, she'd never see him again.

Even if he was pretty damn good-looking. And interesting. And definitely not Brad.

Chapter 6

Zach

Snow and a blast of cold air swirled in when Pennewell left, and Zach saw the docent watch with concerned eyes as the old man drove cautiously away before closing the door.

"He hates to leave," the young woman said. "Especially since his wife passed. He's such a sweetheart, and we all sort of look after him now. But I do worry. He's a bit obsessed with this place. I think he'd live here if the Historical Society would let him." She made sure the door latched shut. "Well. Would you like to go upstairs and change into period clothes before dinner? I'm happy to help you."

Zach figured Verity would scoff and decline, but the historian in him was sort of fan-boying at the idea. He'd been involved in some re-enactments during high school. Living here in New England and being a history nerd, that kind of thing came with the territory. And Hobb had paid a lot for this "experience." Might as well go all in.

Without looking at Verity—he did not want to see her disapproval—he said, "Sure, that sounds like fun."

"I suppose I'll have to wear one of those corset things?"

The young woman, whose name they still didn't know, laughed. "Not quite. Colonial women wore stays. Rich women's stays laced up in the back, as they had servants to help them, but less affluent women's stays laced up in both front and back, making them easy to tie themselves. And they're not super tight. They actually provided back support for more safely carrying heavy things, like buckets of water or heavy cooking pots. I'll be happy to show you how to get them on and off."

Zach waited, holding his breath.

Her smile looked forced when she said, "Oh, why not?"

A reluctant acceptance, but he appreciated her attempt at getting into the spirit of things.

"Great. Mr. Merrick, I don't think you'll have any problems. Men's clothing really hasn't changed much over the centuries, other than the invention of zippers, but if you have any trouble, just holler."

"I've worn period clothes before."

Verity had the grace not to laugh. "Don't tell me. You're one of those Revolutionary War re-enactors who dress up like Minute Men and shoot pretend guns at one another?"

He kept his expression neutral. "Actually, I spent two summers working at the Plimouth 17th Century English Village during high school."

Her cheeks flushed, and she pressed her lips together. "I'm sorry. That came out wrong."

He shrugged. He was used to it.

The young docent cleared her throat. "Dinner will be ready soon. We should probably head up and start the transformations." The brightness in her voice was a little strained, but Zack was determined to make the most of what Hobb had paid for.

Besides. To him, anyway, women looked hot in stays. And there was something about Verity that drew him in. She was smart, interesting, and when she let her guard down, even kind. She'd been very gentle, wiping the blood from his forehead.

And there was something else, something he couldn't quite put his finger on. He found he wanted to get to know her. The real her. The one she kept hidden.

Meghan led them back into the hall and up the narrow stairs to the second floor. The landing opened onto a small corridor. Two doors faced each other, and at the end of the hallway was a third that had to be the modern bathroom Pennewell had mentioned.

Zach headed into the chamber with the sign that said "Temperance Hathorne's Chamber" while the docent and Verity went into the other.

Verity looked nervous, but the upward tilt of her chin bespoke a determination to endure whatever came next. It was almost comical.

Ten minutes later, Zach had dressed in woolen breeches and stockings, a heavy cotton shirt, a long woolen waistcoat and frock coat, and a pair of remarkably well-fitting buckled shoes. He took a minute to use the bathroom, then propped himself up against the wall to wait for Verity.

Out of the corner of his eye, he caught a shadow on the stairs, creaking up, then rapidly descending. He sauntered down the hallway and peered over the railing, but saw no one.

Had it been the docent? Or maybe one of the caterers come to check on their diners?

If it was Meghan, that meant that Verity was getting ready without her help, or stalling. He bet on the latter.

He knocked on the door of the chamber that the plaque outside identified as Mercy Hathorn's room. "Verity? You ready?"

A few seconds later, the docent opened the door and slipped out into the hall. "She's just about there. Do you want to go down and wait for her in the hall?"

Zach shook his head. "No, no, I don't mind. Besides, I think it would be more appropriate to escort her downstairs. You know, like the tales of the twin shadows on the stairs?"

The young woman nodded. "Our overnight guests do mention that a lot. There's loads of references in the guest book about it. Before you and Ms. Dickenson leave, do please leave a note of your own there. It's always lovely to hear how people enjoyed the house during their stay."

"We'll be sure to." He paused, remembering the person he'd seen on the stairs. "I think one of the caterers might be looking for you. When I came out, someone was just coming up. Or going down."

The young woman tilted her head. "Was there, now?" Her tone sounded amused. "Well, I'd best go check. I'll see you downstairs in a few minutes."

She left, and Zach resumed his post against the wall, now glad he had changed. His jeans and sweater had been warm, but it was chilly up here, and the several layers of Colonial garb really made a difference.

Verity's period clothes should be equally warm, at least while they were downstairs, but she'd likely be cold tonight. Temperance's room had a fireplace, which had been set, but not lit, but he didn't recall there being one in Mercy's room. He wondered if he should offer to switch with her. It would be the gentlemanly thing to do.

In his head, he imagined Hobbs telling him that he and Verity should just share Temperance's room. "Oh, go to hell, Hobbs."

The door to Mercy's room opened, and Verity stepped out. "I beg your pardon?"

"Sorry, just talking to..." He trailed off as he took her in. Her gown had a bodice and split skirt of sage green, beneath which a simple white underskirt peeked out, and a white lace fichu had been fastened around her shoulders. Nothing fancy, like well-born ladies of Boston might have worn, but the colors brought out the green in her hazel eyes, and the bodice fit her figure like a dream.

She balked and took a step back. "What? Am I wearing it backwards or something?"

He shook his head. "No, no. You look amazing." God, that sounded lame.

"Oh." She looked down at herself. "There aren't any mirrors, and I wasn't sure." She gave him a once-over. "You clean up pretty good yourself. You look...comfortable."

He laughed. "Like I said, I've done this before." He crooked an arm. "May I escort you down to dinner?"

Her smile reached her eyes. "You can, but given the width of those stairs, it's gonna be a little awkward. There is no way two people can walk down side by side."

He let his arm drop. "Ah. You have a point. Well then, ladies first."

He followed her down to the hall, where the old trestle table had been set with lovely, replica pewterware and cups. A bouquet of red roses sat on the table as well. A merry fire blazed in the enormous fireplace, and Zach noticed the niche on the side contained enough wood to last at least through the next day. Good. That meant no trouping out into the cold for more.

"Oh, thank goodness," Verity said as she perused the table. "I was afraid it was going to be all eat with your fingers, like at the Renaissance Faire."

"Our Colonial ancestors were not barbarians. They had dishes and silverware and all the rest. Wealthy people had fancy stuff, but Temperance and Mercy probably had tableware much like this. Except for the wine glasses—those are modern."

"I'm beginning to think all this talk about the wine cellar is a ploy to get us both drunk."

Zach poured a fragrant red wine he was pretty sure he wouldn't like into the two glasses. "Well, I mean, we're supposed to be on a blind date. I imagine the expectation is that we'll want to, um, how do I say this without getting slapped...lower our inhibitions."

Verity laughed, a delightful sound now that it was more than just politeness. "You mean they want us to get laid."

"That's actually why my friend Hobb set me up for this thing. He thinks I need it." He felt a flush climb up his neck. "Which I don't. Of course. I mean—"

She held up a hand to stop his babbling. "Oh my God, Dana said the exact same thing to me. It's a pain in the ass to have well-meaning friends."

He pulled out one of the ladderback chairs for her. "But also good to have people that care."

With a lift of her brows, she sat and examined the placard by her plate that spelled out the night's menu.

"Good heavens. Look at how many courses there are." She took a sip of wine, then another, as though she needed courage. "We're going to be too full to get it on."

As she spoke, two servers came through the door, bearing a loaded platter, a soup tureen, and broad, knowing smiles.

Chapter 7

Verity

Verity hadn't been joking. Dinner had been six courses. A starter of hearth-baked bread with honey-butter and some sort of pickled apples had been followed by a winter vegetable soup. Then came miniature mushroom and herb pies, roasted potatoes, and something she thought might be turnips, alongside a green salad. The dessert course consisted of pears poached in what the server said was rosewater, sprinkled with candied ginger, and drizzled with crème anglaise.

Verity ate only small amounts of each course, or she'd never have gotten through the whole meal, delicious as it was.

Finally, the young docent came in from the kitchen and poured a deep purple liquid into their cordial glasses. "A little blackberry cordial from the cellars." She stepped back and set the bottle on the table. "And now, I'm off. The catering staff will be back early tomorrow morning to get breakfast set up, which means you'll have the evening to yourself. If you get hungry later, there'll be a selection of cheese, bread, and crackers in the kitchen." She paused, glancing out the window. "It's really starting to pile up. I need to warn you, sometimes when it gets like this, the power lines go down. They usually fix things by morning, though, and you've got the oil lamps and candles. I expect you'll be fine."

Zach poured a little more of the potent blackberry concoction into his glass. "We'll be fine, no worries." He gestured at the piles of firewood with his glass. "And we've definitely got enough wood to keep us warm."

The docent clasped her hands together in a gesture she'd clearly picked up from Pennewell. "Good. Then I'll see you in the morning."

With a cheery wave, she hurried back into the kitchen, and a minute later, they both heard the heavy back door clunk shut.

The crackling and popping of the fire filled the silence that followed her departure. Verity found herself looking out the window into the darkness, wondering if the snowfall continued. She resisted, barely, the urge to get up and press her nose to the glass to check.

"Well," Zach ventured.

"A deep subject," she countered, then put the heel of her hand to her forehead. "Ugh, sorry, reflex. One of my father's favorite jokes."

To her surprise, Zach laughed. "My pop loves that one too. It's almost like a call and response thing at this point." He hooked a long arm over the spindle of his chair. "So. What should we do? Instead of heading upstairs, tearing all our borrowed clothes off and throwing ourselves at each other, like everyone, including Arthur Pennewell, wants us to?"

She gazed around her. The large, yet somehow cozy room felt both strange and familiar. "I wouldn't mind a look at those journals and letters Pennewell talked about. I always figured there'd be some juicy gossip in Mercy's diaries."

Zach scooted back in his chair and hurried around to pull hers out for her. "Oh, thank God. I've been dying to do that myself, but figured you'd think it was boring." He offered her his hand to help her to her feet, and while the gesture felt strange and a little awkward, she allowed it.

In the parlor, they gathered up the bound volumes the Historical Society had printed of Mercy's letters and journals and brought them back into the hall, where it was warm. The rest of the house had become distinctly chilly. Someone had banked the fire in the parlor for the night, although Zach had assured her that if she felt more comfortable in there, he could get it going again.

He was, she began to realize, as at home in the past as he was in the present. Just generally handy.

As they passed the front window, now rimed with frost, she peeked out. "Jeez, there's got to be four inches of snow out there already."

Zach leaned over her shoulder to look as well, and she was acutely aware of his cologne, a spicy scent with notes of leather and musk. She also noticed the way his breath tickled her neck and her visceral response surprised her. She hadn't felt even the vaguest stirrings of interest in a man since she'd walked out on Brad.

To be honest, her reaction to the man himself startled her even more. He wasn't at all the type of guy she usually fell for. Blonds had never interested her, and for some reason, she'd always been drawn to people who objected to her being as tall or taller than them. Nor had she ever dated someone she considered an intellectual. In the world of business and accounting, she hadn't encountered many of those.

And yet here she was, getting hot and bothered by a tall, blond history nerd.

She felt a little disappointment when he stepped back. "Yeah, it's really coming down. We should probably check the weather report."

She shrugged. "Why? Not like we're going anywhere." She pointed to the mountain of logs tucked into the niche of the massive fireplace. "As you said, we have plenty of wood."

He snorted. "Wood. Hah. Sorry. Guy humor. Apparently, I'm still twelve. And you wonder why I'm still single."

She sniggered. "I don't mind guy humor as long as gals aren't the butt of the joke."

"Nope. My mom raised me to be one of the good guys. More Captain America than Homelander."

Appreciating his choice in entertainment, she laughed. "Then you should have no trouble dating."

His grin faded. "And yet, here I am." He cleared his throat and set the volumes detailing Mercy Hathorne's life onto the table. "So, where do we start? Are you an A-Z kind of person or do you go right to the ending?"

"I'm an accountant. Methodical by nature." She brushed off the table in front of her. "I say we start at the beginning."

He pulled his chair around the table and sat down next to her. "Your wish is my command," he said and opened the first volume.

An hour later, they'd gotten through the first few years of Mercy's life after coming to live with her grandmother.

The girl had been a prolific writer, sharing her initial fears of leaving her father's house—though that hadn't been a happy place for her after her father had remarried—her diligence in learning all the things Temperance taught her, in preparation for Mercy one day taking over running the orchard and the business it fed, and her first meeting with the handsome young son of the baker who delivered bread three days a week.

In her neat hand, Mercy waxed rhapsodic about Josiah Thayer. In addition to his bakery deliveries, Temperance had allowed the young man to visit on Sunday evenings, when Mercy would read to both Josiah and Temperance from books of poetry and, of course, the Bible. She enthused about how Josiah loved the same poets as Mercy, how fine-featured he was, the beauty of his green eyes, and how astute were the questions he asked when Temperance would lead discussions about Bible passages.

Then came Mercy's crushing disappointment at her father's refusal of Josiah's suit. How cruel her father had been, and how little Mercy liked the man her father had chosen for her. She spoke of how uncomfortable Benjamin made her feel, and the rumors she'd heard about his tendency to drink to excess and get into fistfights at the slightest provocation. All unseemly behavior. But when she brought these matters to her father, he brushed her off or accused her of engaging in sinful gossip.

As Verity and Zach reached the end of the first volume, Verity pushed back her chair and stood. Stretching her hands toward the fire, she felt echoes of her own soured relationship with Brad. Benjamin's controlling behavior, his fits of violent temper, and his drinking sounded so much like Brad that Verity found her chest tighten and her fists clench in response.

Zach closed the book and climbed to his feet. He touched her shoulder but didn't crowd her. "You okay?"

"That asshole Benjamin just stirred up some ghosts. I'm fine."

"Mercy certainly painted him like a villain. I'm sorry it brought up bad memories." He moved to the woodpile and built up the fire, which had started to burn low. "How about we take a break? Talk about something else for a bit."

Some of the pressure in her chest eased. "Like what?"

"Like...poetry. I admit I'm partial to the romantic period, especially Shelley."

"I do like the romantics, but if I have to pick a favorite, it would be Philip Freneau."

"You've stumped me. I have no idea who that even is." He cocked his head at her. "You're no fan of poor Emily?"

"I should be, given my last name. But no, I think Freneau is highly underappreciated. Have you read The British Prison Ship?"

Zach shook his head. "No. But if you recommend it, I'll give it a go."

The statement hit her as utterly obsequious. If she'd been in a bar, she'd have suspected his motives. Here, now, she didn't. He came across as serious. Genuine. "You might be bored."

"I might. And then again, I might love it. You never know you'll like something unless you try."

"You sound like my dad."

He chuckled. "No, I sound like my mom."

"I think I'd like your mom."

"I think you will too." He stopped, then stammered, "I mean, would. I think you *would* like my mom. I mean, everyone does."

She went back to the table and finished off her blackberry cordial. She found his open embarrassment endearing. Vastly different from the conceit and macho bluster she often encountered in the business world. "Given what we've read in the journal, what do you think happened to Mercy and Josiah?"

He sat down next to her and, hands locked behind his head, stretched his long legs under the table. "You know, I always believed they ran off together. Not to Boston, like Benjamin told everyone, but somewhere no one knew them."

He paused. "Now, though, after reading Mercy's journal, and how many times Mercy talked about what a belligerent bully Benjamin was, and how he made her nervous and afraid, I'm wondering if maybe they tried to leave, but Benjamin prevented them. I absolutely don't believe that old theory that they drowned themselves in the mere."

"I agree that they didn't end happily."

"A natural pessimist?"

She wanted to snap back at him. *You'd be one too if you'd been through what I have.* "No," she finally said. "But *if* you believe in the hauntings, then they can't have run off and lived happily ever after. Or they wouldn't still be moaning and crying and whispering in people's ears here, would they?"

He let his arms drop and faced her with a grin. "You *do* believe! I knew it. I knew I wasn't the only one."

"Oh no. No, no, no. I'm an accountant. I don't believe in ghosts."

The fire on the hearth suddenly whooshed and popped. A log toppled, sending a shower of sparks onto the stone hearth.

Chapter 8

Zach

Zach leaped up to examine the hearth for errant sparks and, fortunately, found nothing. When he turned back to Verity, her face looked pale, even in the ruddy light of the fire. "It's okay, no harm, no foul."

Verity trembled. "See, this is what I like about modern central heating. You can't accidentally set your house on fire."

He kept his tone joking, though he half-believed he was right when he said, "I don't think it's the heating method. I think someone didn't like what you said about ghosts. Better take that back."

For a moment, he thought she'd double down. Instead, she put up her hands, palms out, and gazed up and around. "Sorry, guys. Didn't mean to offend anyone."

Zach felt a chill sweep over him.

The hair rose on the back of his neck.

The presence of Mercy? Josiah? Or had that been the stern old Temperance casting spiritual disapprobation on their dismissal of the house's alleged non-corporeal residents?

He supposed he believed in the concept of ghosts, but had never really given much credence to all those crazy ghost-hunting shows on TV. Surely that was all just hype and entertainment.

And yet tonight, here, he might be persuaded.

"I'm, uh, going to head upstairs and use the little boy's room, and while I'm up there, I'll light a fire in the big bedroom to warm things up. Why don't you top off our glasses while I'm gone? Need anything while I'm up there? An extra sweater or an afghan off the bed?"

She shook her head, still looking a bit uneasy. "No, I'm fine. I might take a look in the kitchen for something a little less alcoholic, though."

"Good idea. Intoxication leads to a lowering of body temperature."

With a wave of his fingers, he grabbed a candleholder with a finger loop and headed up the narrow, creaking stairs as she disappeared through the door into the kitchen, hurricane lamp in her hand.

Thank whatever architect had designed it, the bathroom was tastefully modern. Small. Tiny, really. But serviceable.

He checked his reflection in the mirror by candlelight before he left, half expecting to see a figure behind him. Instead, he just saw himself, pink-cheeked from the wine and the blackberry cordial, hair slightly tousled, and looking oddly more normal in his period dress than he looked in modern clothing. If this were a fantasy novel, he'd step out the door and find himself transported back in time.

In truth, tonight felt a bit like a fantasy novel. The lack of modern lights and heating, the period clothes, the atmosphere of such a storied setting, and the immersion in the mystery of Mercy Hathorne and Josiah Thayer all helped. Not to mention Zach's highly unusual attraction to a woman he'd never before met.

He felt as though he stood on the threshold of a liminal space. A place that existed between his normal reality and somewhere else.

As he fussed with his hair and clothes, he wondered what it was that drew him to Verity. Clearly, she had intelligence and a wicked wit, things he found enormously attractive. And when had he ever met a woman who loved 18th-century poetry? Nor did it hurt that he was a sucker for dark hair and curves.

He gazed in the mirror at the lump on his forehead, which had started to bruise. Damn it, he looked like a cyclops wearing purple eyeshadow.

He didn't stand a chance with this woman.

Giving up on trying to improve his appearance, he stepped out into the hallway and was immediately hit with the mouth-watering aroma of freshly baked bread and the faint scent of apples. Was Verity warming up something left by the caterer? Despite the enormous meal, he could always eat, and homemade baked goods were a weakness.

Verity didn't seem the baking type, but then again, he didn't know her very well. He entered the bedroom that had been Temperance's. Someone had turned on the little electric bedside lamp. He set about lighting the fire in the grate and replaced the modern screen to prevent any stray sparks.

That would warm things up nicely, at least in here. He'd definitely offer the room to Verity. Unless maybe...

No. No matter what Hobb wanted, Zach did not do one-night stands.

As he moved to the door, the little lamp on the bedside flickered, then went out, leaving him for a moment in the dark. Not even a second later, the light came on again, and he breathed a sigh of relief. The docent hadn't been wrong about the power. They'd have to make sure to carry an oil lamp with them at all times.

Exiting Temperance's chamber, he caught a flash of movement, the impression of a shadow crossing the sliver of light peeking out from under Mercy's bedroom door.

What the hell? Could it be one of the staff turning down the beds? But the docent had said they'd be alone. He hurried across the hall and flung open the heavy wooden door.

The room lay empty. And cold. Could enough he could see his breath.

The hair on the back of his neck rose, as it had downstairs. And he sensed...anticipation? Hope?

A voice called up the stairs, breaking the spell. "Zach? You okay?"

Verity, wondering what was keeping him.

He stooped beneath the doorframe and onto the landing to holler down the stairs. "Yeah, just finishing up the fire. If you don't mind, I'm leaving the door to Mercy's room open to warm it up in there, since there's no fireplace."

"Okay. Thanks."

He stepped into Mercy's room again. Still empty. And oddly, much warmer than it had been moments before.

Did he believe in ghosts? Really? Before tonight, he might have said, maybe. Right now, though, feeling as though someone watched him, waiting for something, his "maybe" had gotten a lot closer to a "yes."

He addressed the potential presence. "Look, if you've got something to say, you're going to have to be a little clearer."

Nothing.

Of course, he heard nothing. This was just the power of suggestion. An old house, a ghost story, and a trick of the light. He shook his head. Where had his parents' Massachusetts practicality gone?

As he turned to exit through the especially low doorframe, he thought he heard a whisper.

It said, "Duck."

Chapter 9

Verity

Verity had opened up the second book of Mercy's letters and journals by the time she heard Zach scrambling down the narrow stairs, nearly tripping over his own feet. He glanced back over his shoulder twice, once on the stairs and then again at the bottom.

"Something wrong? A bat, perhaps? Please tell me you're not afraid of bats."

He jerked his attention away from the stairs. "Uh, no. Well, maybe. I mean, I like them in concept. Um. I just thought I heard...saw..." He heaved a sigh, shook his head. "Never mind."

When he resumed his seat, he emptied what was left in the blackberry cordial bottle into his glass and chugged it down.

Verity waited a moment, then folded her hands in front of her. "Okay, spill. What did you think you saw?"

He pursed his lips. "From your tone, you're not going to believe me. I'm not sure I'm up for further humiliation."

Damn. Why couldn't she ever just be nice? She used to be nice.

Breaking all her own rules, she reached out a hand, placed it on his arm. "I'm sorry. I didn't mean it like that." Sitting back, she moderated her tone. "You came down those stairs like the devil himself chased you, as my mother would have said. What startled you?"

His gaze flitted around the room. "It's crazy. I'm sure there's a logical explanation. I keep telling myself it's all this ghost story stuff. When I came out of Temperance's room, I thought I saw a shadow cross the light from under the door to Mercy's room. So I went in there, but of course, no one was there. And then it got super col,d and I felt like someone was in there with me. Waiting."

She could have said it was a trick of the light, or his imagination. A draft. This place was insulated about as well as a child's plastic playhouse. But she didn't. Not only because she was trying for once not to be a bitch, but because while he'd been upstairs, she'd felt that sense of someone waiting too. And smelled, of all things, freshly baked bread, as though someone had just walked in with a basket of baked goods. "Okay. I can see where that might have been freaky. Anything else?"

He reached for his glass and knocked it over. Thank goodness it had been empty. He huffed a breath. "Told you. Clumsy."

"Never mind that."

"Okay. As I turned to leave...you're not going to believe this."

"Try me." She realized she was open to whatever he was going to tell her. Because a part of her had started to believe.

His remarkable green eyes met hers. "As I turned to leave, I heard someone whisper, 'duck.'" He touched his aching forehead. "Like I should have done earlier."

The hair on her arms prickled. "It could have been the wind." She wanted to believe that. Why didn't she? She took a breath. "Okay, since we're sharing fairy tales, while you were upstairs, I was in the kitchen. First, the wind blew the door open." She shrugged. "The caterers probably didn't latch it well, and the weather is really turning." She paused and pointed upward at the sound of the wind whistling through the eaves.

He swallowed. "Not unexpected."

"But after I closed it, I smelled..." She stared down at Mercy's journal. "This sounds ridiculous."

Zach leaned forward. "It's just us here. And neither of us are going to repeat any of this. Right?" His eyes crinkled when he smiled. "In for a penny, in for a pound, Verity."

"Fine. I smelled bread. Fresh-baked bread."

He slapped a hand on the table, startling her. "Me too! Wafting up the stairs! I thought maybe you were heating something up."

A thought popped into her head. "Zach, Josiah was a baker. He delivered bread here to Temperance and Mercy."

He laughed, although not at her, thank heavens. She'd have had to slug him then. "We've gone mad. Maybe the wine was drugged."

"Or maybe it's this place."

"Or maybe, just maybe, all those stories people tell about what happens to them here are true. And Mercy and Josiah are trying to tell us, tell someone, something."

No. Not possible. She was a rational person. There were no such things as ghosts.

Though after what happened before, she wouldn't say it aloud again.

"Look, let's take a break from the past and talk about the present." She gestured at the table. I brought out some cheese and crackers from the kitchen, and a couple of cream sodas I found in the fridge. I know they're not 'period', but maybe we should lay off the alcohol."

He reached for the bottles and twisted off the caps. "Good idea. We're just suffering from a joint hallucination."

And yet she could see in his eyes he didn't believe that any more than she did. She knew what she'd felt, what she'd smelled.

Brushing it aside, she clinked her bottle against his. "Right. So. Why aren't you teaching?"

"Yikes. You don't do small talk, do you?"

"Nope. Waste of time. If I like someone, I want to get to know them."

She watched him lean back and stretch his long legs out under the table. When he deliberately bumped against her, she found she didn't mind. In fact, it sent a little thrill through her.

She noticed he smiled when she didn't pull away. "Budget cuts, mostly. I was teaching at a small college outside of Chicago. Federal funds for non-business-related curriculum are getting cut all over the country, and I hadn't achieved tenure yet. So they let me go." He took a swig of his cream soda. "It sucked more than usual because I really liked it there. The kids were great, and I think I actually reached some of them. Even though a lot of the classes were undergrad level, we had pretty good discussions. That's when teaching becomes magic, when you know you're making a connection and watching them start to reason for themselves."

"I'm sorry. And you can't find another spot?"

He shrugged. "Not yet. Honestly, at this point, I'd be happy just working at some place like this. A place I could just dig in and root."

"I hope that happens. Can't be easy living at home with your folks. I stayed with my dad for a few years before he...moved to his current situation. The roles of parent and child shift as we get older. The transition can be awkward and frustrating."

"Amen to that. My mom keeps telling me to wear my mittens, and my dad assumes I'm there to help him with any chore that crosses his mind. Like I'm sixteen and don't have a life."

"Oh yeah. I get that. Dad wanted to vet every date I went on. I kept trying to tell him I wasn't a teenager anymore, but..." She sighed. "They just do it because they love us."

Zach nodded. "I know." He leaned forward. "You said your dad has moved. But the way you said it felt like you meant something other than to a condo in Florida."

Points for being observant. "He's in a memory care facility now. I moved in after Mom died to kind of help him out for a bit. He wasn't ill then, or we didn't know it. Mom's death...well, it really sucked the life out of him."

"I'm sorry. Truly."

She believed he meant it. "No pity, please."

"None offered. My gran had Alzheimer's. I know what it's like."

They sat for a moment in silence, and when he reached across the table to lay a hand on her arm, she felt the tears come, felt her shoulders drop along with her hypervigilance.

He said nothing, didn't try to hug her, just left his hand on her arm in quiet solidarity while she took a moment to let the feelings wash over her. When she'd mastered herself, she removed her arm and reached for her own soda.

Zach leaned back again, giving her space, and gazed around him. "Why do you think old Pennewell does this? Invites couples here on a blind date once a year?"

"I don't know. Maybe he's just a hopeless romantic. I hear they exist. Otherwise, romance writers couldn't make a living."

"I don't believe you're really that cynical." The man's grin was infectious. The kind that made you feel better, no matter how far down in the hole you were. "Did you notice the picture of his wife on his desk in his office? And how he mentioned Claire earlier? Maybe he just wants others to find the same sort of love he and his wife shared."

"It was sweet, wasn't it? Like her spirit is still part of his life." She wondered if her father still felt the presence of her mother. "Are your folks like that? All lovey-dovey?"

He considered. "In their own way, I guess. I mean, they're typical New Englanders. Practical people. But they have a solid marriage. Like a good house."

He got up, tossed a couple of logs on the fire, and poked at it a bit before coming back to sit next to her.

Surprisingly, she didn't mind. It felt comforting to have him close. She gazed into kind eyes. Eyes that invited her to share, a smile that offered understanding.

She swallowed. "Mr. Pennewell said you were interested in colonial architecture. Why didn't you become an architect?"

He chuckled. "I can't do math. Besides, it's the beauty of the structures, the simplicity and elegance of the designs that I really love. I don't want to build the past or reconstruct it. I just enjoy studying it. Getting into the mind of the people that created those buildings tells you a lot about how they saw the world. That's as close as we'll ever get to understanding those who came before."

Wow. A man who understood himself. She stared down at the book beneath her hands and nodded. "Exactly. That's why I like poetry. To understand how people think. The words, they make you realize that across the vastness of time, people have always been people. We feel the same things, want the same things, love the same way."

She made the mistake of glancing over at him. His face lay only inches from her own, his eyes fixed on hers.

When he leaned in to kiss her, she didn't pull away, though every lizard-brain instinct screamed at her that she should.

His lips tasted like blackberry cordial, and his long eyelashes tickled her cheek.

Finally, he eased back, those green eyes glittering in the firelight, and she saw both pleasure and trepidation in his gaze.

A question lay there. He waited patiently for her response.

She hesitated for only a moment. She knew the answer, even if it turned out to be the wrong one. Sliding her fingers into his hair, she pulled him close for a longer, deeper kiss.

A second later, the room filled with the sweet scent of apple blossoms, but only a part of her brain registered it. The rest of her reveled in the indulgence of his lips, the warmth of his arms around her, and a long-forgotten sense of being alive.

The ghosts, if ghosts they were, could wait.

Chapter 10

Zach

Zach's lips tingled when he finally broke away. He could have stayed in that kiss for hours. Days. Decades. No kiss had ever felt more natural, more effortless. More intoxicating.

Verity sank back, her expression a mix of surprise and, from her drawn brows, puzzlement. "Maybe our friends weren't wrong."

He burst into laughter. Thankfully, she joined in instead of looking offended. He reached for his glass and found it empty. Again.

Verity cleared her throat and looked down at the second volume of Mercy Hathorne's journals and letters.

A clear signal. Time to back off a little. Which was fine. If anything were to develop between them, something he hadn't expected to want, they'd need to take it slow.

He stood. "Before we resume our journey into the past, I suggest we head down to the wine cellar. Might as well take advantage of those expensive bottles of wine we're allowed. Plus, we haven't explored down there."

She wrinkled her nose. "Cellars are musty."

"Don't tell me you're afraid of basements."

"No." She paused. "Not much."

"Well, there can't be anything too scary down there, or they wouldn't have put the wine there. Come on. It'll be an adventure." He offered her his hand, hoping, but not expecting, that she'd take it.

She did, but only long enough to stand. "Fine. But then I want to delve into this. Maybe, if we put our heads together, we can figure out what really happened."

He led the way to the cellar door, located in the kitchen, used the key to unlock it, and flicked the light switch. He wasn't afraid of basements, but no way was he going down there with nothing but a candle.

He'd expected a rickety staircase, or maybe a set of old stone steps, but the construction was relatively new, probably built within the last fifty years, and the handrail was sturdy.

Verity followed close behind, close enough that he could smell her perfume. Something floral with a spicy base note. Different from the sickly sweet scent his last girlfriend had worn.

His train of thought ran off the tracks. Wait. When he and Verity had kissed. He'd smelled...apple blossoms?

"Um, Verity?"

She nearly ran into him when he paused on the stairs.

"What? What is it?" Her voice sounded a little panicky.

"Sorry, I didn't mean to startle you. I just realized something."

She huffed a breath. "Idiot. Don't scare me like that. What did you realize, and it better be important."

"When we kissed. Did you...Did you smell anything?"

Too late, he realized that stupid question could be interpreted in a variety of ways. Like maybe he farted. God, he was an idiot.

She stayed silent long enough that he had to turn around to look at her to make sure she was still there.

Her eyes had widened. "You smelled it too? Apple blossoms? I hoped maybe I imagined it."

There had to be a logical explanation. One that didn't include the legend that when the house approved of a young couple, the scent of apple trees in bloom filled the air. "Shared hallucination?"

"That only works if you talk about it first." She glanced down the stairs. "Let's get this over with. It feels creepy down here."

They trouped down the rest of the way and followed the large signs with block lettering and arrows through several underground spaces to the room designated as the wine cellar.

It lay at what Zach knew to be the back of the house, a rectangular space that stretched the length of the building but narrow in depth. Perfect for a long rack filled with many bottles. A skinny table made from empty wine barrels and a finished oak plank created a space for a tasting table. Tonight it held not little plastic cups, but two bottles on a tray, with a note card and a little heart-shaped box of what were likely specialty chocolates. Clearly, these were the bottles set aside for them.

Verity stepped into the space and gave a low whistle. "This is a serious collection." Ignoring the tasting table, she moved to the racks and slid out a few random bottles just far enough to dust and read the labels. "Jeez. I'm surprised they let us down here." She pointed. "This bottle alone is worth several hundred dollars."

"Then put it back. Before I accidentally bump you and you drop it."

She flashed a grin. "Is that something that's likely to happen?"

"If you haven't noticed, I'm a klutz. One of the reasons my father has relegated me to picking up orders at the lumber supply store instead of actually working on job sites."

"You weren't meant to be a construction worker." She slid the bottle back into the rack and moved along the wall to a different section, where bottles stood upright. "Just like I wasn't meant to be an accountant. And yet here we are. Oh wow. This is a 50-year-old Sandeman tawny port."

"And that's a good thing?"

"It's an awesome thing. Tawny port is my favorite, but even when I splurge on a fancy bottle, I can't afford anything more than a 20-year-old bottle. This thing? Three hundred bucks a bottle. Brad would have had a seizure if I'd ever spent that kind of dough on a 'lousy bottle of booze'."

"Well, Brad," and Zach made a face at the name, "can't control what you do anymore. I say you go out tomorrow and buy yourself the most expensive bottle of port you can find. And toast being rid of him."

"I like the way you think!" She moved back to the tasting table. "Meanwhile, these are excellent choices. I'd expected something on the low end, but these aren't shabby at all."

He felt like a bit of a dunce. "I'll take your word for it. Sorry, I don't really know much about wine."

He loved the way her eyes sparkled when she allowed a genuine smile. They did that now, as she bumped shoulders with him. "As my father says, the only thing you need to know about wine is whether or not you like what you're drinking."

The temptation to wrap his arms around her and pull her in for another kiss nearly overpowered his good sense. "Your father is a wise man."

She stared up at him, unmoving, for a long moment, and he nearly gave in to his desire. Before he did, she swallowed and turned away, reaching for one of the bottles on the table. "Do you like sweet or dry?"

"Um...I like sangria."

She laughed. "Then, probably this Gewürztraminer. Not as sweet as a dessert wine, but also won't parch your throat, like a full-bodied red."

"Sounds perfect." Although tonight, he'd probably drink anything she wanted him to.

She scanned the tabletop and moved the box of chocolates on the tray. "No corkscrew. Someone screwed up. We'll need to search for one."

Now *that* he could do. He wandered down to one end of the room, which would have been the far south side of the rectangular footprint of the house, and found a small 1950s-style kitchen cabinet that must have been here since the 1968 renovation when a wealthy industrialist tried, before running out of funds, to turn Hathorne House into his weekend retreat. Zach knew from his research that it was he who had outfitted the wine cellar.

The freestanding jade-green metal cabinet had an old Formica counter with a creaky drawer and a two-door storage section beneath. Someone had shoved it up against the plaster and, judging from the amount of dust and cobwebs, it had remained there ever since. Another matching upper piece hung bolted to the wall above, and Zach saw that the old plaster had begun to flake off onto the floor.

The other three plastered walls in the wine cellar had also begun to peel, revealing the original fieldstone wall beneath. But this short section at the end of the long room was different. Instead of old-fashioned stone behind the plaster, the wall had been constructed of brick.

How odd. Likely an addition to hide pipes or electrical conduits. Had to have been part of some renovation, though he couldn't remember anything in the architectural drawings he'd skimmed through years ago.

Curiosity had him peering between the upper cupboard and the Formica worktop, pulling away a few empty decanters and canisters to get a better look.

More odd. The bricks were old. Really old. The size and shape were not modern, nor was the mortar. In fact, the mortar had started to crumble.

Well, that was a disaster waiting to happen. He made a note to mention it to the docent in the morning. Someone should probably fix that, or the brick wall might collapse and damage some of those pricey bottles of grape juice.

"Zach? Did you find anything?"

Recalled to his task, he put the anachronism aside and opened the screeching drawer to locate a corkscrew, which he waved at Verity. "Score. First try."

"Good."

Turning, he was about to recommend they take both bottles with them—no point in wasting one if Verity would enjoy taking it home—when the hair on his arms rose, and a shiver ran through him.

He locked eyes with Verity as a faint moaning sound vibrated the air, followed by the sound of a woman crying.

Verity's eyes grew round as coins. "Zach?"

He hurried toward her and hustled her through the cellar to the stairs. They raced up, Verity clutching the wine bottle, while the sad, plaintive sobs followed them. At the top, they burst through the door, and Zach slammed it behind them and turned the key in the lock.

The temperature, even here in the kitchen, with the door to the hall closed, felt almost sauna-like compared to the chill of the cellar. Hurrying into the hall, Zach banged shut that door too before dropping into a chair.

Verity sat too. "What was that?"

He grabbed the wine from her and applied the corkscrew with shaking hands. "The wind."

Her raised eyebrows told him what she thought of that explanation.

"What? I thought you didn't believe in ghosts."

She watched the fire for a moment. "I don't."

He poured a glass of the pale gold wine and passed it to her.

She grabbed it, gulped some. "Well, I didn't. I mean, okay, the wind for the moaning, sure. But the crying? Please tell me you heard a woman crying."

"I heard it." He didn't want to accept that he had. But the sound had been unmistakable. "A cat, maybe? Or a raccoon?"

"I really want to believe that."

"But you don't."

She tossed back the rest of her wine in three gulps. "I don't know what I believe." The wine must have helped her shake off her fear. Or maybe she could compartmentalize better than Zach could.

A gust of wind rattled the front window, and Verity strode across the room and peered out into the darkness before returning to the table. "Well, whatever we believe, we're stuck in here with it. There's at least six inches of snow out there now."

Zach jumped to his feet and looked himself. "I thought it was just going to be a couple of inches."

"Welcome back to Massachusetts. I guess we're in for a Nor'easter."

Why did he feel responsible for this? "I'm sorry. I wish your friend and my friend hadn't signed us up for this. If you want to leave, my truck could probably—"

She scoffed. "Don't be silly. It's dangerous out there. And as you said, we've got plenty of wood." She pointed not at the fireplace but at him.

The comment was so outrageous, and her grin so silly, he laughed. Damn, but he liked this woman.

"Sadly, not at the moment. The crying ghost kind of ruined the mood."

"Maybe later we'll see what we can do about that. For now, we've got a mystery to solve."

She might just be joking about them getting more intimate. But even if she wasn't, he didn't want to come across as a creep. He grasped at her mention of a mystery, and Saturday morning cartoons came into his head. "Does that make you Daphne or Velma?"

She picked up on the cue immediately. "I don't know. Are you Shaggy or Fred?"

He chuckled, took a sip of his wine before setting the glass down on the table. She'd been right. Nicely sweet. Just his type. Kind of like her. "Definitely Shaggy. And you're as pretty as Daphne, but way smarter." He shrugged. "I vote for Velma."

"Well, then, Shaggy, let's see what else Mercy has to say in her journals. If that was her crying, there's a reason for it. And if she's haunting this house—and I'm not saying I'm a believer yet—I'm betting that means she never left with Josiah."

The implications of that statement gave Zach another fit of shivers. "You think she's here? Like, buried here?"

"If there's one thing I know about, it's controlling exes. If Benjamin Fitch thought Mercy was cheating on him, maybe he did what jerks like him often do. Get revenge."

It made a certain amount of cruel sense. And it made him both sad and angry that Verity had experienced even a hint of that. He pointed at the book. "Then let's see if we can figure this out. Maybe if we do, the ghosts will, I don't know, stop crying."

The corners of her eyes crinkled when she smiled and raised her wineglass. "I'll drink to that."

Chapter 11

Verity

What on earth was she doing, making that sophomoric crack about wood? Or proposing they do something about it later?

Yet, as much as she wanted to take it all back, as Zach settled close to her to get a better look at the book of Mercy's letters and journal entries, she felt a tingle of arousal she hadn't felt in ages. And not only that, she felt an actual liking.

He was a major departure from the type of men she'd always been attracted to. Although that could have been her mistake all along—going for the wrong sort.

Or maybe all this attraction came from being in this house, reading Mercy's journals. The house was literally casting a spell over her.

Yes, that had to be it. Or the wine. Maybe both.

She looked at her glass, now only half full. Yeah. Definitely could be the wine.

She stared down at the book, unseeing, until Zach tapped the page. "Oh, now that's a bit salacious."

She read the section, having to gently move his finger out of the way. The touch galvanized her. And him too, if his sudden but gentle intake of breath was any indication.

She read aloud from an entry dated 13 February 1761, the night Mercy and Josiah had disappeared.

"Grandmother left for Boston this morning to visit Cousin Abigail for a week, and I find myself torn. It is Sunday, the day that Josiah always comes to read with us. Last week, we read a poem of Margaret Cavendish entitled "Of Flame and Fire". Grandmother had the volume sent secretly from a relative back in England, as it would cause quite the stir if one of the town elders read it. Cavendish speaks of objects called atomes, tiny particles that, by some philosophers' estimation, are as bricks in the structure of all things. Josiah and I had a quite lively discussion about this—after our Bible readings, of course.

Grandmother pretended to be asleep during this discourse, but I knew her to be awake from the slight smile she would evince. She likes Josiah, yea, even approves of him, despite his family's humble occupation. But Father will not conscience the idea of Josiah as a suitable husband.

I digress, as is wont to happen when I discuss Josiah. He exerts such a strong hold upon my heart.

He is so fair. So kind. So tall. I am forever reminding him to duck under the door lintels to avoid hitting his head. And he looks at me in a way that sends my heart racing. I am sure his feelings for me are twin to my own.

Yet he will not be coming today, as he usually would do, knowing that Grandmother is not home.

Oh, how I long to write him. To beg him to come to me. I am here, alone. Unchaperoned. On a previous instance when this occurred, and he arrived, me having forgotten to warn him, we...we engaged in behavior most unbecoming.

And yet, I would not prevent this again. Oh, the thrill of it. The touch of his lips upon mine sent sparks flying, like the atomes Cavendish speaks of.

I sit here at the table, watching the snow fall on this February afternoon, knowing the light will fade soon. I have pen and paper before me, and Jacob, one of the orchard men, stands ready to deliver it, should I ask him to. He is in the kitchen now, finishing the meal Grandmother left him. I know I should not write. And yet, the quill is in my hand, ready to dip into the ink and set nib to parchment. To set my future in motion.

I want Josiah to come. I want to discuss the new book of poetry Grandmother gave me by another English woman poetess, Katherine Philips, who speaks of love with an eloquence that makes my heart want to burst. And I want to share with him all that is in my heart. The things I cannot say when Grandmother is here, even though I believe she knows. More than anything, I want to sit next to him, hold his hand, and once again feel his lips against mine.

I should not write. I should not...

The journal entry ended there, and the next passage in the book was one of Mercy's letters to her younger half-sister, imploring her to try to change their father's mind about Mercy's impending marriage to Benjamin Fitch.

Verity met Zach's eyes. "Wow. Wasn't that, like, a heinous sin back in those days?"

"Canoodling? Well, I suppose people did it, people have always found a way. In secret, I imagine. But yeah, it was a pretty serious issue if you got caught."

She shook her head at him. "Canoodling? Who the heck uses that word now?"

He flushed, ducked his head. "Sorry. Historian here."

God, she was an idiot. "No, I'm sorry. I didn't mean it like that. I actually kind of like that word." She also found she kind of liked the idea of a little canoodling with Zach. Maybe it was the wine, but she felt just as warm and sparkly as Mercy had. And the kiss that she and Zach had shared still made her lips tingle.

She swallowed and turned to look back at the book. In a parched voice, she said, "I wonder what she decided."

Zach had to clear his throat before responding. "Seems kind of obvious. I mean, Benjamin Fitch said he saw the two of them leaving town that night on the road out of town. And even if he lied, and, as you presume, killed them, they must have met." He spun his empty bottle of cream soda. "Besides, the shadow I saw in your room earlier looked like a man."

She jerked a little. "I'm sorry, what? You saw a man in my room?"

He stiffened. "I told you. When I was up there earlier, I saw a shadow of a man in your room. And I smelled bread."

He *had* said that. And she'd promptly dismissed it. "Sorry. You...you didn't say it was the shadow of a man. That freaked me out a little. I mean, if this were a horror story, that shadow could have been a crazed serial killer, not the sad ghost of a baker's son."

He gave her a crooked smile. "True. We are trapped by a snowstorm in what constitutes a cabin in the woods. But no, no serial killer. The room was empty. The whole upstairs was empty, and there are no closets, nor is there an attic."

She took a steadying breath. "No, but there is a creepy basement. And someone sobbing."

"See? Definitely a ghost movie, not a serial killer flick."

Something occurred to her. "So...I smelled bread in the kitchen, like someone had just waltzed in with a fresh loaf. And you say you smelled bread upstairs and saw the shadow of a man in Mercy's room. Do you suppose that means Mercy and Josiah did more than canoodle? That Josiah spent time in her bedroom? Even the suspicion of that would make Benjamin Fitch angry n. It's one thing to think his fiancée was just spending her Sundays gazing longingly into another man's eyes. It's quite another if they were..."

"Engaging in illicit congress? Doing the horizontal tango?"

"Oh, for pity's sake, at least use a euphemism from this century." She said it without rancor.

He grinned. "Gettin' jiggy with it?"

She playfully smacked his arm. "Gawd." Lifting her wineglass, she gestured at the bottle they'd brought up. "Hit me."

He refilled her glass, and she sipped from it, leafing through the pages of the book. "I wonder if she was right about her grandmother. If Temperance knew, and even approved, do you think she allowed their...canoodling?" She giggled at the word. "Even encouraged it, by leaving Mercy alone, unsupervised?"

"Maybe? Pretty radical behavior for the times."

Verity snorted. "The woman let Mercy read poems by Katherine Philips, a woman whose work could be considered sapphic, or at least sapphic-adjacent literature. Temperance seems more like a woman from today than some stuffy old widow from the 18th century."

"Wow. I have to admit, I've never read Philips. Okay, score another point for you. Still, I'm not sure encouraging Mercy would have helped her case with her father."

"Maybe not. Still, now I need to know."

"I don't think a lot of Temperance's papers remain. Mercy was the journal writer."

Verity frowned down at the book. "Hmm. You know, Mercy bangs on and on about Temperance's Bible. Don't I remember that being on exhibit here? Some people keep notes and things in their Bibles. I know my grandmother did. Family stuff."

He raised his eyebrows. "Color me impressed again. Yeah, the Bible is here. They used to keep it in here, but now it's in a new, fancy glass display case in the parlor." He stood and offered her his hand with a grin. "Zoinks, Velma, I think you've found a clue. Let's go check it out."

Chapter 12

Zach

Zach hated to relinquish Verity's hand once they reached the parlor, but it became necessary. Both of them carried oil lamps in their free hands, and not wanting to step on Verity's idea, he let her set hers down on the little table between the chairs they'd occupied earlier to hover over the small wooden plinth near the fireplace, which was topped with the glass case protecting the Bible.

She tried to lift the case, but it didn't budge. "It appears to be attached."

Zach knelt down and pushed the mahogany front panel, which gave a little. "Thought so. This is a standard design. There's a panel here that hides a locking mechanism which lies beneath the surface and holds the glass cover in place." After applying more pressure, the wooden panel slid down, exposing the hollow center of the plinth. He reached up inside and found the lock and the flange of metal that held the glass case in place.

"I don't suppose you have a bobby pin?"

"A bobby pin?" She stared at him incredulously.

"You know, those little things women put in their hair?"

"I *know* what a bobby pin is. And no, I don't have one. Please tell me that lock can't be picked like we're in an episode of Magnum, P.I. If so, I'm heading out next week to knock over some museums."

He loved that she made him laugh. "No, these are just used in places like these, not real museums. It's an affordable deterrent for nosy tourists or annoying teenagers." He shrugged. "Anyway, the bobby pin thing was worth a try." He wiggled the lock, found it securely latched. "And they did indeed lock the cover in place. So no easy solution."

A slow smile spread across her face. "Wait there."

"Where are you going?"

"I'll be right back," she called as she disappeared into the hall.

He heard a couple of clangs. "Verity? Are you okay?"

She hurried back in, carrying the heavy cast-iron fireplace poker. "I'm fine. Like you, I'm a little clumsy, but I'm a great problem solver. Comes in handy when people hand me that shoebox full of ridiculous receipts for their taxes."

"I am totally bringing you my taxes come April."

That she didn't groan or make a snide comment, he took as a positive sign. Maybe there was hope for him. Them. Whatever.

He nodded at the poker. "What's that for?"

She walked up to the plinth and raised the poker over her shoulder like it was a baseball bat.

"No!" He jumped up and grabbed her arm as she swung. "What are you doing?"

"Let go. I'm getting access to the Bible." She stood calmly, still gripping the poker.

When she pulled away from him, he released her immediately. "Shit. Sorry. Didn't mean to manhandle you."

"Hardly. Trust me, I've suffered worse."

"What?" Now he really hated this Brad guy. "But look, you can't just break in."

"Why? Do you want to solve this mystery or not?"

"I do, but..." He rubbed the back of his neck and paced in a circle. "But we'll get in trouble, smashing something."

She lowered the poker and crossed her arms. "I bet that if we solve this thing, Mr. Pennewell won't care. Zach, he basically set us up to solve this. I'm convinced of that. I think that's what this whole Valentine's Day thing is really all about."

"Really?" He paused, thinking, putting the pieces together in his head. "Huh. Maybe you're right. I mean, it's wacky, but it makes sense."

He looked at the Bible under the glass. "I guess we could say we knocked it over." It actually hurt him to think about smashing the plexiglass. History was something you preserved, not something you destroyed.

She followed his gaze. "Zach, I'm not suggesting we tear the book apart.I just want to get inside the damn thing to explore the book."

"It feels wrong." He struggled in silence for a moment. "Fine. But instead of smashing the cover, let me try using a knife to jimmy the lock. It's less...violent."

She gave him an odd look, as though he'd said something she couldn't quite process. "Non-violent, huh? How novel. Okay, good idea."

This time, he fetched a knife from the kitchen. On his way back to the parlor, he glanced out the front window. Heavy snow, lit by the one small light at the entrance, fell fast and thick. There had to be a foot of the stuff now.

He swung toward the open doorway to the parlor and, from the corner of his eye, caught movement from the stairs.

A shiver rippled across his scalp, and he spun to look in that direction.

For a fleeting moment, he could have sworn a thin, wiry woman dressed in a floral-patterned robe anglaise with a lace fichu over her shoulders stood on the shadowy stairs watching him, a faint smile on her wizened face. She nodded at him.

"Verity?" he called quietly.

She crossed the parlor and stepped into the hall. "Yeah?"

As he pointed at the stairs, the woman vanished. If she'd been there at all.

"Tell me you saw her."

She peered into the shadows cast by the flickering fire. "I...I maybe saw something? Just for a second." When she gazed up at him, he expected open derision, but all he saw in her face was a sort of awe. "Do you think... I mean... could that have been Temperance?"

"Oh, thank heavens. At least if I'm going crazy, you are too." Another movie line came to him. "A full-torso apparition. And it's real."

She groaned. "Please don't start with the Ghostbusters stuff. I don't want to accidentally conjure Slimer." She plucked at his sleeve. "Come on. Let's get this done."

He followed her, both thrilled that she'd gotten his reference and also like his legs would give way. Had he really seen what he thought he'd seen?

Shaking off the nerves, he knelt in front of the plinth. As he worked, slowly because of his trembling hands, he asked her, "She didn't look angry, right?"

Verity stood behind him and put her hands on his shoulders. "No. Not to me. Maybe...satisfied? Approving? Does that even make sense?"

The warmth of her hands on his shoulders aroused sensations that made his stomach flutter for a reason other than fear. *Down, boy. This is not the time.* "Does any of this make sense?"

She shifted, and he could tell she looked over her shoulder. "Hurry. I get the feeling we need to hurry."

That was all the motivation he needed. Seconds later, the latch gave as the wood around the metal flange splintered.

With a little crow of delight, Verity snatched off the cover, and by the time Zach clambered to his feet, she was gingerly lifting Temperance's Bible from the little pedestal upon which it sat.

"We really should be wearing gloves. The paper is fragile and the oil from our fingers—"

She lifted her eyebrows. "Do you have document examiner's gloves on you?"

"No, but—"

She pressed a finger against his lips. "Then we'll be as careful as we can be."

Handing him the Bible, she crooked her finger at him, then scooped up her oil lamp in her free hand and strode off through the door to the hall, which left him no choice but to follow. Not only did he not want to be left alone in the darkened room, but the sway of her hips in that dress beckoned him as surely as her finger. Not to mention the mystery of Mercy and Josiah's disappearance.

He was falling. Hard. Not just for her, but for this ridiculous ghostly riddle.

Yes, he'd follow her. Probably off a cliff at this point.

Which he hoped, once all this was over, was precisely where they were headed.

Chapter 13

Verity

Verity felt giddy as Zach eased the Bible onto the trestle table in front of her. A large, heavy tome, it bore a simple black leather cover, cracked at the edges not only from the passage of time but decades of daily use. The word "Bible" had been etched onto the thick leather binding, perhaps once gilded but now just an intaglio series of ornate letters. A tarnished clasp held the book closed.

Zach hurriedly cleared away the wine bottle and glasses, probably to protect against a spill, and sat down beside her, leaning close. Taking a steadying breath—she had no desire to damage the book either—she unlatched the clasp and opened the volume with trembling fingers, half expecting something to fly out.

But no, the only thing that manifested was the smell of musty, mildewed paper wafting up from the pages.

Zach gave a nervous laugh. "I thought for a minute..."

"Me too. But it's just a book. A lovely old book."

Zach took a breath. "I kinda love that smell."

She faced him. "You're weird, you know?" When his smile slipped, she quickly added, "But no more weird than me because I love it too."

His eyes lit up. "You are a bundle of contradictions, Verity Dickenson. I like that in a woman."

A warm glow suffused her. How long had it been since a man complimented her—and meant it? She could spot phony praise a mile away after three years with Brad, both the passive-aggressive kind and the manipulative sort. Zach's words struck her as genuine.

She broke their gaze and focused again on the Bible. "I suppose I can't hold it upside down and shake the thing to see if anything is hidden between the pages?"

"No!" It came out as a squeak.

"Jeez, Zach, relax. I might be just an accountant, but I'd never do that."

"Sorry. You scared me." His shoulders relaxed. "Besides. If there were anything tucked in there, it would have been found by now. I bet dozens of people over the years have scrutinized that Bible. It was, in a sense, Temperance's only legacy, besides the house and the property." He scratched his head. "As I recall, it wasn't found in the house. After Temperance's death, which happened only a few weeks after Mercy disappeared, Ephraim Hathorne, Mercy's father, gave the house and the orchard to Benjamin upon Fitch marrying Mercy's younger half-sister, Felicity. According to local stories, Temperance's belongings, including the Bible, came into the possession of Josiah's family, whose descendants still live locally. When the Historical Society took over the place in the early 80's, the Thayers donated the items they still had, including the Bible."

"That's odd. I mean, the Thayers were the bad guys, according to Fitch. Their son seduced and absconded with Hathorne's daughter. Why would Fitch give Temperance's things to them?"

Zach shrugged. "No idea. Maybe it wasn't that he gave them as they took them? The Thayers were friends with the elder Hathornes. Nathaniel Thayer,

Josiah's uncle, had been to sea with Captain Hathorne, Temperance's husband."

"You seem to know a hell of a lot about this whole story." She shot him a side glance.

"What can I say? I'm an historian, and I grew up in this town. Also..." He paused, looking down. "I might have been just a little obsessed with the subject when I was in high school and college. I kept trying to prove, or disprove, the notion that Josiah and Mercy had run off to Boston, like Fitch said they did. But like I said before, I found zero evidence."

She didn't believe in hocus pocus or mystical fate. She didn't. But Zach being here, tonight, a person who seemed to know all about the legend, felt a little too coincidental. She wasn't, however, going to say that. "Huh. Well, Mr. I-Have-Hidden-Information, what else do you know about the Bible?"

Disappointingly, he shook his head. "Nothing. Sorry. I just know who donated it. The new glass case is fairly recent. I mean, recent as in the last ten years. It wasn't here back in 2015, which is the last time I visited."

Verity touched the book, almost willing it to speak its secrets. Or were she and Zach just confabulating that the thing had the answers they were looking for?

The pages felt surprisingly sturdy as she turned a few experimentally.

As if reading her thoughts, Zach said, "Seventeenth and eighteenth-century paper was essentially made from rags. Much sturdier and longer-lasting than modern wood pulp paper. And Temperance, being the wife of a prosperous sea captain, would have been able to afford a fine Bible."

"Thanks for the lecture, Professor." She smiled at him to remove the sting of her words.

She leafed through more pages, pausing to read the notes Temperance had written in the margins of various sections. "Temperance really was an independent thinker. Religious but with an almost humanist bent."

"I think when you lived through the kind of losses she experienced, and the struggles she faced to run this orchard without a man, it likely changed her."

"If only she'd been able to change the mind of her son, Ephraim. Then maybe Mercy might have gotten a happy ending."

She flipped more pages, scanning the margin notes for anything even remotely clue-like. The clock sitting on the mantle ticked loudly, counting out the minutes. Zach got up to toss more logs onto the fire, then sat down close beside her again as they pored over the Bible. By the time she reached the Book of Revelations, Verity's eyes were blurry and tired.

"It's nearly three AM. I'm beginning to think my brilliant idea wasn't that brilliant."

"I still have hope." Zach nudged her. "We're on Revelations. What better place to hide a clue?"

That he could maintain optimism, instead of getting grouchy and snappish, made her like him more than she already did. She turned page after page, but found no more notes.

When they reached the end, Zach leaned back in his chair and blew out a breath. "Damn. Nothing. And we broke the damn lock. We're going to have to pay for that, you know."

Verity closed her burning eyes. "No. Not we. Me. It was my idea. I'll pay for it." She jumped when she felt his hand on her shoulder.

"And I used the knife on the lock. And while I'm not exactly flush at the moment, I give you my word I'll pay you back. We're in this together." He paused, and the way he watched her, patiently, inquiringly, made her stomach flutter. "Right?"

Words she hadn't meant to say aloud spilled out. "I shouldn't like you, you know. And I have no business trusting you. I don't ever plan to get burned that way again."

His lips twitched. "But?"

Great. Now she had to finish. "But despite my better judgment, I do like you. And yes, I believe you when you say you'll pay me back."

"Because..." he prompted.

"Oh, fine. We're in this together."

He wiggled his eyebrows. "I really like the sound of that."

She shook her head, looked away, lest she make even a bigger fool of herself. Her gaze returned to the Bible, and she fingered the paper pasted onto the inside of the heavy leather back cover, where Temperance had inscribed in precise and tiny script a list of family names with birth and death dates. Too many had died young. Temperance herself had lost four children.

She skimmed her fingers down the list, recognizing surnames that still existed locally, ancestors of people she and Zach had likely gone to school with.

She'd gotten about two inches down when her fingers encountered a slight difference in texture. Not quite a bump, but an area that felt slightly thicker.

"Zach."

He was still watching her in a bemused fashion. "If you're about to propose something illicit, I'm all for it."

She playfully smacked his arm. "Men, you're all alike. Seriously. Feel this."

When he reached for her, she grabbed his hand and pushed it onto the inside back cover of the Bible. "The book. We'll consider illicit behavior later."

With a grin, he explored the page affixed to the leather binding. "That's odd." His fingers slowly traced a rectangle, and she could imagine them on her skin. "I think..."

She shook off the image. *Focus, woman.* "That there's something underneath. Right?"

He grinned. "Right." The smile quickly faded. "Oh, God. You're going to want to cut apart the back cover, aren't you? Do you have any idea how valuable this book is? Not just in general terms, as an antique Bible from the 18th century, but to this particular historical home?"

"No idea what it's worth. But this could be the clue we need."

"A clue to a mystery we may have made up. What if all of this is just in our heads? What if our wine was spiked with some hallucinogen? What if we're just caught up in the moment?"

How odd was it that in another time and place, it would be Verity asking those questions? She'd always been the cautious one, the one who followed the rules. And here she was, throwing all that aside to solve the disappearance of a woman who'd been dead for over 250 years.

She put her hand over his, where it rested on the names of Mercy's ancestors. "Is that what you believe?"

Zach sighed, went to rub his forehead, winced. "No, that's not what I believe." He pulled his hand away. "We'll need a very thin, sharp knife. I don't suppose you have a scalpel in your purse?"

She laughed. "I'm an accountant, not a doctor." She scanned the table. All the dinnerware had been removed by the caterers. "Where did you find the knife you used to pry open the lock?"

He jerked his thumb toward the kitchen. "Drawer in the kitchen. But that was a heavy blade. If we stand a chance at someone being able to repair the damage to the book, we need something almost surgical in nature."

"Show me where you found it. We can at least look."

They trouped into the kitchen, oil lamps in hand. The place had a creepy feel, made worse by the chill in the air. Shadows shivered in the corners, and Verity felt like she was being watched.

"Damn it, this is ridiculous. Ambiance is great, but we live in the modern world." She went to the light switch near the back door and flicked it up.

The room remained dark.

Zach's voice sounded a little tremulous. "The lights flickered earlier. I suppose that was a sign. I imagine the power lines are down."

A logical conclusion, given the storm, but Verity still felt weirdly threatened. "Are you sure we're not in a serial killer movie?

Zach shook his head. "Nope. Definitely a ghost movie."

"Why doesn't that make me feel any better?"

She winced when he yanked open a drawer and held the oil lamp over it. "I'll look, you stand watch."

A shiver ran through her. "For what?"

"I don't know. The ghost of Benjamin Fitch, pissed off we're acting like the Scooby gang?"

That made her laugh. "Well, half the gang. And minus the dog." She stared around them nervously as he rummaged through what was clearly the utensil drawer. Suddenly, he yelled, "Aha!" And held up a very small, very thin paring knife.

Wasting no more time, they raced back into the hall, shutting the kitchen door behind them. She thought if there had been a way to lock the door to the kitchen, she would have. The hall now felt like a refuge—cozy and far safer than the kitchen.

As they stood over the table, she pointed at the blade. "Do you want to do the honors?"

"Why me?"

"Because you're the historian. You probably know more about old books."

"Yeah, reading them, not destroying them."

She shrugged, took a breath. "Right. Well, since you broke the lock, I guess I'll break the book." She took the paring knife from him and ran her fingers along the edge of the page affixed to the back cover. A small section had begun coming loose at the bottom. Inserting the knife, she slid it carefully between the pasteboard and the page.

Then, using a pair of tweezers from her purse to reach into the opening she'd created, she pulled out a sheet of folded paper.

"Jackpot!" With a grin, she faced Zach.

Zach whooped. "You're a genius!" Grabbing her face in his hands, he kissed her.

Chapter 14

Zach

Zach hadn't meant to do it. But once their lips met, he didn't want to stop.

Still, he knew better. His mother had raised him to be a gentleman.

He pulled back, studying her face. "Sorry. I just got carried away in the excitement."

Her lips curved in a soft smile. "I didn't mind." Then she looked down at the papers she held. Her hands trembled. "But maybe we can save that for later?"

He cleared his throat. Their previous bantering had been one thing. Playful, a little risque. The kind of things you said in a bar or at a Christmas party. But the way she had said that last part made him believe she might actually want there to be a later. "I'd like that. Not just the kiss, but a later."

She met his gaze, and the raw vulnerability in her eyes scared him a little.

Too few moments later, she glanced down again and lifted the paper. "Shall we? I'm almost afraid to unfold it. Like it might just disintegrate in my hands."

Zach got control of himself. "Like I said, paper back then was stronger than modern paper. I think we'll be okay as long as we're careful."

She held out her prize. "Do you want to do the honors? You're the expert."

He itched to take the page from her hands and unfold it himself, but he refrained. "I'm no document expert. Besides, you found it."

"You just don't want to get in trouble again."

That acerbic tone was back, though there was no bite in it. He could see now she used it as a defense, both to keep people out and to project a confidence she might not feel. "Can you blame me?" he snorted a laugh. "You might be some fancy accountant, but I'm just a poor unemployed college professor living in my parents' basement."

Her gaze shot back to him. "You're not really living in the basement, are you? That's going to make spending the night at your place kind of weird."

"Better than sleeping in my old bedroom. Trust me, you don't want to meet my mom on the way to the bathroom before she's had her coffee. At least the basement has its own kitchen and bath. And a separate entrance."

"Good Lord." She laughed before taking a breath. "Okay. Let's do this."

She unfolded the page.

Turned out there were two, one smaller note enclosed in the larger, yellow, brittle paper.

Zach pulled an oil lamp closer so they could better make out the spidery, jittery handwriting on the small note first. Verity read aloud.

Dearest Dolly,

I must be blunt. Time is running out. I do not believe young Benjamin's story. Not one word of it. I know my Mercy, and she would not leave me so. Nor would your Josiah do such a rash and unpardonable thing.

Yet no one will hear me.

To make matters worse, Benjamin has become a constant presence in this house, apparently at Ephraim's behest, to care for me. You and I both know I need no caring for.

And yet I feel so ill, Dolly. Unaccountably ill. And I am fearful. Please, I beseech you. Visit me soonest.

Your most loyal friend,

Temperance

With enormous care, Verity set the note down on the trestle table. The table on which Temperance might very well have written it. "Holy crap. Zach, what did Temperance die of?"

He squeezed his eyes shut, trying to see the photograph of the church document he'd read on microfiche all those years ago. And realized his head was throbbing from where he'd hit it. Stupid klutz. "The cause wasn't clear. Church records indicated the cause of death as "Visitation of God", which just means a person died suddenly and with no apparent cause. I imagine that the family would assume she passed away because she was upset about Mercy and the scandal she had caused the family."

"Which is baloney. Given all we know about Temperance, I cannot believe she would just waste away like an overly dramatic Regency maiden."

He'd never given it much thought, but Verity had a point. Temperance was not the sort of woman to lie down and give up. "True. What I wonder is if this letter got delivered. And if it did, how it ended up in Temperance's Bible."

"Plus, if Dolly, who is clearly Josiah's mother or grandmother, got it, why was nothing done to investigate further?"

"I hate to break this to you, but women couldn't even testify in court back then. They weren't considered sufficiently intelligent to be credible witnesses."

Verity made a growling noise. "That's...Oh!"

Zach held up his hands. "I totally agree, but now is not the time for a mutual hate-fest over the patriarchy. The caterers will be here in..." He glanced at his watch. "Too soon. We need to solve this mystery before they get here."

Verity waved at the window. "I'm going to bet they'll be late. But you're right. Let's see what else Temperance—"

"Or Dolly. Remember, the Bible was donated by the Thayer family. If Dolly received Temperance's note, *she* might have hidden it in the Bible for posterity."

"Good point."

The subsequent page had been drafted in a very neat and tight hand. Verity read aloud again.

My Dearest Josiah,

I write in trembling haste, for my heart is near to bursting. As you know, Grandmother has gone to visit Cousin Abigail and will not be back for at least six days. The house is quiet, and I am alone with thoughts of you—of your voice, your smile, the warmth of your hand when last we walked beneath the orchard trees.

Oh Josiah, how I long for the peace that only you can bring. Every hour we are kept apart by circumstance feels to me a theft of precious time. Come to me tonight, I beg you. Come when the moon rises and the lane lies still. I will tie a white ribbon on the gatepost so you shall know the way is safe.

We shall speak freely, without fear of watching eyes or cruel tongues. There is much I wish to tell you—of dreams I scarcely dare write, and of a hope that grows in me like spring itself. If you do not come, I fear I shall wither beneath the weight of all that remains unsaid.

Hurry to me, my love. Let this night be ours.

Yours in steadfast affection,

Mercy

The stillness in the room lay cold and heavy like the blanket of snow outside when Verity finished.

Zach finally broke the silence. "So...Mercy must have sent this. Right?"

"Unless Temperance found it, unsent."

"But Josiah went missing, and unless he just up and ran off without Mercy, then he had to have gotten the letter and come here."

Verity stared into the flame of the oil lamp. "And they ran off together?"

Zach shook his head. "I don't believe that any more than you do."

"But if Josiah got the letter and came here, how did the letter end up in Temperance's Bible?"

Zach puzzled over that. "He must have left it at home, and Dolly or someone found it. Then they tucked that into the back of the book along with Temperance's letter. Proof of sorts. I found no record of anyone filing a complaint against Fitch, but that kind of thing would likely not have gone through a formal process. If there was such an action, and nothing could be proved, then maybe Dolly kept the documents for some kind of future justice. Justice that never happened."

Verity tapped Mercy's letter. "Until now." She turned to look at Zach. "Until us."

Zach nodded. "And Mr. Pennewell. He knows all this somehow. Or suspects. I'm convinced he's been arranging this event for years, hoping someone would discover the truth."

"That's..." Her derisive expression turned thoughtful. "That's pretty damn smart of you, Professor. I think you're right. Then we're agreed that Josiah came in response to Mercy's letter and—"

"And that bastard Benjamin Fitch killed them."

"And then, based on that note to Dolly, poisoned Temperance because she knew the truth."

Zach sat back. "Which means..." He squeezed his eyes shut. It was late. He was tired. And the wine was probably making him even more so. But no way was he giving up now. "Fitch got rid of Mercy and Josiah's bodies somehow." He leaned forward. "The winter of 1761 was a harsh one. Lots of snowstorms, unusually cold temperatures. That's another reason I've been convinced Mercy and Josiah wouldn't have been on the road late at night. The temps were likely in the single digits. They had a week to plan their escape if that's what they decided to do before Temperance returned home from Boston. They could have waited for a break in the weather. Or found a different way out. I mean, I sure wouldn't drag you out on a night like tonight, no matter how much I wanted to."

She nudged him with her shoulder. "Aw, thanks. Ditto. If the winter was harsh, then Fitch couldn't have buried them outside. The ground would have been frozen. Do you suppose he hid them in an outbuilding?"

"Maybe, but he'd risk one of the men who worked the orchard discovering them."

"But it was winter. Not a lot going on then, I wouldn't imagine."

Zach shrugged. "Maybe. Still sounds chancy."

Verity sat back, finger tapping on the table. "I don't like to think about it, but what if he buried them in the house?" She shivered and pointed down. "In the cellar."

Zach thought about it. "That would explain the haunting. But..." He shook his head. "No. There've been a ton of renovations. They laid concrete down there. And installed plumbing and electricity. Surely if there were bodies, they would have been discovered."

"Maybe they completely decomposed? And besides, if Mr. Pennewell suspected, wouldn't he have tried to find them?"

She wasn't wrong about that, not if their line of reasoning was correct. "Hang on." He shot to his feet. "The brick wall."

Verity stood as well. "What brick wall?"

"In the cellar. The wall behind the cabinet at the far end of the room. It's made of brick, not the stone that makes up the rest of the cellar."

"So?"

"At first, I thought it was a modern wall. Maybe hiding plumbing or HVAC conduits. But then I noticed that the bricks were actually really old. From the colonial period. As was the mortar."

He loved that she came to the same aha that he just had. "You're saying the wall was made during the right time. But after the home was built."

"Right."

"And maybe it's concealing something. A hidden space."

He nodded. "A small space, or it would be obvious." He glanced down. "Unless it was put in by Fitch during the years he lived here, after Temperance's death. Or even later, after the house was sold." He rubbed the back of his neck.

"Are you thinking what I'm thinking?"

He didn't want to be thinking it. They were already in trouble for breaking the case over Temperance's Bible. There'd certainly be a fine, possibly legal charges, maybe even a jail sentence. How would he ever get another job after serving time for defacing a historic home? "You're talking about breaking through the brick wall to see what's behind it, aren't you?"

"Do you have a better idea?"

He felt like he stood on the edge of a cliff. He was a historian. He preserved history. He taught history. He didn't take a sledgehammer to it. He paced away, stomach suddenly churning. Too much wine. Too much rich food. Too much...lunacy and fear. "No. No, no, no. We can't do this. It's desecration."

"Zach, we don't have a choice. How else are we going to find the truth?"

He went to the window to look out, wanting nothing more than to jump in his truck and speed away from this. Without the parking street lamp, the moon, or the stars, the world outside consisted of dim snow-covered shapes in the darkness, amplifying a gnawing sense of claustrophobia. He was trapped, both by the weather and by his own ethics. But if he had no ethics, he could not rightly call himself a proper historian.

His blood pressure rose, and his forehead throbbed as if someone beat on it with a mallet. Things had been going so well.

"Verity, I can't. I can't willingly destroy this place. Why can't we...why can't we wait until tomorrow? We'll tell Mr. Pennewell what we've found. Let him have restoration experts come and take a look. That's a reasonable solution, right?"

She stared at him, her disappointment slowly frosting into an icy-calm anger. Her voice was low, her words clipped and measured. "Fine. You do you." She grabbed the knife he'd used to break open the case holding the Bible. "I don't know why I thought you were different. That things would ever be different. But it's never been clearer that if I want something in my life, I have to get it by and for myself. Every. Damn. Time."

She flung open the door to the kitchen, taking one of the oil lamps with her, and leaving him both literally and figuratively out in the cold.

Chapter 15

Verity

Slamming the kitchen door behind her, she stood for a moment in the dim kitchen, seething. Once again, she'd been a fool. Once again, she thought she'd been part of a team when it was all a fantasy.

But she was done setting aside her own wants and needs, the things that were important to her, for someone else.

Her life had been a never-ending litany of sacrifice. Giving up her lit degree for her parents when her mother became ill, giving up her very soul to be with Brad, giving up her independence when her mother died, and she became her father's caretaker. She loved her parents. Loved her father. But now she was free, and damn it, she was going to put herself first for once.

And what she wanted right now was to solve this mystery.

No, that wasn't quite right. She didn't just want it. She needed it. She felt compelled to do it. Mercy deserved closure as much as Verity deserved this one moment of success.

She spent a moment or two rummaging through the utensil drawer, then the other two drawers in the kitchen, looking for anything she could use to chisel through mortar, but found nothing. With growing frustration, she slammed the last drawer closed and swore.

Well, she'd dig through the mortar with a spoon like the Count of Montecristo if she had to. As angry as she was, she figured she could probably chew through it right now. She crossed the small space to the cellar door and cranked the knob.

The door banged against the frame but would not open.

Her fury burned hotter when she remembered Zach had locked it when they'd come up earlier.

"Zach!" She stomped back into the hall. Finding it empty only fueled her temper. "Zach!"

Silence.

She called a third time and met more silence.

Where was he? Had he...had he left? Gotten in his truck and stranded her here?

She raced to the window, cupping her hands to block out the glare of the inside lights. Scanning the small gravel parking lot, she spotted the hulking shape of his truck, covered in white. The snow had drifted to the top of his tires.

At least he hadn't driven off. But where was he?

As her eyes adjusted, she saw tracks leading away from the front door, quickly being filled by the blowing snow. Then, yes, there. Movement. A figure struggling toward the house.

She hurried to the door and flung it open as the snow-covered figure reached the house.

Yanking Zach—it had to be Zach in those clothes—inside, she brushed the snow from his shivering form, then whacked him on the arm. "You idiot. What on earth were you doing out there?"

He ignored her question for a moment, stomping the snow off his feet and hurrying over to stand in front of the fire. "God, it's cold out there."

She wanted to hit him again, but he looked pathetic enough that even in her current fit of pique, she couldn't. "Duh. Why were you out there? Taking a romantic midnight stroll through the orchard? Or trying to leave?"

He gaped at her, his lips practically blue. "I would never! What kind of asshole do you think I am?"

She pressed her lips together, remembering a night when Brad had left her stranded outside a bar in a freezing October rain for taking five seconds too long chatting with the bartender while waiting for their drinks.

Zach shook his head and stretched his cold-white hands toward the fire. "I went out," he said through clenched teeth, "because I thought I saw someone coming up the drive. I thought maybe one of the caterers had come early to, I don't know, bake bread. Or some young dude who skidded off the road looking for help." He glanced toward the window. "It was definitely a man, of that I'm sure."

Stubbornness and experience made her doubt him. "Then where is he?"

Zach shrugged. "I don't know. By the time I got out there, I couldn't see him anymore. Then I got worried that he'd fallen in the snow, and I searched around for a minute but couldn't find anything. So I came back."

Now it was her turn to gape. The anger bled out of her, replaced by shame. "I'm sorry. I shouldn't have assumed..."

She looked down, feeling like an idiot, and really tired of it.

He approached and gently touched her shoulder. "You had every right to assume. You don't know me, and your ex certainly didn't do me, or any other guy, any favors, from what you've implied." He dropped his hand, careful, she noticed, not to invade her space too long.

She couldn't look at him yet, couldn't face him. "Do you want me to get a blanket from upstairs?"

"No. I'll be fine in a few minutes, although I should probably put another couple of logs on the fire."

She stared into the crackling flames for a time while he went back to warming himself, first one side, then the other. Finally, he cleared his throat. "So, why did you come back in here?"

She knew he was basically asking her if she'd changed her mind. The urge to be conciliatory and say yes almost took over, but she hadn't spent the last year in therapy to backslide now. "I needed the key. You locked the cellar door when we came back up earlier."

His lips, now a normal color again, formed the word "Oh." He patted his left pocket, and she realized for the first time he was left-handed. He reached in and pulled out the old key. "Sorry about that. I forgot."

Damn it, her righteous indignation was dissipating. "Are you often absent-minded, Professor?"

"Story of my life. When I was a graduate student and had to teach History 101, I could barely make it to class on time until my then-girlfriend bought me a watch."

She raised her eyebrows, trying not to be charmed. "Your first watch?"

"Oh no. My mom used to buy me one every Christmas."

She nodded. "Because you kept losing them."

He grinned, though at a reduced wattage. "I plead the fifth."

She took the key from his still frigid fingers. "Well. Thanks. I better get back to it."

She turned and walked toward the kitchen, but halted as she heard his intake of breath.

"Look, Verity, maybe..."

She glanced over her shoulder.

Saw a sort of shimmer in the air between them.

The hair on the back of her arms stood up. The flames in the fireplace shot up. And a voice, a thin tenor, whispered, "Please."

It had to be the wind. Or the fire. Sometimes wood hissed or whined or squeaked.

But to her ears, it had sounded like a young man. Pleading.

Zach's eyes fixed on the shimmering air between them. His mouth fell open, his eyes grew wide, and he took a couple of steps backward.

Fearing he'd fall into the fire, Verity rushed forward through the icy cold shimmer and grabbed Zach's sleeve to yank him toward her.

Disaster averted, she faced the shimmer again—but it had gone. Or had never been there.

Zach stumbled over to his chair and fell into it. "I keep asking this, but please tell me you saw him."

She sat next to him and took his chilly hand in hers. "Which him? I only saw a shimmer. And heard a voice." Although she had no doubt in her mind whose voice it had been. Certainly not Benjamin Fitch's voice.

Zach closed his eyes. "It was the same as the figure I saw in the snow. A young man. Dressed...I think...like I am now. He reached out to me."

Verity saw a shudder run through him. "Josiah."

"It has to be. And he spoke."

She nodded, knowing he needed the confirmation. Heck, she did too. "He said 'please'."

Zach met her eyes, then rubbed his face. "Oh God. This can't be good. My career will be ruined. I'll never get another job. My parents will disown me. A month from now, after Hobbs is sick of me crashing on his couch, I'll be living in a refrigerator box near the train tracks."

She choked back a laugh. Now was not the time. "You will not." She squeezed his hand, felt him tighten his grip and hold on. "Zach, we owe it to Mercy and Josiah. And Temperance, too."

He still didn't believe her. She could see the panicked look on his face.

"Look, remember what Mr. Pennewell said when he left?"

"Vaguely. Something about us taking care of the house. Which is exactly the opposite of what we're considering doing."

"No, you're wrong there. I remember his precise words because it felt odd. He said, 'I have a good feeling about you two. You'll take good care of them all.' He wasn't talking about the house. He was talking about Mercy, Josiah, and Temperance."

Some of the panic left his eyes. "That doesn't make any sense."

"Unless you believe that he believes in the ghosts, too. Which he clearly does."

Zach sat frozen for a moment. She couldn't read his thoughts, but she felt the moment his decision changed. He squeezed his eyes shut, and Verity held her breath, not daring to hope but unable to keep from doing so.

He wore a tentative smile when he opened them. "You know, I've spent my life looking at things that already happened. Being a sort of...voyeur of the past. The past is safe." He scrubbed the back of his head. "I mean, you know how it's going to end, one way or another."

She nodded. She knew about the fear of doing something where you didn't know how things would wind up. Lord, did she know.

"Maybe it's time I actually started living in the present. Maybe Hobb was right. I should get up off the metaphorical couch and do things in the now." He took a breath. "Okay. Fine. Let's do it." He gave her hand a squeeze before pulling away. "But if some undead creature leaps out from behind the cabinet, I'm running straight up the stairs and out into the snowstorm again."

Could she count on him? She didn't know that she could count on anyone anymore. But she'd take his help as long as he'd give it. And if he did chicken out, then she'd just finish the job on her own. Because she was going to see this through. Even if a zombified Colonial crawled out of a hole in the cellar.

She patted his leg and stood. "If that happens, I'll be right behind you. Come on, Shaggy. Let's go solve this mystery."

Chapter 16

Zach

Zach's heart hammered in his chest as they descended again into the cellar. They'd brought three oil lamps, two large flashlights, and two knives from the kitchen, a bag of flour, some salt, and a pitcher of water. The last three items could be used in place of mortar for a temporary fix. It wouldn't hold long, nor would it provide structural support, but it would be a way to fix the wall until real repairs could be made.

The cellar appeared as they'd left it. Zach paused at the bottom of the stairs, listening, but the only sound he heard was Verity's quiet, rapid breathing behind him.

"No crying," Verity said.

Zach whispered in her ear. "Maybe she knows we're coming?"

Verity raised her oil lamp high as they moved deeper into the basement and back to the wine cellar. "Where should we start?"

He gestured at the far end of the narrow room. "When I found the corkscrew, I saw loose mortar behind that cabinet there."

They moved purposefully past the tasting station to the area he'd indicated. As they neared, the air grew icy, and Zach could see his breath. "Oh, man. This place feels wrong. Creepier. Like there's something evil down here."

Verity nodded. "I feel it too. It feels just like Brad when he'd get furious over nothing." She grimaced. "I'm betting that's Benjamin. Probably still trying to hide whatever he did."

When had she turned into a full believer? He wasn't even sure he was there yet, despite everything. He watched her expression harden into frightening determination as she set down the oil lamp on the small counter where Zach had found the corkscrew. Turning to face the empty cellar, she shook the knife she held.

"Do you see this, Benjamin Fitch? This is the knife I'm going to use to expose your dirty secret. And you can make things cold and make scary noises, but you're a ghost, and you can't hurt me. You don't scare me, Benjamin Fitch. No man is ever going to make me feel afraid again. You hear that?"

The remaining wine bottle from the tasting station, the red they'd left behind, suddenly flew across the room and exploded against the wall.

Zach gasped and jumped, putting his arms around Verity protectively.

Verity pushed him away, not aggressively, but firmly. Her tone grew derisive. Almost taunting. And strong. She exuded strength. "Cute, Benjamin. But you have no power over me. No power over either of us." She glanced at Zach. "Come on. Let's do this."

He stared at her, open-mouthed.

She turned back to the cabinet and started unloading empty bottles, glasses, and other items meant for wine tastings. "You gonna stand there all night or help me?"

Her words galvanized him. But even though he began shifting things to the floor, his voice shook a little when he said, "The bottom cupboard is really just a modern free-standing kitchen base. We should be able to drag it away from the wall once it's unloaded."

"Sounds like a plan." Verity's calm tone surprised him. As did her smile. A confident, self-assured smile. He liked it on her.

The ominous presence remained, he could feel that, but it had shrunk back into the far corner of the wine cellar. Zach did his best to ignore it, although he felt eyes boring into his back as he worked.

The unloading went quickly, and Zach muscled the cabinet away from the flaking plaster and crumbling masonry. Once the way was clear, he took a breath, committed himself to heresy, and knelt down with his knife. "You know, you're pretty bad ass, Verity Dickenson."

Would that break what had been growing between them? Was it too harsh? Too forward? Too...off-brand? Did Verity want to be a badass? He was no good at this.

A smile spread slowly across her face. "Thank you."

He grinned at her. "You're welcome. Maybe instead of Velma, I should call you Ripley. You know, from Aliens? Always loved Ripley. Very sexy."

She giggled. An actual giggle. "You know, Professor, your choice of video entertainment defies expectations."

"That's a good thing, right?"

"A very good thing." She gestured at the wall. "Shall we?"

Working side by side, it took them about half an hour to chisel through the decaying mortar and open up a small hole in the base of the brick wall. The opening would fit Zach's shoulders, and if they scrunched down, tall enough for both of them to crawl through.

Still not quite believing, he half expected there to be evidence of the original stone wall a few inches beyond. But the existence of a significant space became evident after removing only a few bricks.

They knelt side by side when the work was done, staring into the gaping blackness. Zach's hands ached, and he'd acquired a number of scratches. Verity wasn't in any better shape.

"Should have worn gloves," he mumbled. He rubbed his hands on his breeches and looked down to find streaks of dirt and plaster dust on his clothing. "Yikes. And you're going to ruin that dress going in there."

"Do you think that's going to stop me joining you? I'm not missing the finale, Zach. I'm no hot house flower."

"I can see that." He motioned at the entryway. "Alright then. Ladies first?"

She pulled out one of the flashlights they'd brought down with them. "Maglites first. And bring one of the lanterns too in case it's true that ghosts can drain batteries."

She ducked down, then looked back. "I'm glad you decided to join me. I know it sounds weird, but I'd rather be doing this with you than without you."

Damn. Whatever happened after, he realized he felt the same. "Me too, Verity. I wouldn't want to be here with anyone else."

Flicking on her flashlight, she aimed the beam in front of her and crawled through the space into the darkness beyond.

The secret room the wall had created measured about 6x6. As Zach crawled in behind her, he swung the flashlight around. The beam highlighted a ladderback chair festooned with cobwebs on which sat something black and book-shaped, a lumpy mess against the far stone wall, and a raised mound against the third wall, marring the otherwise flat dirt floor.

Zach's whisper rang loudly in the confined space. "Really dry down here. I kind of expected it to be damp like a musty basement. I swear they built root cellars way better than modern basements." He held up his lantern, which cast a dim glow a few feet in diameter. "What's that on the chair?"

Rubbing her hands nervously on her gown, Verity took two steps into the center of the room and shone her flashlight onto the object. After a quick swipe of the long sleeve of her chemise, she said, "It's a Bible." She glanced back at Zach. "Creepy."

"Not as creepy as that mound of dirt over there. I've got a bad feeling about what that is."

Verity grimaced. "You think it's a grave."

"I mean, it's not a far-fetched assumption, given our theory."

Verity took another step closer to the pile of rags in the corner, playing her flashlight over the floor. "Looks like maybe straw and some old clothes..." She froze. Put her hand over her mouth. "Oh God. Zach."

Zach rushed over and aimed his Maglite at the floor as well. The beam fell first on what looked like a mass of dark hair attached to a brown leather cap. But it wasn't leather. It was skin. Nor was it a cap. It was the back of a skull.

Zach set his lantern on the floor and crouched down.

Verity's voice sounded young and small. "It's her, isn't it?" she asked. "It's Mercy."

He knew it had to be. But he needed to be sure.

Zach panned his flashlight over the remains on the ground, shivering not from cold but from horror. They weren't looking at a pile of rags or trash. What they'd discovered was the fully clothed body of a long-deceased person. A woman. Dressed in the rotting tatters of what had once been a fine winter robe Anglaise. Some large swaths of the fabric of the outer dress remained over the almost mummified corpse, and her long, dark hair, faded after the centuries, hung in waves down her back.

She lay on her side, one arm stretched over her head, the other tucked across her abdomen. Her leather shoes, with their wooden heel, still covered the leathery remains of her feet.

Her face was turned toward the wall, and Zach could just make out a small, narrow nose above an open mouth, the lips stretched not in a scream, but from dessication.

Verity finally squatted down beside him. "Poor thing. Do you think he just walled her in here to die? Like in the Cask of Amontillado?"

A shudder passed through him. "I don't know. I can't even imagine that." He peered all around the body. "I think this might have been some kind of sleeping pallet she's lying across. If he just walled her in here, I'm not sure he would have provided that. Or the chair. But who knows?"

His flashlight caught a glint of something shiny, and he leaned closer. "Is that a ring or a button?"

Feeling a little sick, he reached under her folded arm for the item that had caught the light.

Verity gasped when Zach pulled back Mercy's hand, the stomacher of her gown, and something that fluttered beneath the stomacher, all stuck together.

From behind them came a gust of frigid air and a howl that sounded like someone wailing "Noooo!"

Zach fell on his ass and crabbed backwards, dropping the mass of glued-together objects.

Verity, clearly braver than Zach had ever been, stood and faced the hole they'd made in the wall. "It's over, Brad. Leave. Move on to whatever afterlife will have you. You have nothing left to do here."

The momentary wind died, and the air grew warmer.

Zach stared at Verity, utterly amazed. Had she realized she'd called Benjamin 'Brad'? Clearly exorcising more than one demon. "You're...freaking awesome."

She snorted. "Thank you."

"Is he gone?"

She shrugged. "I think. At least for now. It feels different down here."

She was right. The oppressive, ominous atmosphere had lifted.

With a dismissive gesture, she squatted again and moved the detached hand gently aside to pick up the stiff triangle of fabric called a stomacher, worn over the front of a bodice, filling the gap between the edges of a gown. Attached to the stomacher, via a mother-of-pearl pin that shone in the light, was a brown piece of paper.

Feeling like a fool and a coward, but now intensely curious, Zach crawled forward and held his flashlight on the page as Verity tried to read it.

"It's a page from the Bible. Corinthians 13. That old passage they read at weddings. You know. 'Love is patient, love is kind?'"

"It's been torn out." He glanced at Verity. "She must have hidden it from Benjamin inside her dress. But why?"

Bringing the page closer to her face, she shone her own light on it. "Look. There. Do you see that? It looks like writing in the margins. And there, it carries onto the other side of the page, too. But it's very faint. Can you read it?"

He glanced around them, still feeling the chill creeping down the back of his neck. "Maybe upstairs?"

She rolled her eyes heavenward. "Fine. But we need to check out one last thing." She shot her gaze at the mound of dirt.

Zach groaned. "I knew you were going to say that."

"You can't tell me you don't want to know. Clearly, this is Mercy. It has to be. Which means that..."

"Has to be Josiah." He rolled his shoulders. "We're going to dig him up, aren't we?"

"We have to. We need to know for sure." She set the page from the Bible beneath the Bible itself to keep it from being swept to the ground and brandished her knife. "Don't suppose you saw any shovels around?"

He wished he had. The thought of digging around a dead man with nothing but a knife and his bare hands made him want to run far and fast. Or be sick. Or maybe both. "No." Making a face, he headed over to the mound.

"Let's get this over with. Meanwhile, we need to figure out how we're going to explain all this to the docent in the morning."

They began to dig at one end of the mound, which proved eerily soft and yielding, clearing a couple of inches of dirt in from a small section in a matter of minutes. Had this floor been exposed to the elements, it might have been hard as a rock. Particularly this time of year. But protected here as it had been, Josiah's grave, if that's what this was, was easy to dig.

Again.

As Verity worked, she said, "We're not going to tell the docent. We're only going to talk to Mr. Pennewell. He'll understand. And he'll be happy. I just know it."

"You are a woman of many talents. We'll just add psychic to that list, shall we?"

His knife struck something hard a couple of inches down. "Verity. I think I just hit bone."

She straightened up, hands braced on her knees. "Brush the dirt away carefully."

It took a little more digging and a lot of brushing. When they'd finished, they gazed down on a bare skull. A little more work revealed the upper spine and shoulders. Unless Zach was mistaken, whoever this was had been placed in their grave face down.

He heard Verity sniff, looked up to see tears running down her now grimy cheeks. "Poor man. Look at his head."

Zach didn't need to look again. The skull had a huge dent in it, one that radiated fractures in zigzag patterns across the bone. He stood and reached down a hand to Verity. "Come on. I think we've seen enough for now. Grab the Bible and let's go back upstairs."

His partner in crime wiped her face with her sleeve and looked askance. "Damn it. I don't usually cry."

"Anyone would cry over this. It's awful." He took her arm gently and helped her to her feet. "Let's go."

"I feel bad leaving them like this."

"They'll get a proper burial soon. And then maybe they can finally be at peace. The important thing is that everyone will know the truth. That's what Mercy wanted."

She nodded, and they crawled out of the chamber that had become Mercy and Josiah's tomb, pushed the cabinet back into place, and, hand in hand, climbed the stairs to the hall once more.

Chapter 17

Verity

The hall, the room where Temperance and Mercy had spent most of their time, smelled of apple blossoms when Verity and Zach settled themselves at the table.

Before, that ghostly scent might have risen the hairs on the back of Verity's neck, but in this moment, it felt like a benediction.

Verity lay the page torn from the Bible on the trestle table and rubbed her face. "I wish we had some coffee. I feel like I just competed in a triathlon."

Competed, won, and with all the odds stacked against her, too. She had surprised herself down there when the vengeful spirit of Benjamin Fitch menaced them. She should have been afraid. Instead, a kind of outrage filled her. She was done tiptoeing around some man's ego. Even a dead man's. Especially a dead man's. Never again would she let a bully stop her from living her life and doing what she wanted to do, being who she wanted to be. She was done being some man's emotional punching bag.

Zach dropped into the chair next to her. "I could sleep for a week." He glanced up at the mantle clock. "It's almost 4 am. What time do we expect the caterers in the morning?"

"I don't remember. Maybe six? If the roads are passable. I haven't heard a plow yet."

"Heh. We might be stuck here for most of the day."

The thought didn't irritate her as much as it might have yesterday. In fact, the idea of snuggling up in bed with Zach while the snow piled up held a dangerous appeal. But no. She pushed that thought away. First, Mercy's message.

She pulled close a couple of the oil lamps and gently smoothed the page. "It's really faded. Temperance's letters weren't this hard to read."

"Do you want me to try to read it?"

Feeling suddenly protective and a little selfish, Verity shook her head. "No, I need to do this. It's somehow important that her words, likely her last words, be spoken by a woman. Is that crazy?"

"Not at all." He leaned closer and put a hand on her back. Not in possession, like Brad had, but in solidarity. Support.

Taking a breath, she peered at the page, recognizing the hand from the letter Mercy had sent Josiah. It was shakier, more cramped due to the limited space, but clearly Mercy's. She read the young woman's final message aloud. As she spoke, the fine script seemed to glow on the page.

"I write upon my knee, for he has taken the table away, saying I have no further need of it. The light is poor and the candle gutters, yet I must set these words down, using the pin Josiah gifted me... two nights ago? Three? I no longer know. I write in my own blood, as I have no ink, speaking the truth, lest I perish and leave no mark that I was ever here.

Josiah is gone.

He lies only a few feet away, in the shallow grave Benjamin dug for him, leaving my beloved's corpse to keep me company as I languish here in the cellar. Some madness in me wishes to dig Josiah up and hold him, but it is a selfish impulse.

Let him rest where I cannot. There was a warmth in me when he yet lived, a small answering flame that now has gone cold, as if quenched by the very earth, his shroud.

Benjamin came below this morning. He spoke gently, which frightened me more than his anger ever did. He says he will keep me here until I fall to his will. When I cried out, he struck my cheek and said I would learn gratitude, for he had spared me much shame. I think he believes what he says.

This afternoon, he built a wall. No door, only one brick lacking so he can peer in at me while the mortar hardens and ask me the same question over and over again: Do I love him? He says I will be free if I say the words, but I shall never do so.

Now he is gone, the final brick in place. I have wept until my tears ran dry, here where the mortar smells of sorrow and despair. There is no true night, only the long waiting. I have prayed until my words feel thin as breath on glass.

If anyone should read this, know that I did not run. I did not forsake my father nor my name. I loved Josiah Thayer with a whole and willing heart, and he loved me in return. There was no sin in it but joy, and no disobedience but hope."

An inch of blank space separated the previous section from the next. The handwriting grew shakier and harder to read.

I know now I shall not leave this place. My body grows weak, and the cold settles into my bones. Yet I am not afraid of dying, only of being forgotten, or worse, of being remembered falsely.

If there is justice beyond this life, I trust it will find Josiah and me. If there are spirits that linger, perhaps we shall linger too, until the truth is spoken aloud and believed.

The candle is nearly spent. Only the silence of the grave remains.

Josiah, my love, if there is any place where words still travel, know that I am coming.

Verity sobbed as she read the last sentence, feeling Mercy's grief as keenly as if Josiah had been her own true love.

Zach had to clear his throat before he spoke. "Dear God. Walled in with the body of your lover? I can't even imagine the hell she went through."

"I can." She didn't realize she'd spoken aloud until Zach tipped her tear-stained face toward him.

"I'm so sorry."

He meant it. She could feel his sincerity. And while she had enough sense not to throw herself into his arms, she did lean against him, taking in the warmth of his body and his caring.

Zach almost growled his next words. "I hope Benjamin Fitch is enjoying his much-deserved reward." He wrapped a loose arm around her and rested his chin on her head. "I'm not particularly religious, but if there is a hell, then I hope he's roasting on a spit there."

The words Mercy had written on the page had stopped glowing, becoming little more than faint scratchings again. "She wrote this in her own blood. In the hope that one day the truth could be told."

"She was a helluva woman. And poor Josiah. Fitch must have caught him unawares. From the damage to his skull, it appears he was hit on the head with something from behind."

"Do you think they got to see each other, or did Fitch kill him when he was on his way?"

Zach shrugged. "I don't suppose we'll ever know. But I like to think he caught them enjoying an evening together, heads bent close by the fire, trying to figure out a way to be with one another."

"I like that image." It was, in fact, exactly what she and Zach were supposed to have been doing tonight.

Her eyes burned with exhaustion, and she realized dirt and plaster dust covered her hands, her dress, and, from the feel of it, even smeared and dried on her face. "I'm beat, but I'd really like a shower. Do you suppose without power we have hot water?"

"Maybe. But probably only what's in the tank. Should be enough for at least a sponge bath for both of us if we're careful."

She eased away from him. "Why don't you go first, and I'll stoke the fire in the bedroom."

He raised his eyebrows. "Bedroom?"

"Easy there. I'm not suggesting anything, just that it'll be warmer if we both sleep in the same room." At the slight droop in his expression, she added, "Not that I would be opposed to, um, heating things up under other circumstances, but I'm too damn tired and achy and grungy for that kind of thing right now."

He gave her that grin, the one that lit up his eyes. "As you wish."

Recognizing the line from one of her favorite movies, she couldn't suppress a smile as she held out her hand. "Come on, *Westley*. Let's get a little sleep before the cavalry arrives."

Chapter 18

Zach

When Zach awoke, bright sunlight poured through the narrow window. Outside, sparkling snow decorated the apple trees in the distant orchard.

Verity lay curled up next to him, dressed in the warm woolen nightdress and stockings Meghan laid out on Mercy's bed, a wiser choice than the thin pajamas Verity had packed. He wore a similar garment but had chosen his own Nordic-patterned alpaca socks to wear on his feet. He chuckled at the image he must have presented before he dove under the mountain of blankets that covered them. Put a stocking cap on his head, and the two of them would have looked like the couple in the poem, The Night Before Christmas with Mama in her kerchief and him in his cap.

At his movement, Verity stirred and blinked. "Gawd. Why do I live in this climate? Damn, but it's cold."

"Sorry. Fire's gone out. I'll light it." He started to move, felt her press her hand against his chest.

"No, don't. You're warm."

"But if I leave, it'll get warmer."

Okay, that wasn't entirely true. If he stayed put, he was pretty sure he'd spontaneously combust. Especially if she moved her hand any lower on his torso.

"What time is it?"

Loath as he was to do so, he pulled his hand from under the covers to look at his watch. "Holy cow. It's nearly noon!"

He scrambled out of bed and grabbed his shaving kit, jeans, and sweater from the day before, extremely conscious of the fact that the nightdress really did little to hide what lay underneath, particularly with the sun shining through the window. "Be right back. Stay there until I get the fire going again."

One hand yanked the covers over her head, and she burrowed back under. "Good plan."

Out in the hallway, the sounds of clinking drifted up from downstairs, a clue that the caterers had arrived. That meant the roads had been cleared, although he hadn't heard any plows during the night. Then again, once he'd fallen asleep, he'd been out for the count. He couldn't even remember dreaming.

In the bathroom, he stared, appalled, into the mirror. His hair was a mess that even a brush might not fix, he had a scrape on his cheek he had no memory of acquiring, and the bruise on his forehead was dark purple and looked like a tumor.

Prince Charming he was not. Oh well. Their little dalliance had been fun while it was dark and romantic.

When he returned to the room, he found Verity already dressed, poking at the embers in the fireplace, feeding the few licks of flame with kindling.

"Is there anything you can't do?"

She turned a smile on him, and if he'd been ice, he'd have melted into a puddle. "Oh, lots of things. I burn eggs, I've never met a sewing needle that didn't draw blood, and I can't drive stick."

"But you've pretty much got everything else covered?"

"Oh God, no. But I manage okay." With a wave of her toiletries bag, she hurried out.

In her absence, Zach tossed his remaining belongings into his overnight duffel and reluctantly zipped up the bag.

When she returned, he said, "Is it weird that I kind of don't want to leave?" He turned to face her as she packed a few things into her wheelie. "I've really enjoyed spending time with you. Getting to know you."

"Despite finding two dead bodies?"

"Maybe that was part of the magic. Solving a mystery together. A nearly three-hundred-year-old mystery. We..." *In for a penny, in for a pound.* "We made a good team. I thought. Think. Gah." He rubbed the back of his neck. "Sorry."

She crossed to him and took his hand.

"Words," he stuttered. "Not my strong suit outside of a classroom."

"You're fine. I know what you mean. I feel like that too." She looked away, scanning the room as though looking for a place to focus her attention. Anywhere but his face. When her eyes found his again, he felt like he could see straight into her soul.

"Last night was amazing." She laughed. "I usually mean something different when I say that."

He took her other hand in his. "Me too."

"I know your friend Hobb and my friend Dee didn't get exactly what they wanted, but maybe we could do this again sometime."

"Solve a mystery and uncover some dead bodies?"

She yanked one of her hands away and smacked his arm with a grin. "No, you idiot."

"Oooh. You mean spend the night in a haunted house, get snowed in, and lose electricity."

Another smack. "You are incorrigible."

"That's what my mother says. All. The. Time."

“Your mother must be a saint.” Her lips twisted in exasperation. “Clearly, I’m going to have to do the heavy lifting here. Men are useless. Zach Merrick, would you have dinner with me next weekend? And since you’re unemployed, I’ll pay. But only the first time. After that, we can go Dutch until you find a new job.”

Had he heard that right? “I think I need you to pinch me.”

“I’m not into kinky stuff.” Her tone bit, but he could see her holding back a smile.

“I just mean...oh, never mind. Yes. Yes, I would love to have dinner with you.” He gestured at the hallway. “I think the caterers are here with breakfast. May I escort you downstairs, Mistress Verity?”

“I’d be honored, Master Zachariah.”

In the hall, silver domes covered a multitude of breakfast delights. Eggs Benedict, thick-cut bacon, sausages, oatmeal, fresh berries, orange juice, coffee, and a selection of teas. A lovely, if not period-accurate, smörgåsbord.

They both filled their plates and sat down, eating in companionable silence for a few minutes.

In fact, it seemed too silent. Where Zach had heard the catering staff clanking about earlier, now no noise at all emanated from the kitchen.

And then he noticed something else. “Verity.”

She glanced up, her mouth full of eggs. “Mm?”

“Didn’t you leave the Bible on the table last night? With Mercy’s note tucked inside?”

She scanned the table, her eyes growing wide. She swallowed quickly. “Yes. Right there.”

There. An empty spot.

“Maybe the caterers moved it to lay out breakfast.”

They both inspected the rest of the room. Zach even got up to check the kitchen, which was indeed empty.

No Bible.

Both whirled as a figure appeared in the doorway to the parlor.

Chapter 19

Verity

Verity gasped as Arthur Pennewell cleared his throat and held up the Bible with the letter on top. "Good morning!" The attorney beamed as he came toward them. "You had a busy night, I see. I am thrilled you were able to find this letter."

Verity glanced at Zach. She knew there'd come a reckoning, but hadn't planned for it to be this morning. She hadn't prepared her defense yet.

Pennewell approached Zach and shook his hand. "My dear boy. Well done." Then he moved to Verity and clasped her hand in both of his. "And Miss Verity. I cannot thank you enough. I knew you would be the ones. Claire had her doubts, but I told her, this time was it." He moved to a chair, his hands shaking a little as he gingerly placed the Bible onto the tabletop. "Please. You must tell me everything. But first, a cup of coffee. The doctor says I should eschew caffeine, but one cup isn't going to kill me. And after this, well, I deserve a little celebration." He reached for the silver coffeepot with palsied hands.

Verity beat Zach to the pot. Points for him that he didn't just wait for her to do the serving. She figured pouring Pennewell coffee was the least she could do before telling him how they'd vandalized the house.

Pennewell closed his eyes and took a long drink from the cup while Verity and Zach seated themselves again. "Ah. The things you don't know you'll miss."

Opening his eyes again, he fixed them both with a piercing, almost manic gaze. "Miss Verity? Would you like to begin?"

Her stomach dropped. "You'll likely think we're deranged."

"Nonsense. I have spent more time in this house than anyone alive. I have experienced a plethora of unexplainable things. I've held séances, I've talked out loud to our three departed friends, I've enlisted one of those ghost hunters to bring in their fancy voice recorders to get them to tell me their secrets. Back when I was young enough to do so, I dug in every room in the cellar to see if I could find Mercy and Josiah's bodies. All to no avail. I knew the key was to find two young people, such as yourselves, to whom Mercy and Josiah would reveal themselves."

He sat back with a satisfied smile. "And finally, after all these years, the miracle has happened. Thus, no, I will not think you deranged. And you must tell me every little thing, every detail. I am desperate to hear it all."

Zach cut Verity a nervous look. "Maybe I should start with the laughing. When I bumped my head. I think that was the first thing."

Verity smiled in relief. "After you, Professor."

Zach launched into their tale, pausing to let Verity add things. It took two more cups of coffee, and then a glass of water, when Verity judged the elderly man had indulged in enough caffeine, for them to finish.

When the tale was complete, Pennewell clapped his hands in delight. "Oh, what a night. What a perfect night. And you smelled apple blossoms when you came upstairs. Wonderful. They can be free now. We finally know the truth and have the evidence to prove it. Best of all, they approve of you. Couples only smell apple blossoms when the ghosts give their blessing."

Draining her own coffee cup, from which she was now vibrating, Verity felt compelled to point out the negatives. "Well, you're going to need to get a stonemason in to fix that wall. We tried to minimize the—"

"Oh, pish. Minor damage. In fact, we'll need to widen the opening to remove the remains for proper burial. I've a mind to get rid of that horrid construction altogether. It doesn't belong, it never did. Such a heinous thing."

"And the case holding Temperance's Bible..."

"Easily replaced, Miss Verity. I'll take care of it. We'll need a second one for Mercy's Bible. And something to preserve her letter to Josiah and her final message. There is much to be done to make sure every visitor knows the truth." He braced his hands on the table and looked toward the stairs.

Toward, Verity realized, the spot where they had seen the faint image of Temperance the night before.

A small smile appeared on Pennewell's face. "Yes. A time for endings and a time for beginnings, Mistress Temperance." The man grew a bit dewy-eyed, and Verity raised her eyebrows at Zach. Was the man okay?

Zach cleared his throat. "Mr. Pennewell?"

The attorney started, then refocused on Zach. "Yes, yes. Much to be done and little time to do it." He climbed slowly to his feet. "I'll take both Bibles, the letters and such with me, hand them over to the document expert who helped me with Mercy's journals. And tomorrow, being Monday, I'll contact an archaeologist who'll work with the coroner's office to collect and prepare the remains."

Verity, suddenly inspired, stood as well. "Could we..." No, she couldn't include Zach. He was broke. "Could I help pay for a memorial service? Maybe in the spring, when the apple trees are blooming? I'll bet the whole town would come out for it."

"What a splendid idea!" He crossed to the window and looked out at the snow. "The roads are fairly clear." He chuckled. "If I made it out here, you should have no problem getting home. I'll wait until you're quite ready to go, then lock up after you."

Go? Verity exchanged a glance with Zach.

She hadn't wanted to come. Had basically been dragged here by Dee. Yet now, she didn't want to leave. She didn't want to leave what she and Zach had shared. Leave this feeling of camaraderie. It had been a long time since she'd felt able to trust anyone. To let anyone in. She didn't want to leave a place and a time and a feeling she feared they might not get back.

Zach must have felt something similar because he said, "We could lock up for you, Mr. Pennewell. It's the least we can do."

"No, no. You two toddle off. But there's no rush. I will be in the parlor, warming my old bones by the fire and reading a book. Although I admit I will never be able to read Poe's story about Fortunato with the same relish again."

As Pennewell wandered off into the parlor, Zach walked around the table and reached for Verity's hand. He looked every bit the absent-minded professor then. A little muddled and unsure. "I suppose this is it, then. Mystery solved."

Her lips quirked up. "Yeah. Old Man Fitch would've gotten away with it, too, if it weren't for us meddling kids."

Zach laughed, then sobered. Looked down at his feet. "I kinda don't want to leave."

She squeezed his hand. "Me either."

Before she could think of all the reasons she shouldn't, she leaned close and kissed him.

Not a tentative thing. Not a peck on the lips. A fabulous, full-on, run-out-of-breath kiss. When she finally stepped back, she felt dizzy.

Gloriously, perfectly dizzy. She reveled in it, realizing she wanted more. And not just more kisses but more Zach. More of his cheesy movie quotes and deep dives into history. More of his silly grins. More of his tender concern. More of the way he looked at her with his heart wide open.

As for Zach, he looked dazed himself. And the tips of his ears were pink, either from arousal or embarrassment. Either way, it made her heart melt.

She wiped some lipstick off his face. "You're cute when you're thrown off your game."

Shaking his head, he said, "Verity, I don't have a game."

She let go of his hand and headed for the stairs. "Well, you better get one by the time we have dinner next weekend."

She was aware of him watching her head up the narrow stairs with that dopey grin on his face. She'd need to get some game herself and wondered how many Bellinis she'd have to buy Dee for her friend to help her out. It had been way too long since Verity had dipped her toes in the dating pool.

The number, she later learned, was five. Plus, the promise of a spa day in the spring.

Chapter 20

Zach

The day for the interment couldn't have been more perfect. A balmy sixty degrees in early May with sunny skies and a slight breeze wafting the delicate and ephemeral scent of lilac through the old cemetery. Zach stood next to Verity at the graveside while the local pastor finished up, the crowd dispersed, and the cemetery men lowered the small casket containing both sets of remains into the earth.

He'd been a little surprised at the turnout. Dozens of townsfolk had shown up to lay Mercy and Josiah to rest in Temperance's grave. There had been no room for a new plot nearby, and Verity had insisted that the two be placed close to family here in the old part of the cemetery. Near both families, as it happened. Dolly Thayer, who was indeed Josiah's grandmother, was only a few grave sites away, and after some Verity-style persuasion, the cemetery had agreed to reopen Temperance's grave. A fitting resting place, all things considered.

Zach found himself tearing up as the pastor walked away. Sad not only for Mercy and Josiah's awful fate, but that the adventure was over. Verity, who seemed to notice everything, and not in a bad way, quietly handed Zach a tissue from the pocket of her black suit. He wiped his cheeks, blew his nose, and shot her a grateful look.

"Allergies, you know."

She rolled her eyes. "Uh huh."

He reached for her hand, something he found himself doing with increasing frequency these days. Holding her hand, holding her, felt so right. "Do you want to stay until they finish?" He pointed to the cemetery men, who were moving aside the large standing display of flowers provided by the town council in preparation for filling in the grave.

She shook her head. "I imagine they'd like to do their work in peace. And we've already said our goodbyes."

He smiled, remembering their first visit back to Hathorne House once the restoration had been completed. Mr. Pennewell had given them a free night there to make up for the romantic evening they didn't get on Valentine's Day Eve. Funny, but Zach thought that their tumultuous night of discovery had been pretty romantic after all. Then again, he was a history nerd. Or probably just weird. Still, Verity had thought the same thing, so maybe not that weird. Or they were just meant to be weird together.

Even though Mercy and Josiah's remains had been securely stored offsite by then, the two star-crossed lovers had made an appearance as Zach and Verity sat 'canoodling' by the fire in the parlor. A ghostly giggle, and the scents of apple blossoms and fresh bread accompanied a whoosh from the fireplace and a sudden guttering of the oil lamps.

After both their heart rates had returned to normal, Zach had gotten up to fetch another bottle of wine, and as he passed into the hall, he felt a touch on his hand and heard two voices say, in unison, "Thank you."

Six months ago, he'd have thought he was crazy, but the fact that Verity had heard it too and didn't run screaming from the house made him feel better. A shared kind of crazy.

In fact, over the last few months, they'd shared almost everything. All the dark moods and previous relationship baggage, the lost dreams neither of them were willing to let go of, and a crap ton of pizza and movie nights. It had been unlike any relationship Zach had ever had.

He didn't want it to stop.

And he worried that after laying Mercy and Josiah to rest, it might.

At Verity's sniffle, Zach handed her the fancy handkerchief from the suit he'd borrowed from Hobb, not having a clean tissue. After a quiet moment, he said, "I'm surprised Mr. Pennewell didn't show. Do you think he's ill?"

"Maybe? He's been looking tired lately. And he is in his eighties."

A voice at her shoulder startled Verity, and Zach felt a sudden chill breeze. They turned to find Arthur Pennewell standing beside them.

"Lovely service, wasn't it?" He beamed at them.

Zach nodded at the older man. "It's all thanks to you, sir."

"Pish. You did all the work. I just set the wheels in motion. And what a result we've achieved." He sighed contentedly. "Well. You two take good care of each other, but then I know you will. I've got to go, Claire is waiting for me."

Zach exchanged a worried glance with Verity. Was Pennewell sliding into dementia like Verity's father?

Pennewell continued. "It's your turn to mind the house, now. I'll be watching."

And on that mysterious statement, he walked away.

Before Zach could react, someone else approached, and he was forced to turn away.

A younger version of the aging attorney, Robert Pennewell, had his grandfather's smile and blue eyes but stood six inches taller with wiry ginger hair. Zach and Verity had worked with him to make the arrangements for Mercy and Josiah, while the senior Pennewell dealt with the basement restoration team.

"Good morning. It was a lovely service."

Given the work he and Verity had done to honor Mercy and Josiah's story, Zach felt pleased both Pennewells thought so. "That's what your grandfather said."

"He was really looking forward to being here today," He sighed. "You probably haven't heard, but I'm sad to report that he had a heart attack the night before last." His eyes welled up.

Verity stiffened. "Oh no! Then what on earth—"

Zach touched her arm in warning, suddenly understanding. The chill. The elder Pennewell's odd reference to his wife. "We're sorry to hear that."

"The doctor assured us his passing was sudden and painless. His housekeeper found him in his bed, a smile on his face. I don't think you can ask for a better way to go."

Verity stood silently, shaking her head. Zach saw she couldn't quite process what Robert was saying. She glanced around, and he knew she was looking for the man who had just walked away. The man whom they'd both spoken with.

But Arthur Pennewell was nowhere in sight.

She turned wide eyes to Zach. He gave her a slight shake of his head, then said, "We really appreciate you coming, but I feel bad taking you away from your family at this time."

"He would have wanted me to come. He grew to be quite fond of you both over the last few months." He winked. "He had big plans for your wedding...whenever that happens."

Now it was Zach's turn to react. He felt the blood drain from his face. "I..."

Verity's customer service skills kicked in. The woman, he thought, could be lawyer-smooth. "He is, or rather was, a die-hard romantic."

"Absolutely. And we loved him for it. Well, I should get back. Mom's a little lost, and I have arrangements to make. Thank you both for everything. You have no idea the peace you gave my grandfather. I know he could be a bit crazy about this whole ghost thing, but in the end, he really just wanted to know the truth. And you gave him that."

Zach took the hand Robert proffered. "It was our pleasure. Please let us know if there's anything we can do for you and your family."

Robert nodded. "Thank you. Oh, I'm not supposed to know this, but since I work with the attorney Granddad used for his will, I suspect I'll see you at the reading. Something to do with the management of Hathorne House. But you didn't hear that from me." He took Verity's hand and shook it as well. "See you both soon, and thank you again."

With a wave, the younger Pennewell turned and headed toward his car.

When he'd driven away, Zach gave a low whistle. "What the heck just happened?"

"The part about a bequest from Mr. Pennewell or the fact that we saw Mr. Pennewell just minutes before we found out he was dead?"

Zach grabbed her hand and led her away from the grave. "May we live in interesting times. You remember the last thing Pennewell said before he walked away?"

"Not really."

They reached her Acura, and Zach opened the driver's side door for her. "He said," as he went round and climbed in the other side, "'It's your turn to mind the house now. I'll be watching.'"

Verity thought about that. "I bet he wants us to take over managing the house. Stepping into his shoes. Which means…" She grinned at him. "You'll probably have a job. For life."

"Oh! I hadn't thought of that. I was more focused on that last part. He'll be watching. Meaning, we might have gotten rid of Mercy and Josiah's ghosts, now they've been put to rest, but we're now saddled with Arthur's spirit. Watching us." He put his head in his hands. "Watching us do things. Like, private things."

Verity laughed. "Like canoodle?" He loved that she still giggled when she said the word. Reaching across the console, she squeezed Zach's hand. "Oh, he wouldn't do that. All in all, I don't think having Mr. Pennewell watching over us is such a bad thing."

Zach squeezed back and decided to test the waters. "As long as we keep him happy and stay together."

She pushed the button to start the car. "Pretty sure that's not going to be a problem."

Yes!

It wasn't an acceptance of a marriage proposal—they weren't ready for that. But it was progress, and at least for now, the future felt as bright and fresh as apple blossoms in the spring.

About Nan Sampson

Nan Sampson has been creating new worlds and peopling them with quirky characters since she was old enough to hold a crayon. Convinced she was an alien, she spent her adolescence reading SF/F, watching Star Trek, and waiting for her real family to arrive in a spaceship to take her home. Since that didn't happen, she now happily lives through her fiction, where she can time travel, pilot spaceships, cast powerful spells, ride clockwork horses, and find magical macguffins, always finding love along the way. When forced to exist in the mundane modern world, she is an avid history nut, a terrible but earnest gardener, and consumer of many cups of tea and coffee. She likes to imagine she lives in Roger Zelazny's Amber, but it looks remarkably like the suburbs of Chicago. Who knew?

Connect:

Website: www.nansampsonauthor.com

Amazon.com/author/nansampson

Facebook.com/nansampsonauthor

Instagram.com/nansampsonauthor

Thank You For Reading

Please consider leaving a review on Amazon, Goodreads, Lulu, or your favorite book retailer. Reviews help readers discover new stories, and they mean more to authors than you might imagine.

If a particular story touched your heart, made you smile, or stayed with you after the final page, please reach out and connect with the author. Your support, kind words, and enthusiasm truly make a difference in our lives.

Thank you for reading and for celebrating love with us.

www.ingramcontent.com/pod-product-compliance
Lightning Source LLC
LaVergne TN
LVHW091112080826
845145LV00008B/1887

* 9 7 8 1 9 5 1 6 0 8 2 1 7 *